Sandra Cassandra

Shawna Lewis

Clink
Street

Published by Clink Street Publishing 2021

Copyright © 2021

First edition.

ISBN: 978-1-913962-53-1 Paperback
978-1-913962-54-8 Ebook

This novel is dedicated to
The Arvon Foundation

1

She had once heard herself described as lumpen.

Lumpen. What a word.

None of the other girls on the pitch was lumpen. She'd heard Marianne Reid described as svelte.

Now there *was* a word. The way Marianne sped smoothly down the field, silky black hair flowing out behind her... svelte was exactly right.

But Sandra was lumpen. She'd looked it up in a dictionary, but it wasn't there.

Lump...lumping...lumpy...lumpfish, but no lumpen.

She knew what it meant though. They did it in English in Year 7.

Suffixes.

If wood + en = wooden, meaning made of wood, and ash + en=ashen, meaning made of or pertaining to ash, it stood to reason that lump + en= lumpen, meaning made of lumps.

And that just about summed her up.

She allowed herself to ponder upon her body. In magazines, the girls were slim, tall, with thighs the circumference of baguettes and pretty much the same length. She didn't know how the photographers found so many skinny girls. The only ones like that at her school were anorexic or hadn't started their periods yet.

No, most girls she knew were gently rounded, lithe and glowing with health. They had energy and style, limbs that could fling themselves around with abandon and still look good. In the showers, they had breasts pert as peaches or heavy and promising like those little, golden-coloured melons she admired in Asda.

Her own breasts were like two lumps of pale dough stuck to her chest, like on the biscuit ladies her Gran used to let her make from spare pastry when she was baking. Gran had died when Sandra was eight, so she didn't make biscuit ladies any more. She missed the mess and warmth of her grandparents' kitchen. The one at home was always neat and tidy.

Sandra's bottom was flattish where it should have been rounded and broad where it should have been narrow. And as for her thighs! Well, tears sprung up in her eyes as she contemplated their girth. It wasn't so much that they were fat: they were very firm and strong. But in shape they were something like ice-cream cones – including the various ridges round the top. In fact, they were lumpy, despite their athleticism.

Lumpen.

She pushed herself off the goal-post. It looked as if the ball might come up her end soon. That Rachel Goodison was a cracking forward but as a stand-in left-back she was rubbish.

An auburn-haired girl was winging her way past Rachel, ball deftly controlled at the end of her stick. Sandra readied herself for the shot. When it came she dived to the right, anticipating the arc perfectly, kicking the ball clear out of the D. Marianne Reid gathered it on her stick and made off down the pitch.

Sandra returned to her position on the right-hand goal-post. At least no one could see how lumpen she was when she was in goal. The body-protection and pads made everyone look the same size and the face-guard covered the spots pretty effectively. That was the only reason they'd managed to talk her into playing hockey in the first place; she enjoyed the game, but no way was she ever going to bare her legs in those little pleated skirts like the others. Some of them even turned the skirts over at the waistband, to show off their tight little bottoms in their tight navy knickers as they ran.

You daren't do that when you were lumpen. Didn't want to.

It had been Mrs Hardisty who'd called her that a couple of years ago, when Francine Hardisty was getting married and was short of a bridesmaid. She'd wanted three, but they could only find two teenage girls who looked good in the frocks. Sandra, being lumpen, wouldn't have fitted the image, so she didn't get asked. But Sandra had heard Mrs Hardisty discussing it in the bread shop with Mrs Hope, the bridegroom's mother.

Sandra worked in the bread shop on Saturdays. There were some very lumpen loaves in there, so she felt quite at home. She got to hear an awful lot of gossip as well.

When Mrs Hardisty died a year after the wedding, there were a lot of pursed lips that told Sandra all had not been as it seemed in the Hardisty household. No one would tell her just what Mrs Hardisty had died of; something to do with the gas oven. An accident. Had she inhaled too much ovencleaner? Had the cooker fallen on her? Did it explode when she was cooking a casserole? No one would say.

Sandra picked up snippets, though; gossip about Mr Hardisty's appetites. Well, his wife did used to buy a lot of bread and would always go to the butcher's next door straight afterwards. Maybe she cooked a lot of casseroles and bread-and-butter pudding because he was always hungry, and the cooker got worn out and that's why it killed her.

Mr Hardisty had become quite friendly with Dad. Well, Dad said they were business acquaintances but Dad wasn't a businessman so that seemed a daft thing to say. He was manager of the bingo hall on the High Street now, ever since the cinema had closed down because of the multiplex they'd built out of town.

Mr Hardisty was in finance. So they said. And whatever that meant.

Mr Hardisty didn't seem to mind that she was lumpen. He used to come and watch her play hockey quite regularly. Kind, Sandra's mother called it; showing an *avuncular* interest. Sandra didn't have many real uncles so it was quite nice really.

Mr Hardisty said Sandra was well-built and ripe. She'd heard him tell Dad that she was burgeoning. Sandra didn't think Dad knew what burgeoning meant and nor did she, but she hoped it didn't mean lumpen. One day she'd look it up in the dictionary but she was scared it might mean ugly.

Sometimes Mr Hardisty would carry the keeper's pads in for Sandra at the end of the game. The other girls would stare and giggle, and ask who the old fellow was, but Sandra kept her cool and said he was just a family friend.

She was flattered, if truth be told. And Mr Hardisty had told her once that she was very special to him … she supposed because he had no daughter left at home since Francine got married. In secret, she used to pretend that Mr Hardisty was her boyfriend – gentleman-friend, really. That sounded so much more sophisticated … wouldn't half make the other girls sit up and take notice. Such a better class of relationship than they had with their acne-ridden lads from school. God, it made her want to puke sometimes to see how they stuck their tongues down each others' throats. And the things they said they got up to on Saturday nights after they'd been to the pub! Sandra's parents were very responsible people and would not let her go out with the others in town: under-age drinking was the only evening activity on offer in Wraith, so Sandra stayed in and watched a lot of television.

Sometimes on a Saturday night Mr Hardisty would come round and they'd all play Trivial Pursuit. Mind you, they'd played the game so many times that they knew most of the answers already.

She wondered if he'd come round tonight.

Mandy Davies had invited her to a party but she wouldn't go. In fact, she hadn't been to a party since Eleanor Jackson's when they were eleven. They'd been playing Hide and Seek, and Sandra had squeezed herself under a bed. Eleanor's big brother Steven, thirteen at the time, had squeezed under it with her. It had felt quite nice at first, but then he'd started squeezing various bits of Sandra and that wasn't quite so nice. So she'd decided that if that's what parties were coming to, she'd stay away. She'd liked it best when there were Musical Chairs and Iced Gems, Pass the Parcel and sausages on sticks. To hear the girls talk now, every party was an alcoholic orgy. In Wraith! There was some talk that Eleanor's even older brother, Tim, sometimes brought Blow.

Blow what? Sandra wondered. Yeah, they had drugs education and sex education in school ... had done lower down, anyway ... but it was about as real to Sandra as the history lessons on the American Midwest. Sure, it happened, but not here, not now. It wasn't relevant to her life.

The ball hit the backboard like a rifle's report. Jolted from her thoughts, Sandra stooped to retrieve it and passed it out to Rachel. 7-1now. At least the other team had scored, so they wouldn't feel so bad about losing.

Sandra didn't like people to feel bad and never joined in the girlish gossip with the others. But most girls were really, really nice. They only said hurtful things when they were true, like about Sandra having no waist. It was absolutely spot-on. She did bend in the middle, but she didn't curve in much the way most girls did. And about her hair being mousy!

Next door's cat, Ferdie, had brought a mouse in the other night and it was exactly, *exactly* the same colour as her hair. So when Andrea had made that comment, she was just being accurate; observant, really. It was flattering, in fact, to think that Andrea, so pretty and popular herself, had taken such an interest in Sandra's appearance. Sandra was quietly pleased to have been noticed.

The whistle blew and Miss Haggard picked up the ball. A fine drizzle was blowing at them as they trooped indoors, and Sandra was glad of her track-suit bottoms as she bent to un-strap the keeper's pads and kickers. All the other girls had long, shapely legs, reddened now like warming embers. She wouldn't want Mr Hardisty to see her legs – her lumpen legs – when he helped take her gear off.

Because ... he'd arrived on the touch line just fifteen minutes before the final whistle, in his camel overcoat and leather gloves and oatmeal suede shoes, looking distinguished. Miss Haggard looked at him quizzically but didn't comment. Sandra liked that word: *quizzically*. She'd only just learnt it and was glad of an opportunity to try it out, even in her head.

When she'd showered and changed and waved goodbye to the others, she started walking towards the bus stop. There'd be a ten minute wait, but never mind. She leant against the metal pole, mind empty. Soon, a sleek grey car drew up alongside her. The passenger-side window opened silently and Mr Hardisty leaned over, smiling.

"Want a lift, Sandra?" He patted the breast pocket of his camel coat. "I'm just popping round to see your dad. It's no trouble."

The drizzle had intensified and water was trickling down inside her collar, so she was glad of the offer. Once she'd climbed in, Mr Hardisty helped her remove her sodden anorak. The zip got stuck a bit but he fiddled about until it freed itself … kind of him to take the trouble, really, she supposed

The Mercedes purred as it slid along the lanes towards Sandra's home, slowing behind a flock of sheep being moved from one field to another. The farmer ignored the rain and the queue of cars as he strolled amiably along, whistling to the black and white collie bitch and occasionally shouting at her headstrong, rangy offspring, who was still learning the ropes.

Sandra's dad got impatient when they were delayed by livestock, but Mr Hardisty didn't seem to mind, even though the sheep were filthy and bumped along the sides of his car, which was all clean and lustrous.

Mr Hardisty switched off the engine.

"We might as well just wait until they've all gone into the field," he said. "Let's just sit here in the quiet, enjoying the countryside."

'Enjoying the countryside?" she thought. 'And it's raining. And it's February!' But to Mr Hardisty, she just smiled compliantly.

He put his left hand on top of her right one – which was lying on her thigh. Smiling, he reminded her, "I've told you that you're special to me, haven't I?"

"Because Francine's married and lives in Selby, do you mean? Like another daughter?"

She reddened. God! His hand was on her thigh…well, nearly. Quickly she lifted her right hand to brush back a lock of hair that had fallen forward, but that made it worse. Mr Hardisty's hand rose with hers and brushed heavily against her right breast … her lumpen breast! Embarrassment flared up her throat and swelled it to silence but *he* seemed unperturbed. Perhaps he hadn't noticed. She'd better stop being so silly. Over-sensitive, her mother called her.

"No, not like a daughter," Mr Hardisty went on. "I see you as a woman of great promise, Sandra, great, great promise. And I think I could help you to fulfil that promise."

A woman: women tend to be plump, while girls tend to be slender. That must be it.

"I don't understand, Mr Hardisty," she murmured. "It's my A Levels next summer and my teachers don't think I'm showing much promise in *them*. In fact I'm not even sure whether to bother applying to university at all."

"That's not what I meant. And if we're to be friends, you should start calling me Fergus. No, a woman like you will have no need of A Levels or university if you let me mould you as I know how. I could make a real woman of you."

A real woman, not a lumpen girl? He must be a magician. She looked at him wonderingly.

'Fergus,' she mused. 'Unusual. Hmm.' But how would he do it? And what would Mum and Dad say?

"Let me explain." His smile was suave. "You know that I'm a widower. My dear wife Enid died in tragic circumstances and of course I miss her terribly. But life must go on. One must look to the future, not the past."

"I suppose so." Sandra was still puzzled.

"Well, I see you as part of my future. No, don't look shocked. *I* can see your promise, Sandra. To your father you're still a schoolgirl, but I can see the real woman inside you, straining to get out. The reason for my visit to your father this morning is to seek his permission to ask for your hand in marriage."

He was talking like someone out of a nineteenth century novel, she thought, paralysed into silence. Her mind wouldn't work.

"What do you think, my dear? Can you give me an answer?"

She managed to gasp out, "Don't know … surprise … don't know."

"Well, think about it. I won't press you for an answer now, but I will speak to your father so it's all above board. You'd make me a very happy man, Sandra, and I know what a kind-hearted girl you are."

He turned the key in the ignition and the engine throbbed gently. The sheep were all safely gated in, the lane ahead clear where it could be seen through the steamed-up windscreen and drizzly mist.

On reaching home Sandra bolted in, leaving the front door ajar for Mr Hardisty … Fergus … to follow. She leapt heavily upstairs and shut herself in her room. The school anorak, wet uniform, shoes and tights were left in a steaming heap on the carpet. Taking her red candlewick dressing gown from the hook behind the door, she looked at herself afresh. She was a burgeoning woman, not a lumpen girl … although she still looked the same in the mirror.

Her bed beckoned, the Barbie cover left over from childhood a warm reassurance that she need not face adulthood quite yet unless she wanted to. Did she? Did she want to? She lay hugging the duvet, thinking, surrounded by girly pinkness. If she said yes she'd have to learn to cook, to cook a lot more than she could imagine. She'd have to satisfy Mr Hardisty's appetites and wondered if he liked Yorkshire Puddings. She could make those alright, out of a packet; very cheap, if you bought the supermarket's own brand.

Voices from downstairs told her that Mr Hardisty had found Dad. Jovial-sounding laughter drifted up. She heard her mother's voice asking if anyone wanted tea or coffee.

"This is a special occasion, Pamela." That was Mr Hardisty's voice. "Haven't you got anything stronger?"

What special occasion was that? Sandra wondered. Perhaps next door's tabby had had its kittens. They were about due. She rubbed her hair dry, climbed into jeans and sweatshirt and started downstairs. If the kittens had arrived, she was keen to see them.

When the lounge door opened, Mr and Mrs Pogson and Fergus turned to greet her. They had glasses in their hands. Sherry glasses, with sherry in them. Mr Hardisty took care not to spill it on his coat. A lot of fuss over a litter of kittens, she thought.

"Congratulations, my darling." Her mother rushed over and hugged her tearfully. "Well, fancy you keeping all this to yourself!"

Sandra stared at the three adults in turn.

"Dad's just been telling me that Mr Hardisty, Fergus, wants you to be his wife! Such an honour! Quite the successful businessman, he is. You've done well for yourself. You'll want for nothing."

Mrs Pogson thought smugly of Sally, her friend Josie's girl, engaged to that Gary Gentry who was no more than a road-sweeper, though he did call himself an Environmental Operative. *And* she was pregnant, Mrs Pogson was sure. They mostly were, these days…if they bothered to get married at all, that is. Half of them were living over the brush and proud of it, but not her Sandra. Not now. What a weight *that* would be off her mind.

"The wedding will be lovely," she went on. "I'm so looking forward to it; something happy to look forward to after all the funerals."

Three of Sandra's grandparents had died in the last eighteen months, plus Uncle Archie – Dad's uncle, he was. Yes, it would do Mum good to have a wedding to plan.

Sandra was still unable to speak. Her eyes sought out her father's. He was looking rather emotional but saying nothing. His complexion was normally florid – something to do with high blood pressure – but now he seemed pale. His eyes glittered. Malcolm Pogson's voice, when it came, was hesitant; hoarse.

"Yes love. Congratulations. You must do all you can to make Fergus happy … and I'm sure he'll do the same for you."

"Indeed, indeed." Fergus's laugh was bombastic.

"There's just one proviso, however," Dad went on. "I really must insist that Sandra finishes her schooling. The wedding must wait until after her A Levels."

"But that's over a year away," said the groom-to-be, his left hand hovering over his breast pocket. "I don't think I can wait that long. And Sandra will be eighteen in September, so we can marry then, with or without your consent, Malcolm. But I will agree to her staying on at school until the exams … no reason why not. She'll have plenty of time for studying while I'm out on business. It will keep her occupied so she won't miss Mum and Dad too much." He smiled indulgently.

Malcolm Pogson was silenced. Was it his daughter's imagination, or did he look crestfallen?

He seemed to be avoiding her eyes. Why was that? She thought the world of her father; would do anything to please him. His face was smiling, but not at her. It was as if a pane of glass had slid down from the ceiling, cutting him off from his daughter.

Silence filled the pause.

At last Malcolm seemed to rouse himself; he stepped forward to put an arm around her shoulders and propose a toast.

"To my little girl: may she be happy in her life…" he choked on his words, "…with Fergus."

The husband to be oozed radiant satisfaction.

"She's not your little girl any more, Malcolm, but from today, my womanly helpmeet."

He crept up behind Sandra and laid his hand on her bottom.

She gulped. He pressed. His fingers kneaded the flesh through her jeans, just a little, just enough for her to notice. A shiver passed up her body.

What was that? What should she do? Did she like it? Was it allowed? More to the point, was she engaged? And how had this happened?

An hour ago she'd been standing in the goal mouth thinking about Ferdie and the mouse. Now, an engagement had been announced ... before *she* had given her answer. At least, she didn't think she'd given an answer. She supposed she must have done, though. Mrs Fortune at school, her History teacher, was always saying that she must make her meaning clear. Be more explicit. Well, it looked as though she'd been more explicit than intended with Mr Hardisty. Would she ever get used to calling him Fergus?

She'd have to. She'd given her word. She must have done.

Sandra took the glass her mother offered and sipped the sweet, sticky liquid. God, she hated sherry, although she'd only had it once at their Alison's wedding. Alison was her cousin who worked at the building society. She was tall and slim, with lumps only in the right places. Mind you, Rory, her husband, could be described as lumpen ... if you could use that word for a man. Boy, really. That's all he was. Not like Mr Hardisty: mature.

She wished there was a bottle of Coke instead but she knew there wouldn't be. Bad for the teeth, Mum said; wouldn't have it in the house. There was always lemon barley water if anyone wanted a cold drink.

Three sips and the world started spinning. The warmth of the room, the hugeness of the occasion overwhelmed her. Pins and needles pierced her face. Lips became taut, fingers rigidly contorted. Constriction crept up her throat. A ball thudded about in her upper chest, her breath shallow; throaty; fast. She fell heavily, knocking her shoulder on the corner of the table, and lay prone on the carpet.

Dimly, she noticed the design which filled her view. The Axminster, down for years, was well cared-for: browns and beiges in a traditional pattern; very serviceable; very sensible. Wouldn't clash with anything; wouldn't go *with* anything, either. This thought lodged in her mind as reality tried to impinge itself on her consciousness.

Mum was all a-flutter, but Fergus took control.

"Just overcome with emotion, my dear," he smarmed, helping her to her feet.

Nevertheless, between them Mum and Dad helped her upstairs, leaving her on the bed to rest. Dad closed the door quietly when he left the room, still without eye-contact, and Sandra drifted into a light doze, not sure what to think or feel.

In the sitting room Malcolm concentrated on the carpet. Hardisty stared through the window. From his breast pocket he extracted a small square of paper between finger and thumb.

"You knew the deal, Malcolm." His tone was cold. He waved the paper in front of his lips.

"Not my fault if you didn't know what you were doing! The proof is here in my hand … a nice little addition to any family album." He wandered round the room, picking up ornaments here and there as if appraising their value.

"Where do you keep yours, then?" He slid out a drawer in the polished unit. "I could always make another one to share with your family if you like, since I'm keeping the video for my own entertainment."

He laughed in the knowledge that he held Pogson in bondage.

In the kitchen, Pamela Pogson cleared away the glasses and busied herself in the next room, wiping surfaces that were already spotless while her mind ranged over wedding-related matters.

But not love. It never crossed her mind. If anyone had asked her she'd have said yes, of course she loved Malcolm and he loved her. It was a fact, not an emotion. The question of whether Fergus loved Sandra, or Sandra loved him, did not arise. They were getting married. Love was assumed. No need to delve any deeper. And Sandra would be well set up. Secure. The best anyone could hope for.

The dress would have to be carefully chosen, to hide Sandra's figure. She took after her father in the build department: hefty. Not fat exactly, just big-built. Better have little bridesmaids so they wouldn't be any competition for Sandra. Love the girl though she did, Pamela's honesty wouldn't permit any false vanity over her daughter's face or figure. She'd long ago faced up to the fact that Sandra was plain lumpen and that no man would ever want her for her looks, as Mrs Hardisty had said.

Sad though this was, she couldn't resist a glance in the little red-rimmed mirror, placed on the window ledge behind the taps so she could check her hair if the doorbell rang while she was washing up. One glance confirmed that she, Pamela, on the other hand, was pretty; always had been. Nothing flashy, you understand. Understated, she liked to think. But even now, at fifty-five, there was a neat symmetry to her features that pleased her. She kept herself nice. Clothes from Marks and Spencer, hair done once a month at Justine's on the High Street (highlights every other visit). Quite slim, though that was more of a battle since the menopause, but she hadn't let herself go. A tidy woman in every way: controlled; efficient.

She hoped she'd passed on the control and efficiency to Sandra, even if she hadn't passed on the trim figure. Still – it didn't matter now. Mr Hardisty would mould the girl into the wife he wanted. Quite a catch, he was. Sandra would be a wealthy widow one day.

She wiped out the fridge, running the cloth over the eggs in their tray even though they were only bought yesterday. Jade would be a nice colour for the bridesmaids' dresses. She'd just nip round to Josie's to tell her the news.

2

Malcolm Pogson traced the pattern on the carpet with his toes. This was a situation he didn't know how to handle. Hardisty stared through the window. The man held him in thrall.

"You knew the deal, Malcolm." Hardisty's tone was cold.

"But she's seventeen; an innocent. I'm her father."

"That boy on the boat was seventeen. And no doubt he had a father. What's the difference? At least this will be legal."

Shame silenced Pogson. How had he let this happen? His blameless life ruined by a few minutes' indiscretion.

"Sandra will do me very nicely," the older man continued. "She's docile, compliant, good-natured, and she's burgeoning. I can see that in a few years' time she'll be quite a voluptuous woman, and I'm still an active man: very active." His grin was salacious. "I'll show her the way to fulfilment."

From his breast pocket, Hardisty extracted the small square of paper between finger and thumb.

"You knew the deal," he repeated coldly, tapping his lips with the paper.

Groaning inwardly, Malcolm said nothing. The clock ticked on the mantelpiece. A wedding present, it had stood on the same spot for nineteen years, a symbol of stability and normality. For that's what the Pogsons were: stable; normal.

Malcolm and Pam had married quite late in life. Neither had much of a past, romantically speaking, and when they met at a French Conversation class it seemed quite natural, as the only two unattached students in the group, for them to share text books and lifts. Their courtship had been conventional and managed, and they wed a year after the class had closed for the summer. A honeymoon in Le Touquet was chance to try out their French: Deux tasses de thé, s'il vous plait.

47 Mulberry Crescent, a bay-windowed semi built of rustic brick between the wars, had been their home ever since. Malcolm kept it neatly decorated – they were very fond of magnolia – and the garden neat, with a conifer by the front door and bedding plants round the border in the summer. Pam was handy with a sewing machine and ran up lovely curtains with fabric bought quite cheaply from the market in town, where they went once a month on a Saturday morning. They were pleased with their life together, for it was satisfying in its own small way. When Sandra was born after two years of marriage, their little unit was complete. They never failed to thank God for the blessing of their daughter, each having believed that the chance of parenthood had passed them by.

And so life continued, the parents delighting in and protecting their sweet-tempered though un-prepossessing child. They taught her about standards and morals. They protected her from the general seediness of life in the late decades of the twentieth century. She would not be subjected to the constant smut and violence that seemed the lot of most children nowadays. Her tele-viewing was carefully monitored. They taught her that Virtue was a virtue; that Kindness was a kindness; that Sin was a sin, and so she had grown up, safe and confident that she was loved, that the world was good, its inhabitants generous and protective. She need have no truck with the few who were not. But *he* had changed all that. In order to protect her from the truth, Malcolm must acquiesce to this marriage. That was the deal, and he was a man of his word.

Looking up from the carpet, he caught Hardisty's gaze. Fear pattered like a caged rat in Pogson's chest. Sweat broke out on his lip. His tongue was tied.

"Let's make it early August," decided Hardisty. "That's plenty of time to make the arrangements. Good month for the honeymoon, and the girl will be back for the start of term in September." For an instant, he flashed the picture in Malcolm's face. "I expect Pam knows all about it, eh? I'll book St Peter's. The Reverend Jackson owes me one."

Malcolm wondered what indiscretion Reverend Jackson had committed but remained silent as the other man moved into the hall, donned his costly camel overcoat and left, calling a terse goodbye to Pam. Hearing his footsteps crunching down the gravel drive, Malcolm crouched down beneath the front room window, hiding in the folds of the green brocade curtains so lovingly sewn by Pam, desperate to obliterate himself from this life, this home, this betrayal.

*

Sandra rolled over in the bed and studied her bedroom, familiar as a womb.

Being an only child she'd never had to share, apart from a tent on a Girl Guide camping trip. She'd found that quite embarrassing, really, because puberty had come suddenly and unexpectedly one night and had been difficult to cope with in secrecy.

Getting married meant sharing a room. That would take

some getting used to. She expected she and Mr Hardisty would have twin beds, like Mum and Dad. She never saw the point of a double bed. How could you expect to get a good night's sleep with another person's arm or leg taking up your space?

She knew what went on in bed. God! You couldn't get away from it. She wasn't exactly afraid, just couldn't imagine anyone wanting to actually *do* it. Must be blooming uncomfortable, she thought. Anyway, she doubted she would have to worry about that because Mr Hardisty … Fergus … was surely past it. When he said he wanted to marry her, he didn't mean in *that* way, that was for sure. He wanted a companion, someone to go shopping with, someone to keep the house nice and to have his tea on the table when he got in from work. Like Mum and Dad.

She'd like that. She'd always liked playing house when she was little. Of course, Mr Hardisty already had a house – quite a big one, according to Dad – but he'd let her change things and buy stuff for it, she was sure. It would be like having a doll's house, but for real.

Tucked in one corner of her room, next to the white melamine desk where she did her homework and beneath the poster of a kitten peeping out of a basket, was her own doll's house, made by Granddad from plywood when she was five. He'd used matchboxes covered with remnants of curtaining to make a settee and arm chairs. Other bits of furniture had been added over the years, bought with pocket money or given as stocking-fillers at Christmas.

Throughout her childhood, Sandra had used the dolls' house as the setting for her games of pretend. She would move the furniture around, occasionally fitting new carpets and curtains when there were off-cuts available, and populate the dwelling with imaginary friends and relatives … even a husband, sometimes. Now the husband could have a face, although the ones in her games had been much younger than Mr … than Fergus.

Of course, at seventeen she was too old for dolls' houses and had lately turned her attention to the room itself, wanting to make more of it. Last year she'd persuaded Dad to emulsion the walls in Rose White rather than magnolia. He'd taken some persuading – 'you can't go wrong with magnolia' – but declared himself happy with the result. She'd quite like to get rid of the Barbie duvet cover, but Mum said there was plenty of wear left, so it stayed. When that was in the wash there was a grey and pink one picked up cheaply at the market.

Recently she'd begun creating a little nook that pleased her. A triangular whatnot of stripped pine that had come from Uncle Archie's house stood in the corner, to the left of the door. On it she laid her collection of pebbles, pretty ones she'd collected from the various north-eastern beaches when they'd been out for Sunday drives. The stones never looked as good when they'd dried out, but Sandra liked the feel of them in her hands. She recalled the smell of the sea and the grittiness of the sand as she picked them from the tide-line and rinsed them clean.

The stones were on the lowest shelf, arranged on a length of blue muslin left over from a bridesmaid's dress. She'd draped the gauze from the top shelf, where it was held in place by Copper's bowl. She kept the water clean, the glass bright and shiny. Copper swam his (or her) life away, fed regularly, watched occasionally. His colour pleased Sandra: deeper than an ordinary goldfish. More bronze, really, she thought.

To the left of the bowl was a ceramic burner in blue and white, with a concave top for water and your aromatic oils. A hole in the side created a miniature cavern to take a tiny candle or tea-light. As the candle burned and the water evaporated, the aroma of choice filled the room. Aunty Valerie had brought it back for Sandra from a holiday in Somerset, along with three little brown bottles containing essential oils: juniper, lavender and something called ylang ylang. Sandra like that one best, but couldn't say why. Behind Copper's bowl, stuck upright in a lump of plasticine, were two pheasant's tail feathers she'd found on the moors near Goathland.

A plant pot covered in seashells occupied the middle shelf, a short stem of ivy trailing from its perpetually moist soil. Sandra had only just begun to appreciate plants and had begged a cutting from Dad. She was hoping the ivy would fill out and trail properly right down to the floor. From the ceiling above, suspended from a cup-hook found in the kitchen drawer, a bamboo wind chime wafted and tinkled hollowly. This had been Sandra's gift to her Granddad on the birthday before his death. It made her feel connected to his love.

She hoped Mr Hardisty would be able to find space in their room for her whatnot; it meant a lot to her, although she knew it held nothing of value. Except Copper: all life is valuable, she reminded herself.

Sandra was coming round to the idea of marrying Mr Hardisty. It would be nice and secure. She liked security. And it wouldn't matter too much about her A Levels if she was married; married to Mr Hardisty. She remembered what she'd asked for when she got the wishbone last Sunday dinner: a gentleman-friend like Mr Hardisty. Wow! This was even better.

Rising from her bed she crossed the room to kneel in front of the whatnot and examine, one by one, the objects displayed. She prodded the soil in the plant pot, testing for dampness. The pebbles rested comfortably in her palm, reassuring in their solidness. She played the feathers across her cheek, poured oil into the water in the burner, lit the candle and stared into the flame. A whiff of lavender scented the room, soothing and pleasant. As she relaxed into her imagination, Sandra conjured up images of what being married would be like.

The white dress; the bridesmaid; the bouquet; the church decorated with summer flowers. A honeymoon somewhere abroad; lights twinkling on a night-time sea as she and her husband strolled hand in hand on a white sand beach, pausing to gaze into each other's eyes when the love became overwhelming. She couldn't quite see the husband in her mind's eye, though she tried very hard to see him in the guise of Mr Hardisty. All she could see was a silhouette, and she had to admit to herself that it was the silhouette of a much younger man: quite tall and slender, whereas Mr Hardisty was of only medium height. Not fat, yet there was definitely a middle-aged look about his shape. But Sandra did not dwell on this. She was lucky to get the chance of such a fine husband; might never get a better one. She would be foolish to turn it down, especially when Mr Hardisty was obviously so keen.

She made up her mind to do it. Mum and Dad definitely liked the idea, and Sandra had spent her life doing what they asked of her, always willingly. This would be no exception, and if she missed out on some fun on the way, so what? Fun had not featured much in her life; she barely knew what it was. Most of the time, fun seemed to lead to trouble, with over-indulgence in some form playing a major part. This was not the Pogson way. Nor, she felt sure, was it Fergus Hardisty's way.

Her thoughts were interrupted by her mother, proffering a cup of tea. Mother and daughter sat together on the bed, sharing a silent closeness.

"I'm very happy for you, love," said Pamela. "You'll be well set up with Fergus. Never have to worry about money or a job. There'll be plenty of time for yourself. You'll make him a good little wife"

Even as she said the words, she knew she should have been asking herself, 'But will he make her a good husband?' but the thought was not allowed to surface. This way, Sandra would not have that sinking feeling as, through her twenties, she watched her contemporaries walk up the aisle. She would not experience the loneliness, in her mid-thirties, of watching their children grow while she remained a spinster. For in Pamela's eyes, things had not changed for the better with Women's Lib and the sexual revolution. The prevailing belief that no marriage was better than a bad marriage had not found favour in the Pogson household.

Little more was said between mother and daughter, save some reference to there being a lot of planning to do and guest lists to organise. Nothing about what it meant to be married, nothing to prepare the girl for the momentous change she had agreed to. Sandra must learn from following her mother's example. She had been learning thus all her life and was, Pamela proudly admitted to herself, an admirably willing pupil.

3

Unobtrusively, the mother-in-law-to-be provided Fergus with a seldom-worn signet ring of her daughter's and within a few days he appeared with an engagement ring of exactly the right size, a solitaire diamond set in white gold. The diamond was small and, to be honest, quite insignificant. This was not a ring designed to dazzle or make a proclamation of love: it was a ring that did the job. If Sandra had ever given it much thought she would have opted for something more striking: a ruby or an emerald set in a cluster of diamonds. But Sandra had been brought up not to attract attention and to be thankful for what she was given. It was unthinkable to voice dissatisfaction, so she smiled gratefully as the ring was slid onto her finger with an accompanying peck on the cheek.

She only wore the ring to school once. Her heart had fluttered as she entered the form room, wondering who would be the first to notice. Because someone would notice, she was sure of that. Why, only the other week Mr Wilson, the form tutor, had come in without his wedding ring one day and by break the whole school was buzzing with the news that he'd left his brand new wife. It later transpired that an outbreak of dermatitis on the teacher's hands had been the cause of the ring's removal, but the observational skills of teenagers and the efficiency of the school grapevine were shown to be as effective as ever.

Sandra had chosen a bad day, as it turned out. Just after Mr Wilson walked through the door carrying the register, the air was pierced by a deafening, intermittent hooting from the fire alarm. He waited until all had filed out towards the nearest exit before shutting the windows and following down the stone stairs, shushing his pupils from behind.

Eight hundred young people, assorted teachers, office and kitchen staff, caretakers and other personnel strolled casually out to the assembly area, situated beneath the trees at the edge of the playground behind the school. Lines formed, youngsters moved about their length trying to arrange themselves into alphabetical order. The Deputy Head urged silence through a loud-hailer and teachers walked down the lines checking registers. Being two minutes to nine, however, there were many gaps. One school bus had not turned up yet and latecomers regular and irregular were still making their way through the streets. It was impossible to tell if there were any 'bodies' that might need rescuing. Disgruntled staff muttered darkly about what they'd do if they got their hands on the little beggar who'd set off the alarm. Senior Management made executive decisions about treating the whole thing as a real drill and following correct procedure. No one must move until a thorough search of the premises had taken place.

Sandra stood in line next to Darren Pavior and Adam Quentin, two boys who were anathema to her. She had never exchanged a word with either, except once when she was in the same Drama group as Darren in Year 8. And so she stood, her moment of glory snatched from her, disappointed yet stalwart.

The buildings were not big enough to house the 800

pupils comfortably, yet they were big enough to take an hour to search, and the problem was compounded by the arrival of delayed bus from Snellington fifteen minutes after the search began. The teacher delegated to await its arrival and divert the disembarking passengers to the assembly area had herself been diverted by an irate parent demanding words with the Headmaster on the subject of earrings. Repeated statements that the Head was at a meeting with the Education Authority and likely to be out of school all day did not go down well. By the time the harassed teacher managed to soothe the complainant, the latecomers had scattered to the hundred-odd corners of the buildings, bemused at the emptiness and silence yet reassured that, yes, school was open today, because the special bus had turned up and all the usual crowd got on it.

By the time all the missing bodies had been accounted for or abandoned as absent, fifty minutes had elapsed. The silent, orderly lines of nine o'clock had disintegrated into chattering huddles. Teachers wandered hopelessly up and down the lines, urging their charges to be quiet and to stand in line. But what was the point? Staff members had no problem with enforcing rules, as long as they understood the reasoning behind them, but what was to be gained by keeping hundreds of kids standing outside in the cold March wind and rain, when they all knew there was no fire and, most probably, no bomb. It was obvious that some recalcitrant with a grudge had set the alarm off on purpose. Names of possible perpetrators buzzed through their minds; there would be much speculation in the staff-room at lunch time.

For now they were forced to stand outside, getting crosser and crosser. Planned lessons would have to be abandoned, throwing the whole week's schedule out of kilter…in some cases, the entire term's planning. Backs started to ache, muscles to tighten, clothes to get damp and tempers to fray.

At last the school was dismissed back to class and with time to make up, break was abandoned, lessons conducted in a rush by tense and irritable staff, with low levels of student concentration adding to the strain. There was no moment when Sandra's classmates noticed her at all, let alone glance at her hand. As the day wore on, she lost any hope that for once, she might be the centre of attention. It probably served her right for wanting to show off. She should have known better. Sandra never wore the ring to school again.

She kept quiet about her engagement until the end of the Summer Term. At home-time on the last day, Sandra stood with Andrea Scarr outside school, waiting for her father's car to arrive. Sometimes, the Pogsons gave Andrea a lift to her grandparents' home a few doors away from Number 47.

The girls spoke casually while they waited.

"Are you doing anything special over the summer, Sandra?" Andrea expected the usual shake of the head.

"Well, actually, I'm getting married!" The bride-to-be was relieved to spill the beans at last.

A stunned silence followed, before an incredulous, "What?" in a rising tone.

"I'm getting married to Mr Hardisty, who my dad works for."

She was blushing deeply now, unsure of the other girl's response. Was she laughing? Andrea, for once, was speechless. She forgot her manners and failed to wish Sandra good luck, much happiness or anything else. The engaged one waited for some sort of congratulation, some excitement, but there was none.

For the truth was that Andrea did not believe her. Steadily, Sandra went on to tell of the wedding arrangements, where and when it would take place, but Andrea took it in silence. Her mind was racing over who she should ring up first to find out the truth; over why Sandra, (a pleasant, harmless enough geek) would make up such a story. She must really have flipped …unless, of course, it was true. But no, it couldn't be!

Little was said on the journey home, Andrea not wanting to pursue the matter in front of Mr Pogson, sure it was a fantasy which Sandra would regret inventing. Malcolm noticed and wondered about the tension in the car, but assumed it was due to some girlish disagreement. When they reached Mulberry Avenue, Andrea hopped out of the car briskly and ran up the street to her grandparents' bungalow.

Malcolm turned to Sandra.

"Did everyone wish you good luck for the wedding, love?"

"Those who knew about it did." Not exactly a lie.

Andrea reached her grandfather's shed, bursting and breathless to find out what he knew.

"Well aye, Andrea love. Reckon your Nan did say something about that Sandra lass getting wed. Can't say I was listening, though. You'd best ask her yourself."

Which Andrea did, and was amazed to be told the facts of the matter as the elder Mrs Scarr knew them.

*

By the day of the wedding there was hardly a student at the school who didn't know. A few of them clubbed together to send her a card but it was hard to decide what to write in it, not knowing the name of the groom and not really considering marriage to an old man worthy of congratulation. The card showed a pair of silver bells and the message, "Wishing you happiness on your wedding day". Not a lot for twelve years of shared schooling.

None of Sandra's schoolmates was invited to the wedding; it never occurred to her parents that she might want them there. There was family enough on both sides to make a good crowd. No point in paying out good money on a reception for people you hardly knew.

The days sped by. There were clothes to be bought, the bridesmaids to be schooled, the rehearsal gone through, and Sandra was looking forward to her big day. She knew it was wrong of her, but she really, really wanted to be the centre of attention for a short while; it was not that she didn't get plenty of attention from her parents: she did. But she did not get admiration. Surely, on her wedding day, she would outshine the rest … or at least be noticed. Sandra trusted her mother's judgement and was confident that, on the day, she would look her best ever.

And of course, she would be the centre of Fergus's attention for as long as he lived.

4

Pamela looked lovely in lemon. She'd been to Meadowhall for her get-up and had chosen well: classy. A knee-length shift dress with matching three-quarter length lace jacket. Her brown hair, cut into a bob by Justine, hung sleekly under a broad, white-ribbon-edged hat brim. She'd kept the handbag small: neat; pale grey, with court shoes to match. Yes, the bride's mother looked good.

Malcolm Pogson sweated in his top hat and tails. The pin-striped trousers he'd hired were much too long in the crotch ... nearly reaching up to his armpits. He'd experienced a moment of profound panic, until Pam showed him how to use the waistcoat to create a new waist. All done up, he looked quite smart. Sweat beaded his scalp and a trickle ran down his inner thigh, but no-one noticed.

This was Sandra's day. They'd gone for a simple design in the end. Make the most of her good features, Mum had said. Sandra had nice eyes and her hands weren't too bad. So the dress – white ribbed satin – was a clean cut. Quite plain, it skimmed her body and fell to ankle length before its only touch of frivolity: a broad band of guipure lace. They wanted to draw attention to the bride's eyes, so the veil was held on by a pearl head-dress with tendrils curving over her forehead.

The bride was quite pleased with the result, knowing that 'you can't make a silk purse out of a sow's ear', as Josie had said. Justine had given her a manicure and varnished her nails in pale mauve. Sandra's mother always said she had shapely nails, for her size.

The bouquet was nothing fancy … a spray of white lilies, interspersed with ferns.

'Funereal', thought Simon Fownhope as he watched them coming out of the church. He was balanced on his bike, leaning against the bus stop opposite. He couldn't get his head round the idea of Sandra Pogson marrying a bloke of fifty-odd. It'd be like him marrying his Nan. Perhaps funereal was appropriate. Sandra was certainly going to miss out on life.

Simon liked Sandra. Didn't know her very well, but she'd always been about, a couple of years ahead of him all through school. Once, when he was eight, she'd stopped some bigger boys picking on him and he'd liked her ever since. Sometimes he had to go to the bread shop on a Saturday for his mother, and he was always glad when Sandra served him and gave him a special smile as she handed over the iced buns.

Simon eyed Fergus Hardisty suspiciously. What did he want with a girl like Sandra? O.K., she was no oil painting, but she was nice. That Hardisty fellow was an oddball. He didn't live in Wraith but was often seen driving through late at night in his sleek silver Merc. Hardisty didn't always drive through, though. Sometimes he stopped on street corners or could be seen chatting conspiratorially in dark corners with men of dubious reputation. Simon knew because he often joined the under-age drinkers at the Dog and Pullet. His dad and mum worked odd hours, so his comings and goings were not closely monitored. Not that Simon knew anything definite about Hardisty, mind, but he had his suspicions.

He made a silent promise to keep his eye on Sandra, and protect her as she had protected him years ago.

The bridegroom, tiring of the photographer's monopoly, decided the time had come to move towards the wedding cars. Grasping Sandra's hand firmly, he tangled up the satin ribbon from which dangled a silver cardboard horseshoe, presented by the littlest bridesmaid. Impatiently he snapped the ribbon and tossed the gift aside. Sandra opened her mouth to protest but found herself ushered into the waiting car, a white Rolls Royce.

The grey-liveried chauffeur, Bob Fownhope, tucked the hem of the bridal gown out of harm's way. He'd known Sandra, by sight, all her life. His son Simon had once been protected by the girl from a couple of bullies. He couldn't understand Malcolm Pogson letting her wed this unsavoury bloke.

Folding his lips grimly together, Bob started the engine and the car moved off.

*

She had really fancied Tenerife, but Fergus said it was too hot, too busy, too noisy. Jersey was the place for their honeymoon. Sandra had never been but thought it sounded dull, like the grey jumper she used to wear for school when she was younger.

"Where's your jersey?" her mum would ask if she came home from school without the regulation pullover.

She enjoyed flying over the sea, looking down at the small ships and huge container vessels on the English Channel below, and was excited to recognise the outline of the islands, a living green and grey-blue map edged with sandy strands, coves and sloping green cliffs as the aircraft circled prior to landing, but by the time they'd passed through the little airport she was beyond caring. Tiredness overwhelmed her. She needed to sleep.

What with the hectic preparations and all, she had never given a thought to her first night as a married woman. It had all been about the wedding; nothing about the marriage.

Mr Hardisty ... no, Fergus ... hadn't said much to her all day. Not to *her*. But she didn't mind. You needn't talk all the time when you loved someone. Actually, now she came to think about it, he hadn't said much to her at all, not since that day after the hockey match. Until now, events had swept them both along, caught up in plans and arrange-ments. But they had the rest of their lives to talk. As long as the love was there, she told herself.

The hotel was grand; she had never seen such opulence. A flunky in grey and gold carried the luggage to their room, unlocked the door with a plastic card and stood back for Sandra to enter.

First impressions were stunning. Done out in shell pink, mirror-panelled walls glittered with two hundred tiny lights, waving in a line across their breadth. To the right, on entering, another door led to the bathroom. They moved past this and saw, on the right, a kidney-shaped bath big enough for two. Not an ordinary bath. It was sunk within a pink marble ledge, the salmon-tinted mirrors reflecting the new arrivals from every angle. More tiny lights illuminated, reflected and twinkled in the fittings of gold.

"The Jacuzzi, Madam," indicated the flunky, briefly demonstrating the controls.

God! A Jacuzzi! Sandra was stunned. Why wasn't it in the bathroom? She'd caught sight of another tub as she passed the door on the right. Why two baths in one suite? And who would use the Jacuzzi with someone else in the room? Or were you supposed to wear your swimsuit? She'd bought a nice new one from town especially for the honeymoon, though she hadn't thought about wearing it in front of Mr Hardi ... Fergus.

Moving forward, her eyes alighted on the true focal point of the room. A huge fibre-glass scallop shell in marbled pink slanted eight feet into the air. At its lower, hinged end, a mountain of pillows, white, lace-edged, lay on an oval bed. Around the rim of the bed ran a marbled ledge to match the Jacuzzi. A mirror on the wall behind reflected both the twinkling lights around the room and the bizarrely-canopied bed itself.

Through the darkened window Sandra could see lamps both dim and bright sparkling along the Jersey coastline.

There was only one bed. Oh, God!

5

Ten months later, nothing mattered anyway. They filed into the examination hall, tension cutting thought and knowledge. Smoothly, breathlessly, they found their places. A rattle of pens, a shuffling of chairs, throats cleared.

Sandra's head swam with random facts and quotations. She was not well-prepared, despite the many evenings spent alone with the characters in the exam texts, read over and over as an escape from existence, their cares so normal, it seemed, in comparison. For her, the texts were escapism, her response not criticism. She could believe the characters were at Fergus's house … she was not yet able to call it home … waiting for her return. Needing to believe that the protagonists were real, Sandra was unable to analyse the author's style, language or purpose.

The start and finish times were displayed on the blackboard at the front of the hall. Mrs Fortune recited the regulation rubric, then,

"You may begin."

Opening the paper, Sandra knocked her pen to the floor. It fell several feet from her chair. Mrs Fortune, senior invigilator, moved stealthily between the rows of desks and bent to pick it up. As she passed it back to the candidate, their eyes met. The teacher halted mid-action. The girl was crying. Tears flowed freely down her cheeks from brimming, lost eyes. They ran from her nose, dripped from her chin, dampening the paper. There was nothing to be done except hand back the pen and walk away.

On one level her mind was thinking, "That won't do much for the department's results."

On a deeper, truer level, it said, "We *knew* it."

Miss Haggard and Mrs Fortune were friends as well as colleagues. The one had told the other of her unease about the older man who often watched the Saturday school hockey matches. All members of staff were on the look-out for unwelcome visitors, intruders in school, but it was very difficult to vet spectators. Then the staffroom grapevine had revealed the reason for Sandra's change of name during the summer holidays. Sandra Hardisty was the first married woman to be on the school's roll. It just didn't feel right. A communal shudder had shivered through the female staff. The male teachers with daughters felt uneasy. Few took it without reaction.

It was not their job to react. They had to accept. But it didn't stop them caring.

The questions on the paper were those she'd been prepared for, but Sandra's flow was stemmed. Her answers, short, trite and superficial, were not enough. She knew, but she didn't care. Yes she did. This should have been her best paper. The rest would be worse. They were.

Her hopes faded. She had seen, as a dim light through mist, the prospect of escape through qualifications. She'd thought Fergus might allow her to study for a degree at the local college as long as she spent most of her time at home. That way, she might have reclaimed some of the youth she had allowed to escape. But she needed results for that.

She knew she had condemned herself to hell. No hidden hope could douse its fire or outwit its master.

*

As the months wore on, Sandra grew accustomed to those things she'd found so hard to accept.

Fergus had made it clear from the outset that she had a clearly-defined role. This included managing domestic matters without interfering with the cleaning woman's routine, accompanying him on visits to his several aged relatives, preparing meals when he was at home and being compliant: verbally, emotionally and sexually.

Although sex had, at first, seemed gut-wrenchingly wrong, in time she was able to close down her mind during the act. Fergus savoured her innocence and inexperience. It made him feel freer, released him from the squalor that had become his life. And he was not unkind. Not at first.

He had not always been sordid. As a young man he had been idealistic, open and loving. His relationship with Enid had begun in their teens; she was pretty much the same age as Sandra at the time of their marriage. They wed with the same hopes and aspirations as most young couples of their day.

But somewhere along the line, he changed. Sometimes, when maudlin, in his cups, he would try to trace the roots of the transformation. It probably began with his win on the pools. The money gave him entry to another sphere of life, the society of clubbers and gamblers, artificial stimulants and illicit sex. Enid had never wanted to join him in these jaunts, and it became pretty easy to pull the wool over her eyes with trumped-up excuses. He bought a share in a night-club, became friendly with free-loaders, people with boats and private planes, people who always had something to buy or sell but no receipts for their purchase. He bought a bingo hall; a run-down casino.

The money lasted because he invested in others' weakness.

At first he did this almost innocently, but was soon caught up in its addictive pattern. Before long, he was an expert in relieving men of their self-control and self-respect, bending them to his will without scruple.

His friendship with Malcolm Pogson was an anachronism, like part of his past that he could cling on to, for the Pogson family represented the trusting innocence of the people he'd grown up amongst. He envied their simple lives and small satisfactions. He wanted to taste these again, but the craving for the drug of excess overwhelmed him.

Given the chance, he would destroy Malcolm Pogson, for sheer spite.

Sandra knew nothing of this. Her husband's business affairs, other than the bingo hall where her father worked, were only referred to in the most general of terms.

They were of different generations. That was probably why he kept things from her. Not for secrecy's sake, but because he still considered it the man's role to make money and support the home. These thoughts worked in her mind as she mooched round the house one evening. It was late and it was dark; the heavy August heat had not abated with the setting of the sun. Bored and lonely, she tried to justify Fergus's neglect. Sandra didn't feel like a bride of less than a year.

She found the door of Fergus's study open and wandered in. Why did he call it a study when he never did any studying? Usually, the door was locked, even when he was in the room alone. Important business, she supposed. Now, perhaps she'd give it a tidy for something to do.

Idly she plumped up the cushions on the captain's chair behind the desk, and on the small, regency-style sofa opposite. A used whisky glass and an empty bottle stood on the floor beside it. The door of a mahogany cabinet behind the desk was slightly ajar. It had looked like a filing cabinet, but now she could see that it concealed a TV and video player.

Protruding from the slot in the VCR was a tape. She turned her head sideways to read the handwritten label. 'Pogson,' it said in black ink. She remembered how, just before the wedding, Fergus had brought his video camera round to Mulberry Avenue and filmed some footage of her parents. This must be it. Why hadn't he told her about it? They could have watched it together. That would have been nice.

She pressed REWIND and waited until the machine clicked, then picked up the remote control from the cabinet top, switched on the TV and pressed PLAY.

Yes, the opening shots were of Mulberry Avenue. Sandra was there, arriving home in school uniform on the last day of her exams. She looked younger, somehow; much younger.

More footage of inside the house: Mum in the kitchen, smiling and turning away in embarrassment when the lens was directed her way; Sandra coming downstairs in a beige mini-dress, the only one she possessed, revealing her lumpen thighs; a game of Trivial Pursuit, Dad and Mum in one team against Sandra and a missing Fergus, who was busy wielding the camera, filming pictures of tame domesticity.

Suddenly, a few moments of blizzard on screen were replaced by shots of somewhere she didn't recognise. It looked like some sort of cabin ... the inside of a yacht, perhaps. Yes, there was the ship's wheel; charts on a table; a glimpse of horizon through a porthole; then her father's face again.

She didn't recall hearing about dad going on a boat.

The cameraman must've been at the pointy end ... the bow, was it? She could see bunks curving outwards, a small sink and cooker area, more seating either side of the map-covered table. Dad, bare-chested, sat on the left. Daylight shone brightly down from an open hatch cover. A set of upright steps led up through the hatch to the deck.

The camera focused on the steps and hatch. A pair of feet appeared on deck. They turned round. A left toe pointed downwards, searching for the first step on the ladder. As it took the weight, a slight, smooth calf descended into view. Next came the right toe, heel, calf; and so the legs descended. Bare legs, higher and higher, until a pair of tight young buttocks filled the screen.

Sandra was stone. Who was behind the camera?

The buttocks were male: a boy's – a youth's. As his feet touched the floor, he spun round.

Immediately, the shot changed to one of Malcolm. He was florid, eyes glazed, balding head tousled, half-lounging on a side bunk. His bare chest was visible, his lower half obscured by the table. From beneath the table protruded a head; a blond, cropped head; a youthful head. What was happening? Had the boy dropped something under the table? Yet Sandra knew it was not so.

Sandra's gorge rose. She pressed the OFF button. What next? Had the tape been stopped at a particular spot? Fergus must not know that she'd been in this room; that she'd seen what she had seen.

Shaking, she tried to return things to the way they'd been ten minutes ago. The cabinet door, the tape ejected in the VCR slot, the glass and bottle.

But she knew nothing could ever be like it had been ten minutes ago.

Her mind obliterated all but what she had seen. She saw it in the door as she stumbled through; in the handle she turned, remembering to close it. She saw it in the kettle, the taps and the water that shot and sparkled into the vessel. This was one crisis that could not be calmed by a nice cup of tea, she knew that, but the instinct of her race drove her on.

She chose her mug carefully, aware that this moment would remain with her for the rest of her days. Anything bright or frivolous would jar her electrified senses, would sear the burn into her soul. She chose one that stood new and unused on the top shelf of the cupboard. It had a silver rim, silver inside. But the body of the cup was deepest midnight blue: strong, glossy and dense. Sandra stared at the blue, seeing the light reflected in the glaze yet absorbed into its depth. It took her mind with it, away from numbness, away from pain, into the deepest, darkest recesses, the deep blue cave of misery.

There to lie and wallow, to be engulfed as the tide rose, unstoppably; to be swamped; to hope to die but, agonisingly, to live on.

She moved into the garden, lured by the sky which matched the cup. The air was warm and still, but a chilling waft stirred the shrubs and rustled the deepening, late-summer leaves of the trees above. She moved on, automatically, to the pond, with its nakedly artificial waterfall. Choosing her spot with care, she stepped into the deepest part of the pool and sat down where the cascade entered the water.

The water reached her breast. The bottom of the pond was slimy, hard and uneven, with fronds of water weed, baskets holding lilies, weighted down with pebbles. She drew up her knees, made herself comfortable, still clutching the silver and midnight blue china beaker. Her life depended on the cup and its contents, at that moment.

As she sipped, water ran down her back, over her shoulders, wet her hair, her clothes; washed, but failed to clean, her soul.

*

Fergus found her there when he returned much, much later. Seeing the kitchen door wide open, lights blazing, bed empty, he searched the garden for his wife. *His* wife. That was the important word: *his*.

She was still awake, despite the chill and the passage of time. She did not respond to his call, his command or his questions.

"Good God, girl. Have you been drinking?"

Nothing.

"Get out of there. You'll upset the fish …and ruin your clothes. Have you no sense?"

Silence.

He began to feel some concern, although his mind was rather opaque. He was not an abstemious man and it had been a long evening, but something was amiss. He, Fergus Hardisty, could tell. Sandra had never caused him any trouble before.

He had a shallow fondness for the girl. She was proving a dutiful, if unenthusiastic, wife, who was only slowly beginning to recognise his appetites. He wished her no harm and was ready to offer cheque-book generosity to keep her well-turned out, but in his self-obsession her happiness … or unhappiness … was not an issue. If confronted on the matter, he would have shrugged and said, "She never complains." He did not look into her eyes and see the deadness there.

After tonight, the deadness would putrefy.

The cooler air began to clear Fergus's mind. He must get Sandra out of the pond to avoid having another death on his hands. There had been too many raised eyebrows, pursed lips and approaches side-stepped after Enid's suicide. The woman had been unstable for years, he was certain. Not his fault at all. He, Fergus, was blameless. Even the police had not bothered him for long. Another death which could be construed as accidental, however, would bring him to their attention again. He didn't need that.

It was necessary to step into the pond to lift her out. He carefully removed his shoes and trousers before doing so, placing the folded garment on a bench nearby. Gingerly, he lowered his foot into the greening murk. His foot touched mud and slime. Koi Carp slid ponderously from his touch. Struggling, he pulled his wife forward, wriggled to get behind her, reach his arms under hers and lock fingers. She was a heavy girl and Fergus, a slight and ageing man, was a stranger to such exertion. He could not do it.

Suddenly, without warning, Sandra rose from the water and silently clambered out. Trailing pond-weed she crossed the lawn, stepped through the patio doors, up the stairs and climbed, sodden, into bed.

*

Simon Fownhope had started cleaning windows to earn a bob or two. His dad's mate Clive had a round and had been looking for a chance to take a few weeks' rest, so customers had been transferred over to Simon temporarily. He was good lad, and with business thriving, Clive was happy to share his income with the Fownhopes for a few weeks.

It wasn't a bad job, Simon thought. Although he wouldn't like to do it permanently, it was fine for filling the time waiting for his GCSE results. He knew many of the customers already. In the small Wraith community he would see the same faces at every school event, church gala and sporting fixture but, usually, he didn't know who lived where, so it was interesting to identify the one answering the door when presenting his bucket to be filled with clean water.

The first time Simon had gone to the broad-fronted, detached house in Snellington, he'd been taken aback when Sandra Pogson answered the door. Sandra Hardisty, he meant. He'd last seen her a year ago on the day of the wedding. She seemed slimmer – though that was no bad thing; shapelier. Gone, however, was the friendly open smile. She seemed less … less herself, somehow, though Simon didn't quite know what he meant by that.

Now, four weeks later, there was no response to his knock, although the front door stood open. He could see along the burgundy-carpeted hall to a lavishly-appointed kitchen, and through that, an open back door leading to a garden.

Feeling that he knew Sandra well enough, he went round the side of the house calling her name.

He heard no response. She must have popped round next door: they'd have locked the doors otherwise, even out here in Snellington. He disconnected the hosepipe from the outside tap, filled his bucket and went back to start on the front windows. His ladder was propped beneath a first floor window.

He began on the ground floor, trying to avoid looking through the glass but always aware that the rooms were empty of life: tidied and formal. Up the ladder, the windows of the master bedroom; the en suite, a second bedroom. To the rear of the premises, a third bedroom, a landing, the main bathroom two decades out of fashion with its aquamarine suite, shell-patterned tiles and matching wallpaper. At the side, a smaller window overlooked the gravel drive.

The young window cleaner could not know that this was the one room in the house where she felt secure. It was Sandra's own place. Initially, Fergus had suggested she use the fourth bedroom as a sewing room.

"'What a quaint idea!' she'd thought, confirmed in her impression of her husband as some nineteenth-century, philanthropic master of the house. The room did indeed contain a sewing machine, an ancient Singer which had once belonged to Enid's mother. In a corner stood a daunting tailor's dummy covered in red velveteen. She wasn't sure about dress-making, but Sandra could easily see herself making curtains like her mother had always done. She'd thought maybe they could go to the market and choose the fabric together. That would have been nice, but Fergus had squashed that idea. The curtains in place were profession-ally and expensively made, expertly draped and flounced, but they were not Sandra's choice. Nothing was. She rarely saw her parents now.

So the sewing machine stood unused on a deal table. In another corner Sandra had positioned Uncle Archie's old pine whatnot, adorned with the bits and pieces she'd brought from home. Copper was no more, replaced by a pale, slimmer-looking fish won by hooking a duck at a church fete. This new pet had no name: Fergus said it was ridiculous to give a fish any name more elaborate than Fish, but in her head, Sandra called him Osric.

The ladder rattling against the wall beneath the window did not rouse Sandra, who knelt in front of the whatnot as at an altar, hands clasped in silent invocation. The need to pray was within her, but to whom or what she did not know. Her mind emptied when she contemplated the mementoes of her previous existence: the pebbles; the trailing ivy, now spilling out of its pot with vigour; the pheasant feathers; the goldfish in its gleaming bowl. Only the wind-chime and Copper had not survived the move.

Simon peered in. Was she alright? He wondered? The notion of prayer was unknown to him. Sandra's lips were moving, he could tell, and strained hopelessly to read her lips.

Inside Sandra, oblivious, was uttering pleas to whatever deity ruled her destiny.

"Please, make it better. Help me. Tell me what to do."

Having gently and silently polished the window more

than necessary, Simon descended the ladder, slid the upper half down to match the lower before struggling to balance it across the seat and handlebars of his bike. The dirty water he emptied over a bed of begonias, before hesitating. Should he knock again, or simply leave a card to say the windows had been cleaned, payment to be collected later?

He opted to knock and rattled the knocker several times before pressing the bell, which chimed with a flourish. He sat on the step to wait. Two or three minutes passed before he heard movement and, turning, saw Sandra coming down the stairs.

Her eyes seemed spiritless until she caught sight of him standing on the doorstep. Instantly, a beam of recognition and warmth shone from them – a glimpse of that vitality and honest simplicity which had made people, for years, refer to Sandra as 'a lovely lass'. Sadly, the girl had never heard this; compliments were seldom offered openly in Yorkshire. To those who had really known Sandra in her childhood, her podgy build and plain features were like the covers of a well-loved book: they contained much that was worthwhile and valued, yet in themselves were insignificant.

Simon caught the beam with his own eyes and held it for long seconds. The years since she had rescued him from the bullies disappeared, and a current of understanding flowed between them. She knew that he knew. No words were necessary.

Reaching for her purse, she picked out the eight pound coins needed for payment. Their hands touched briefly as the money passed between them. Neither shrank away, but neither did they linger. Only their eyes, their souls, met fleetingly, before Simon turned away and heard the door close behind him.

6

Fergus was losing patience with Sandra. What was the matter with the girl? She had barely looked at him since that episode in the pond. No explanation had been offered, no forgiveness begged. An apology was due, at the very least.

It was time to put his foot down. She was not shaping up as well as he'd hoped. Refusing to communicate was evidence either of having a mind of her own or having no mind at all. Fergus didn't want a moron; he wanted a mind moulded to match his own.

He could not imagine what might be wrong. He gave his wife an allowance of money to spend; she had no need to work; she lived in a lovely house which was cleaned for her. Even the garden was tended once a week by a mute, biddable woman in her sixties. Both women had been instructed not to disturb Mr Hardisty's wife during working hours.

Sandra had been wrong when she assumed Fergus to be 'past it' sexually. The veiled comments she had overheard two years earlier about Mr Hardisty's appetites had been clumsy attempts by Enid Hardisty's confidantes to share their common fears and disgust. At her lowest ebb, Enid had told her friends, separately, of his harsh and crude love-making since he'd come into money. This had come at a time in her life when she wanted to withdraw from concerns of the flesh, and so had been intolerable. Like most women of her generation she did not elaborate, but her friends knew an abused woman when they saw one: abused both physically and emotionally.

Knowing of and enjoying Sandra's inexperience had been satisfaction enough for Fergus at first, but a year had now passed and he was tiring of her unresponsiveness.

He tried to dominate, to demand, but she withdrew even further. Not often a violent man, he itched to shake her, to force her to do his bidding with a show of enthusiasm. There was, however, still a grain of civilised behaviour left which restrained the urge.

Due to his involvement with the run-down casino near the docks in on the Humber, Fergus spent a lot of time away from home, rarely returning until late at night. Sandra continued with her childhood habit of early nights – there was no reason to stay awake. She understood that business affairs kept Fergus out late, but forlornly examined her own conduct in search of an explanation. A more inquisitive investigator would have unearthed a different story.

Perhaps the house was not as tidy or as homely as when Enid was alive. Perhaps Sandra was less attractive to him than when he had proposed, although Sandra preferred the look of her more slender self. Maybe Fergus found her boring or unintelligent, or her cooking was not up to scratch. She tried harder to be a satisfactory wife yet the more she tried, the more she failed. She knew not what was wrong.

After the revelations on the videotape, she withdrew still further. What must Fergus think of her now? Without understanding the full implications, she knew that what she had seen was bad. The shock and revulsion which had driven her to find cleansing in the pond had been replaced, over time, by a numb, mental blindness. She could not recall the detail of what she'd seen; just knew that nothing was as it seemed. Her beloved father was tarnished, sullied forever in her mind. She thought perhaps it would be better if he ceased to work for Fergus. Whatever happened, her husband must not be corrupted by association. Whoever was misleading her father would contaminate Fergus, given the chance. She was sure of it, though she was also certain that her husband was too strong-willed and righteous to be drawn into anything unsavoury. But then … she'd thought that of her father. She could no longer think of him as Dad.

Seeking some sort of comfort she turned her emotions to Fergus, yet dare not reveal what she had seen. A loving arm around her, a shoulder to cry on, a "There, there," were all she craved, but Fergus was not a tactile or empathic man. Faced with her tears, he would pass the box of tissues and suggest she pull herself together; she had nothing to be depressed about. Although she had found the evidence in Fergus's own study, it never occurred to Sandra that he was to blame for the video's damning contents. Fergus did not own a boat, as far as she knew, but he probably had many business acquaintances who did so. It had been a kind, loving gesture to build up a video record of her family's life, and she had no doubt that Fergus would have been horrified at the appearance of the naked young man. Upset that the video intended for his bride had been defiled in this way, her husband must have been trying to edit out the offensive material when he was called away. Sandra didn't know where he'd been called away to. He didn't tell her everything. There was no need, he said.

It was her own fault, she told herself. She had no right to intrude into her husband's private space. She wouldn't like it if Fergus messed around with the trinkets on her what-not. Fergus had hardly set foot in her special room. She had plenty of privacy. No. If anyone was to blame it was her father, for going on board someone's boat without telling his wife about it. For Sandra didn't like secrecy; couldn't understand it. As far as she had known, Mum and Dad shared everything. There had never been an occasion when one had undertaken a major excursion without the other.

Yet the video told her different.

The video tape: the one that Mum must never see.

It was physically impossible for her to re-enter the study. Perhaps Fergus kept the door locked more regularly now. Sandra could not know. Her feet refused to halt in front of it.

Passing down the hall, it seemed that her feet sped past the entrance to the room. Her hand refused to lift to test the door handle. She had no way of knowing the tape's whereabouts. She could not ask Fergus. Every attempt to seek a solution ended in the same, helpless message.

Mum must not see the tape.

Saturday night: her husband was out looking after his business interests. She was pleased he was so diligent but wished he'd let her help, yet Fergus always insisted she needed her beauty sleep. She wished he'd tell her what looking after his business interests involved. She knew how to type and was quite well-organised, she'd told him. He only had to ask, but no. He preferred to be the breadwinner: in control. Sandra wasn't to worry about the world outside this house. The home was her realm…

… as long as she kept things the same.

Fergus didn't like change. The house had been extensively and expensively refurbished and refurnished before he and Enid moved in, what? Twenty years ago? Twenty-five, maybe? And she'd kept it lovely, give the woman her due. Not a scratch on the polished mahogany, not a scuff on the moulded skirting boards. He still checked from time to time, but was keeping his dissatisfaction with Sandra's efforts to himself for now. He had other things on his mind.

This Saturday night in late September, Sandra's spirits were low as she climbed the stairs. *Business interests:* what did that *actually* mean? She knew that Fergus's business interests paid for her lovely home and comfortable existence, although neither was what she'd have picked from a glossy magazine at the hairdresser's. How lucky she was to have everything provided for her. No need to bother her young head thinking about where the money came from.

That's what Fergus said. He'd been married before, so he must be right. Sandra counted her blessings as she had been taught to do, but her spirits failed to lift.

A hot, slow bath with perfumed foam, a cup of cocoa, a book: not a typical Saturday evening for an eighteen-year-old. She wondered what her old classmates would be doing now, but she'd never seen much of them out of school so the scene was difficult to conjure up in her imagination. Sandra even wondered what Simon Fownhope might be up to with his mates, although they were only kids, really. She'd heard that her fellow sixth-formers had mostly done quite well in their A-Levels, and would probably be making a farewell tour of the pubs in the villages round about. There'd be lots of noise and laughter, she bet; some quarrels too, a scuffle, maybe. She was better off out of it.

That's what Fergus said.

She was lucky, he told her. She had no need to worry about leaving her familiar surroundings or finding her feet at college or university, having to meet new people and learn new things. No! He insisted. She was more fortunate than any of them. Her future lay right here. Granted, her exam results hadn't been up to much … but, chin up! She wouldn't need qualifications to succeed as Fergus's wife. What more could she want or need? He asked her that quite regularly although, Sandra had to admit, the words came out as a statement of fact rather than an enquiry.

When the water had cooled to tepid, she dried herself on a towel and smoothed talc over her still well-covered body. Less lumpen, it seemed, more shapely; more fluid in its curves, but still not a body to flaunt. She enjoyed the fine smoothness of the talc on her skin, its silkiness. She rubbed lotion onto her feet, allowing her fingertips to massage the nail beds, explore the spaces between the toes. It felt satisfying.

Dry now, she buttoned the jacket of her poly-cotton pyjamas over her breasts, and noticed for the first time that they had shape; a womanly shape; no longer two lumps of dough stuck to her chest. Sandra didn't dwell on this – it wasn't proper to do so – but felt a small wave of pleasure in the discovery.

Briefly she went to the sewing room, knelt in front of the what-not and fed Osric a sprinkle of tiny grains. The pebbles seemed to cry out to be handled. She rolled them in her cupped palms, held them to her cheeks, took a match from the box and lit the tea-light; stole half an inch of water from the goldfish bowl; transferred it to the top of the burner and allowed three slowly-shed tears-worth of ylang ylang to fall. She watched the liquid heat and evaporate. Slowly, the aromatic oil pervaded the room, sensual, evoking yearnings Sandra did not recognise. She knelt, inhaling, eyed closed, her mind emptying of its own accord – except for that one, lone and lead-heavy mantra: Mum must not see the tape.

And then it was gone. Her eyes opened briskly, her head was clear. She rose, blew out the candle and left the room.

In the bedroom, she sat at the dressing table and brushed her hair. It was still mousy; still shoulder-length and almost straight. Perhaps she should go to Justine's and ask for a new style, some colour, perhaps; nothing startling – just a hint of auburn or gold. With this thought in her head she climbed into bed, turned out the light and was fast asleep by eleven.

*

Car doors slammed, footsteps crunched on the gravel; she heard loud male laughter and shrill feminine giggles; the clatter of milk bottles kicked from the doorstep. Shrieks and more laughter; the loud rattle of the wrong keys scraping the lock on the front door; a thumping on the mahogany panels; a voice above the clatter of the letter-box, amplified as it flew up the stairs.

"Come on Sandy! I've brought someone to see you. It's a surprise … open up!"

Sandy? No one ever called her Sandy. Fergus never had, yet it sounded like his voice. Was it an imposter, maybe? She hid her ears beneath the pillow. What was going on? She had woken at the first sound of tyre on gravel and the flare of the security light on the wall outside; had lain awake trying to make sense of it all.

The shouted instruction was repeated, sounding cross this time rather than jovial, but Sandra was still dozy, unable to respond. Eventually she struggled herself upright. The duvet encumbered her feet. Her slippers eluded her. The candlewick dressing-gown, rose-pink- a scarcely-used one of Enid's which Fergus liked her to wear, he said – was snatched from its hook behind the door. Hair awry, eyes bleary, mouth sour as summer milk, she stumbled heavily downstairs.

The shouting went on, less intelligibly, but she knew it was Fergus; knew he had brought a guest home for the first time since their marriage. She must pull herself together and be a good hostess. She twisted the lock and stood back as the door fell open. Her husband shoved himself through the door, turned and reached his hand back to grasp a bare female shoulder. He pulled its owner towards him before thrusting her forward into the hall.

Sandra was not *so* bleary-eyed that she failed to recognise the owner of the shoulder. The sleek black hair, the long, slender limbs, the lithe torso: it was Marianne Reed, the svelte one.

Svelte still, but no longer the Madonna of the hockey pitch. In the harsh light of the hallway she looked much older – or rather, as if she had made herself look older. An orangey-tan make-up patched her naturally fair complexion; eye brows plucked to a fine line curved above lids heavily-shaded with pearly-plum eye-shadow. The curled lashes were heavy with mascara, cheeks glittered with blusher. An unsteadily-drawn line of deep maroon –edged lips of vibrant red.

Sandra did a double-take. Why the dreadful mask? Marianne was so lovely to look at, unadorned.

"Hiya Sandra! Bet you didn't expect to see me, did you? Your old school pal, eh? Fergie thought it'd be a nice surprise for you."

Fergie? How did Marianne know her husband at all, let alone be on first name terms with him? *Fergie?*

Fergus cupped his hand proprietorially around Marianne's shoulder.

"Marianne's been doing a bit of work for me at the club." He winked. "I thought that, as she's such a fun girl and an old friend of yours, we could have a good time together." He was laughing in a way Sandra had never seen before.

She was suddenly conscious of the candlewick dressing gown and tousled hair. What must Marianne think of her?

"I'd have thought you'd be out around Wraith saying goodbye to everyone. I believe they're all off to university soon. Are you going?" she asked.

Marianne screeched with laughter. Was she perhaps a bit tipsy, Sandra wondered, immediately ashamed of herself for thinking such a thing. Fergus wouldn't employ a drunkard, she was sure. Sandra *was* puzzled, though. What sort of work had Marianne been doing for Fergus? She wished he'd asked her, his wife, to do it. She'd have leapt at the chance, whatever it was.

The fine strap of Marianne's red satin mini-dress had slipped off her shoulder allowing a curve of breast to fall forward, but its owner did not attempt to set the strap in place. She kicked off her high-heeled sandals, drawing attention to the long, slim legs, nearly all of which were visible before the briefest of flared hems flicked and tossed around her upper thighs. They were lovely legs, Sandra had to admit. Maybe with legs like that she would have dressed more adventurously herself.

The screeching subdued to a suffocated giggle as the girl tried to compose herself.

"No Sandy, not me. University of life, that's the only one I'm likely to go to. I've had my fill of book-learning. Your Fergus offered me a job and I took it. I'm a working girl now."

How odd that Fergus hadn't mentioned taking Marianne onto his payroll. Sandra wanted to ask in what capacity, but something held her back. 'A working girl'? That sounded pretty menial, not like a secretary or Personal Assistant, she thought. No, Marianne was probably employed to clean the bingo hall or give out the prizes. Nothing wrong with that; Sandra had not been brought up to be snooty, but she'd always imagined that Marianne Reid would have a more glamorous career.

Not wanting to embarrass her guest, she kept her thoughts to herself and concentrated on making Marianne feel at ease. Not that Marianne needed much help, by the look of it.

"I'll make a cup of tea," Sandra muttered.

Returning later with a tray of mugs and biscuits, she was

taken aback to see Fergus with eyes closed, knees bent, feet firmly planted on the carpet. On his left knee, exposing a curve of smooth bottom, sat Marianne, her right arm around his neck as she gently caressed his ear-lobe. The well-manicured fingers of her left hand held *his* age-spotted right hand close to her chest. *Very* close to her chest, it looked to Sandra.

She stopped, choked on her breath, the toppling tray only just saved. Hearing the rattle of cups, Marianne stretched out and smiled disarmingly.

"We all like a cuddle now and then, don't we?" She paused. "Fergus is so sweet. He's like a dad to me." She winked naughtily. "I call him my Sugar Daddy."

Fergus opened his eyes.

"Come and join us Sandra, my dear," he beamed. He was not in the least fazed by Marianne having draped herself all over him. Even though she was slim she must be quite a weight, Sandra thought. Actually, this was taking advantage of her employer, but Fergus was probably too polite to put Marianne in her place. Fergus's wife was affronted on his behalf, but didn't like to make a fuss.

She stirred sugar into her husband's tea, thinking to herself, "Sugar Daddy?" She couldn't place the phrase. Sugar Mice, Puffs, Plum Fairy ... perhaps a Sugar Daddy was something like a Jelly Baby only bigger.

The man patted his vacant knee. "Come and sit here, Sandra. We can all have a good time together."

Sandra perched gingerly on the stringy thigh. She and Fergus didn't go in for much cuddling – it was a bit embarrassing, really. And what was that smell? She was used to a faint whiff of alcohol, but as Fergus pulled her head close to his she was drenched in the stench from their mouths. For the first time, she allowed herself to admit the possibility that both Fergus and Marianne were drunk. She didn't think she'd seen a drunken person before, though she'd heard there were a lot of them in Wraith on a Saturday night. Marianne and Fergus seemed to be having fun, but Sandra was sure they'd both feel quite shamefaced in the morning.

"Would Marianne like to stay the night? It's very late. She could sleep in Francine's old room," she suggested.

"She could, aye!" Fergus chortled.

"I'll lend you some of my pyjamas," Sandra offered, "although they might be a bit big."

Marianne snorted.

"There'll be time for bed later. I brought Marianne back for two reasons." The red-lacquered nails ran softly down his cheek.

"First, I thought you might like a bit of company your own age for a change. Second, I want Marianne to show you how to make the most of yourself. She knows how to get all she can out of life ..." his smile was leering, "... and how to put plenty of life in a man."

Instinctively offended and on her guard, Sandra's naive self struggled to point out that, actually, Fergus was being incredibly kind and thoughtful. Fancy that! He was prepared to be mauled by that drunken girl just to help his wife, Sandra herself, to get more out of life,

She fought to suppress an inner rebellion, an urge to shout that she didn't need Marianne Reid to show her how to enjoy herself, but knew she was not on firm territory. She had never seen her husband looking so relaxed, having so much fun. Fun was something Sandra didn't know much about. Perhaps she *did* need showing, yet it was an insult to be shown by a drunken Marianne Reid.

But no! Sandra could not allow herself those thoughts. Those thoughts were disloyal and harmful. One must always think the best of people, especially one's husband.

A wife must be loyal. No disloyal thought must be entertained. Mum had always extolled the virtue of loyalty and its place in a marriage.

Sandra's thoughts flicked briefly to the videotape; she opened her eyes so as not to see the images which still flashed in her brain at unexpected moments. She forced her mind back to the present moment, away from the dimmest of festering ideas that there might possibly, just possibly, be some link between Marianne's appearance at her home and the film shot on someone's boat.

"Just watch Marianne and pick up a few tips."

The young wife did as she was told.

Marianne's left knee bent up; her bare toes wriggled themselves beneath the puny thigh. While the fingers explored the earlobe, the black, silky hair leant close. Red lips caressed the Adam's apple. The tongue tip flicked itself with relish up the chin to the ungenerous lips. Hot breath followed the tongue's course. Fingers stroked and kneaded where there was flesh to be found.

"Now you do it." He was smiling serenely. "It would make me happy."

It was a wife's duty to make her husband happy, so Sandra did it … for a while.

It felt unnatural; forced. She wanted to cry, but knew it wouldn't *do* in front of Marianne. Sandra desperately wanted to acknowledge the kindness in Fergus. Hadn't he promised, when he proposed, that he would show her how to be a real woman? And surely, that's what every girl must want?

Trying to be rational, she analysed what it was that made Marianne, at eighteen, a real woman, while she, Sandra, was still a girl. It didn't seem to have much to do with the wedding ring on her finger or her role as a housewife. She tried to rationalise it, but failed.

The tears welled up in her eyes even as she tried to imitate the brunette beauty on her husband's other knee. Before they overflowed she got up and, with a curt goodnight, went to bed alone.

*

Sandra tossed and turned. Fergus had not followed her up to bed. The numbers on the radio alarm clock glowed vividly in the dark: 2.43; 3.12; 4.05; 5.17, until eventually the cold light of dawn gleamed dully through the curtains. The cold light of dawn also shed its pale spectre on Sandra's awareness. Until now, she had clung stubbornly to her naivete, refusing to countenance the notion that all was not as well as it seemed. She had been brought up to see the best in people. Why should anyone behave in a way they knew to be wrong or hurtful? Why did Marianne and Fergus think it was OK to mock her? What had she done wrong?

A late-developer: that was what some people called Sandra. She knew it, but had never been able to understand why. She'd been ahead of her classmates in height and physical development; her academic intelligence and common sense were on a par with her peers'. What was late about her development?

As daylight dawned she sighed and writhed in the bed, another dawn beginning in her understanding. The antics downstairs had been alien to her. To sit on Fergus's knee seemed silly, yet she *was* his wife. Marianne, whom he barely knew, had no inhibitions and clearly found the whole carry-on fun. Even more astounding was that Fergus had clearly found it fun too, and wanted more.

He'd said that Marianne was there to teach her a lesson. What *exactly* was the lesson she had to learn? Sandra had been reading lots of cookery books and tried to make tasty meals, but it seemed Fergus was thinking along other lines. She *wished* she could understand, though she had to admit that the wish was conjured from fear of disapproval rather than excitement at a happy prospect. She feared that it was something to do with sex, and her suppressed urge to run away.

Sandra forced her chin up and shoulders back. It was time to buck up her ideas and satisfy her husband... or what?

Her feet felt heavy: leaden and immovable.

She didn't like the word, preferred not to think about it. Growing up in the 1990's, it was impossible not to be familiar with all the terminology, mechanics, variations, dangers and optimum frequency, but to Sandra that's all it was. She knew...she felt...that it was supposed to be something to do with love, but the school lessons, magazines and TV adverts seemed to regard it as more of a commodity. Not unlike hair conditioner. You could live your life perfectly well without it, but most people said it was necessary, there was a lot of it about offering many different options, and it made things feel nice.

The chill of dawn was within her. Her toes ached with it. The chill realisation that she wanted a little of what Marianne possessed was in her heart. Not the menial job, whatever that was. Not even the long legs and silky hair, though they would be nice. No. She wanted to be awakened to the pleasures of physical contact; to be able to caress someone's ear the way Marianne had done, because it was loving and pleasurable. To sit on someone's knee out of love; to fondle, to smile, to hug, laugh, tease and play.

Sandra had never done any of those things. She had never seen her parents do them, so did not associate them with marriage. To her, marriage was keeping the house nice, cooking tea, shopping on a Saturday and planning your holidays. Fondling Fergus, though, was not part of the picture. It didn't feel right. In fact if she was honest, it made her shudder. It would be unnatural, like fondling her father.

She pushed the thought away; didn't like to think about Dad too much nowadays. One day she would have to face up to what she'd seen … but not yet. She pushed open the sitting room door. Fergus was still in his armchair, head lolled back, mouth gaping and snoring resonantly. On the carpet at his side: an empty whisky bottle and two empty glasses. Seated on the floor between his legs, head resting on his thigh, Marianne slept quietly. They looked serene; spent. Neither stirred as Sandra turned off the TV and lights. Her heart raced within her.

Blood suffused her cheeks, venom sped to her spleen. Fervently she tried to suppress its rising surge; fervently she remembered her upbringing – to think well of people. They would not wish *her* hurt or harm. These were people who cared for her. They'd just fallen asleep, that was all, so why did she feel so viciously resentful? If only Marianne were not so lovely to look at. But envy was a sin. She must not give it headroom. If only she didn't feel so upset. Stop it! Be nice. Be kind. Put the kettle on. Be a good wife. Be a welcoming hostess. She was horrified by the malignity of her thoughts.

Deciding that she must face the day brightly, she ran a bath and dropped in some invigorating Oil of Lemon. A refreshing soak, her hair newly-washed, clean clothes … *then* she would wake the sleepers. She must try to make more of herself. *That* was what Fergus wanted. *That* was what she must do.

Half an hour later, calmer and briskly cheery, Sandra chinked the crockery loudly as she brewed a pot of tea. Talk radio filled the void. Drawing back the heavy brocade curtains in the sitting room, brisk and breezily she commanded,

"Wake up! Wake up! It's morning. Time for a cuppa"

She forced herself to smile as she watched the two sleepers dopily rouse themselves, tasting their own sourness. Asleep, they'd looked pleasantly tranquil. Now, they looked bleary and bloated, unkempt and unsavoury. Marianne's seductive dress, provocative by night, looked cheap and tacky by day. Mascara and eye-shadow smudged her right cheek, red and creased where it had rested on her boss's leg. His greying hair fell back to reveal the receding hairline, something he normally took pains to conceal. The unfastened waistband allowed his paunch to protrude like a four-month pregnancy.

They had at least, the grace to look abashed and after some mutterings and mumblings the guest stumbled out of the room in search of the bathroom. Fergus fastened his trousers surreptitiously, while Sandra contrived to act as though nothing had happened. Smiling, she handed him the cup of strong coffee.

Like unevenly-balanced scales, her intentions and emotions swung up and down. For the first time in her life she felt malice. Briefly, she allowed it to well up in her soul. It had no direction, no focus. It brewed, it fermented, it bubbled, gave off poisonous vapours within her. She was afraid of these vapours, wanted her old self back again; could not tolerate this invasion of her spirit by malevolent impulses.

She bustled about the house with ferocity, pressing breakfast on the hung-over pair, wiping down cupboards, scrubbing the kitchen sink as if it were part of her daily routine, and all the while the pounding in her upper chest refused to be stilled. Faster and faster it went, rose to her throat, an upheaval of panic. The pins and needles struck her upper lip, fingers became rigid, her breath short and raspy. She remembered the last time – the day Fergus had proposed. What had these two days in common? As the kitchen swam before her, the answer came: she did not know what to do.

No one came to her aid this time. No parental hand guided her to bed. She sat on the cold, tiled floor, back resting against the fridge, as the panic attack passed and her composure returned.

At last she felt able to make her way upstairs to the sewing room. She knelt in front of the what-not, lit the candle and poured some calming Oil of Lavender into the burner. She longed to ask for help, but her mind was vacant. What help could there be? Was there another way she could live? Was there another way she could *be*? How could she become a better person, a better wife? What must she do?

No answers came, yet still she knelt, allowing her mind to pass back to the occasions when the pebbles had been collected: this one from Whitby, from Bridlington, Runswick Bay, Filey. Another from Criccieth, the time they'd gone to Wales for a week because Uncle Archie's mother had been Welsh. The feel of the stones was reassuring. It earthed her; reminded her of her true self. The goldfish swam pointlessly round; Sandra followed its circuits as if therein lay her salvation. She stroked the pheasant feathers, blew off the dust and decided that it was time she bought another wind-chime. Fergus could like it or not. *It was not up to him.*

She did not let this thought linger.

Slowly she regained her spirit; she was once more Sandra Pogson, or Sandra Hardisty the new bride; the unsullied Sandra; the un-awakened one. The Sandra who had felt the cold chill of dawn was firmly locked away.

If only she had thrown away the key.

7

Justine's was closed on Mondays, so on Tuesday at 9am Sandra phoned for an appointment. Business was not booming and there was space the following afternoon. She mentioned something about colour, although she had only the vaguest idea of what she wanted.

She had never messed with her hair the way most girls did in their 'teens. Sandra smiled as she recalled some of the disastrous colourings she'd seen on her classmates: Anna Steeping with purple corkscrew curls; Tracey Brownlow with a snow-white crop above her dark Mediterranean complexion. No. Mr and Mrs Pogson wouldn't have liked Sandra to tart herself up like that. A good shampoo, a trim every three months – these were enough. Mum had permitted a touch of lipstick on special occasions, which were, admittedly, few and far between, but no. There would be nothing garish for their girl. She might be nothing special to look at but she was wholesome, and that's how they wanted to her to stay.

A bit like the granary cobs sold at the bread shop. That was their Sandra.

She was quite excited when she arrived at the hairdresser's. Perhaps, with a new look, Fergus might be tempted to take her out sometimes. Maybe she'd even get to visit his club. He had always implied that she was too young, but if Marianne worked there … why was that?

At five to three she pushed hard on the door of Justine's salon. A second push was needed, the damp weather having swelled the woodwork, and Sandra's entrance was not as smooth as she'd hoped for. Stepping inside, she was welcomed by a cacophony of music from a local radio station, the chatter of female voices, hair-driers blowing, the telephone ringing. The air, warm and moist, smelt of shampoo and perm lotion, female sweat and damp umbrellas. She felt an embracing, superficial warmth, yet to Sandra it felt like love itself. The contrast with the silent, dated smartness of her home made itself felt, but remained unacknowledged.

The girl on the desk was speaking into the handset and noting down an appointment. Sandra waited.

"Hello Sandra. Cut and blow, is it? Oh no, I see you're down for a tint this time. Cheryl's doing you today but she's had to pop home for a minute. Their Ryan's fallen off his bike or something and wouldn't stop crying, so her husband came to fetch her. Sit there for a minute – she'll be back soon."

Nicky went back to the appointments diary. Nicky Elder: she'd been in the year above Sandra at school, another of the faces that had always been familiar. Always there in school assemblies, at sports day, on Sunday school trips … part of the wallpaper of Wraith life.

Sandra settled herself in one of the three upright chairs cushioned in peach and turquoise chintz, which lined the wall beneath the salon's window. Its colour scheme changed every few years but the basic layout had been the same as long as anyone could recall. Six large, rectangular mirrors, evenly spaced, hung on the side walls; in front of each, a chair upholstered in black vinyl. At the rear of the shop, two aquamarine basins provided uncomfortable backwash facilities for the clients. A pair of hair-driers stood adjacent. The peach and turquoise theme, its finish somewhat scuffed and scarred, would be due for replacement as soon as Justine could spare the time. A flounced blind in cream muslin emphasised the femininity of the establishment which had always seemed alien to Sandra, as if she didn't deserve all this prettiness.

Beneath each mirror, small wall-mounted shelves held the tools of the trade: curling tongs, always plugged in, set upside-down in a hole made specifically for the purpose; combs, styling brushes, hairsprays, hand mirror and scissors honed to razor-sharpness.

Round-bottomed girls in tight black trousers, standing in line like dancers at the barre, snipped and chatted to each other and clients at the same time, the twentieth century equivalent of women filling ewers at the well or washing clothes on some Asian river bank. It was as much a social occasion as a job to be done. The radio blared and rattled in the background. Someone was having highlights, the grotesque rubber cap pulled tightly down over her ears while the stylist used a crochet-hook to tease lengths of hair through the holes which punctured the cap. Oblivious to her comical appearance, the middle-aged client laughed and joked as she regaled the room with tales of their Deborah's latest boyfriend and her mother-in-law's dementia.

These people were alive, Sandra realised. Needed. They both gave and received nourishment from the tolerant closeness. She told herself that Fergus needed and nourished her. That's why he married her.

She knew it was a lie.

These women were involved and busy; they loved one another for this hour or two, whether they liked them elsewhere or not. They touched, they brushed, pressed fingertips firmly into scalps as they shampooed. They sniffed and stroked and twirled and tweaked, gauged expressions in the mirror and made adjustments accordingly. They were *in tune.* Sandra felt that she had never been *in tune* with anyone.

The door opened and she looked up, expecting to see the errant Cheryl returning. Instead, she was reminded that Justine's was no longer a unisex establishment as Simon Fownhope entered, had a brief word with Nicky at the desk, and sat down to wait his turn. The local youths tended to drop in on the off-chance and were usually willing to hang about, waiting for a lull in the main business of the salon.

Seventeen just the other day, Simon had reached that stage in his development where even his mother had to start calling him a young man rather than a boy. The gangly, spotty fifteen-year-old of two years ago had started to fill out and need a more regular shave. His shoulders were broadening, his voice deepening, but his composure was not yet that of a man. Sandra could sense it as he took the seat next to hers. His eyes were open but he did not see. Self-consciousness washed over him. Despite having sisters, in such overtly feminine surroundings he wished he could dis-appear into himself. Yet he desperately needed a trim – his Mam had sent him, with instructions not to go home until he looked decent. And Slaughter Slater, the men's barber in the next village, was on a two-week cruise in the Caribbean.

'Must pay well, this hair-cutting lark,' he thought. Another possible career option, maybe.

It was several minutes before Simon realised that Sandra Hardisty was also waiting.

She leafed through a hairstyles magazine, searching half-heartedly for something – anything that might look good on *her.* The problem was that none of the models had mousy hair and a lumpen body. Why *was* that? Were the magazine's editors trying to make the readers feel bad about themselves? It wasn't fair … or did they just not realise?

She began to feel uncomfortable at Simon's proximity. It was hard to concentrate on the photos. A strange sensation provoked her body, as if an electric current were passing gently through it. She became pleasantly aware of her own heartbeat but did not allow herself to look up from the magazine until she heard his voice.

"Sandra! Didn't realise it was you. It's good to see you. How're you doing, then?"

Sandra may have been inexperienced, but she realised that as Yorkshire lads' chat-up lines go, this was pretty strong stuff. The chatter in the salon seemed to hush, as all waited on her reply.

It was widely known that Sandra Pogson had married that middle-aged widower of Enid Hardisty. Not much was said, but tacitly most thought it was a rum do, a queer carry-on. They were good-hearted women, in the main, but couldn't resist a bit of eavesdropping.

"Oh, not so bad," was the expected reply, duly delivered. "Just feeling a bit low. Maybe a new hairstyle will cheer me up."

Simon's face sobered. He ran his hands through his own hair as if to say, "Me too." His eyes lifted to meet hers and share her sorrow. He understood, but what could he do?

For the merest flick of time, Sandra felt in tune.

"Will you be going out tonight then, to show off your new image?" he smiled. "Is your husband taking you somewhere special?"

"Oh, I don't think so. He works most evenings so we don't get out much."

"A bit dull for you though, isn't it? Isn't it lonely in that big house?"

He was pushing it now, anxious to make the most of a rare opportunity. "Do you have your friends round, like?"

"Not really," she said softly, "although he did bring Marianne Reid home the other night for a bit of company."

"He brought *her* home, did he?" A note of disbelief (or was it indignation?) made his voice rise. Beneath his breath, he couldn't help adding, "The bastard."

Sandra was nonplussed. Had she heard correctly? What could Simon mean? She was too embarrassed to ask.

"He wanted to give me some company of my own age. It was a really kind idea, but …"

As she heard herself speak, she knew she didn't believe the words. She knew Simon didn't believe them, either.

"Marianne works for Fergus," she went on. "I'm not sure what job she does." Her voice was brittle.

"No, and I wouldn't be too keen to find out."

Simon instantly regretted his frankness. Changing the subject, he told her about a local band that practised in the back room of the Dog and Pullet. Had Sandra heard them? All its members had been to their school and they'd be performing in the pub on Saturday night. Simon and his mates would be there … in fact a load of Sandra's old classmates too. Why didn't she come along? No need to ask – just turn up. There was bound to be someone she knew and even the chance of a lift home if she needed one. Surely her husband wouldn't object? He would be pleased that she'd found something to do while he was at work.

Sandra thanked him soberly.

"It's not really my scene. Besides, it's my birthday on Saturday and I'm not sure what Fergus has planned for us."

They both knew she was lying.

Her eyes lowered, her face flushed. A tension yoked them, a tension of understanding, a sameness of vision. They could not explain or articulate the feeling; there was just a silent acknowledgement of the bond between them.

The salon door burst open, a gust of wet air blew in, followed by a damp but cheery Cheryl.

"Men! You can't leave them for five minutes. He was

supposed to be looking after the kids today while mi Mam's out shopping, so he's only let our Ryan have a ride on his bike. I ask you! The kid's only seven … on a man's bike! So of course, he falls off and breaks his front tooth, doesn't he? Lucky for him it's a baby tooth – due to come out soon anyway. But he screamed as if his head had come off!"

And so Cheryl chattered away as she led Sandra to a chair in front of a mirror, fingered her hair and began talking highlights, colours, tints permanent or semi-permanent.

They decided on something semi-permanent in Golden Chestnut, "Just to give it a bit of a lift," as Cheryl said.

Sandra gave herself up to the new experience, bathing in the feminine trivia which the salon represented. Yet was it trivial? She pushed away fear; fear that Mum would think the conversations were unsuitable for Sandra's ears and purse her lips disapprovingly. She reminded herself that Mum need never know. Probably, *would never* know. Sandra kept quiet, listening.

Forty minutes later came the moment of truth when the chemicals were washed off and choice of cut was discussed. Mum had always made the decision before, and there was nothing in the style catalogue that seemed to fit the bill for someone like herself, she thought. What if she'd arrived for her Saturday job at the bread shop looking like some of the models in the magazines? Wistfully, she realised how much she missed that little job, but as Fergus had said, she had no need of the money and if was only fair that some other, less fortunate young girl should have the chance to earn a bit of cash. It *had* been quite tiring and her legs ached by the end of the day. Of course Fergus was right. She did miss talking to people, though.

Her mind was not really on Cheryl's advice. She nodded from time to time and agreed in a daydream, for Simon Fownhope was being attended to in the chair next to hers.

Justine herself, the salon's thirty-something owner, had squeezed him in between an eyebrow tint and a child's trim. Her fingers ran through the fair, silky strands which hung from a central parting in the 'curtains' style currently fashionable among boys of a certain age. Sandra could only catch the odd word but heard the number three mentioned; maybe a bus he was planning to catch?

It looked as though Simon's hair felt nice, the way Justine was running her fingers through it, folding it this way and that across his head. Sandra tried to imagine what it would feel like. Then she imagined doing the same thing to Fergus, like Marianne had done on Saturday night. The first thought gave her a warm glow that felt a little bit naughty, whereas the second held no attraction at all. She mustn't allow herself to think it would be unpleasant. That would be disloyal.

Such thoughts were not worthy of her.

Cheryl snipped and styled with practised dexterity, seemingly with a firm idea of what she meant to do to Sandra's image. All the while she kept up a barrage of questions and observations, variations on themes used every day of her working life.

"Have you had your holidays yet? Isn't the weather awful? Did you see that accident on the A19? Has Sally Maycock had her baby yet? Her mum's a friend of your mum's, isn't she? Our Donna's expecting next month but she's got blood pressure so they've taken her in for bed-rest. My Gran died last month … it's terrible in them homes, isn't it? Mind you, they were lovely to her at The Spinney. It's a lot better than most of them …"

On and on she prattled, Sandra hearing but not listening. Instead, she revelled in the light, deft touch, the physical contact, comforting, but not sexual, like a mother's caress.

It soothed and warmed her, made her feel human, part of society. Until now, always the odd one out; here, now, she felt included and whole.

The pile of Golden Chestnut hair on the floor grew deeper without her noticing. From time to time, the work experience girl swept a desultory brush around Cheryl's feet. Simon got up to leave, bent in her direction and said a quiet "Cheerio." Sandra stiffly turned her head, her eyes widening in surprise. The soft, fair locks were gone; in their place a shorn head befitting a paratrooper. The boyish good looks were transformed into a harder manliness. When he reached home, his mother would weep at the final disappearance of her 'little lad'. There was no doubt now that here stood a man. Still a little ungainly, perhaps, the nose too big for the face, but he had the makings of a handsome chap.

The surprise must have shown on her face, but Simon forestalled her response with,

"You had the same idea as me, then? Your old man's in for a shock when you get home. I think it'll look great, though. See you!" He waved his hand awkwardly as the door closed behind him.

For the first time, Sandra noticed her image in the mirror and was silenced. Cheryl's vision for her had been radical. The Golden Chestnut had been left on just a touch longer than the manufacturers recommended, leaving the hair more golden than chestnut. That alone was quite startling to a girl who had always been plain mousy, but the cut took Sandra's breath away. Nowhere on her head was there a strand more than four centimetres long. It clung closely to her head, brushed forward to fringe her face in feathery wisps; was shaped around the rather pretty ears, trimmed close to the nape of a comely neck.

She could barely recognise herself; wasn't sure if she like the transformation. She looked like a stranger but stared at the reflection, seeking out her own identity. It was a bit drastic, she had to say, but actually, she felt a current of … was it excitement? Yes. A shiver ran down her spine. Sandra could not suppress a smile.

Cheryl's eyes caught hers in the mirror

"What do you think?" Confident in her own skills, she added, "I think it looks great. It really suits you."

The looks and murmurs from the other clients concurred. They were glad to see 'that poor lass' taking a pride in herself. The near-tangible chemistry between Sandra Hardisty and the Fownhope boy (*such a lovely lad*') had earlier set off a chain of winks, smiles and nudges from under the driers. Not one of the women, whether twenty or eighty, would blame the girl for fancying any man who was *not* Fergus Hardisty, although it would take more than a new hairdo for Sandra's life to change. After the smiles, their eyes exchanged glances of sorrow. The man's predilections were common knowledge: Sandra's future was unlikely to be a happy one. No words were spoken. Unheard within the salon, malevolent supplications were sent skywards, for they wished no harm to befall the girl.

Sandra was not used to being the centre of attention. Colouring slightly, she dared a smile, catching the eyes of the old ladies under the driers as she glanced around the salon. A shiver of pleasure ran down her spine. Cheryl applied a few finishing touches, a quick squirt of hairspray and untied the protective cape.

"Oh, it looks lovely! He'll have to keep his eyes on you now, Sandra!" Someone even dared to suggest, "There'll be plenty of lads after you now!"

She made her way to the desk to pay feeling light, free, chilly about the ears and even liberated, as if this were a new beginning.

The beginning of what, she could not imagine.

She gave the door an extra tug on the way out. The rain had slowed to a fine drizzle; people had made up their minds that this was as good as it was going to get, stopped sheltering in shop doorways and gone about their business.

Sandra's car, a Mini given to her as a wedding present by Fergus and rarely used (for she had nowhere to go), was parked a hundred metres down the street. She walked towards it slowly, reluctant to re-enter her world of domestic isolation. The car would transport her from one set of realities to another. She acknowledged that she was happier in the High Street realities of superficial chat and human interaction than in her lifeless, loveless home.

She was beginning to understand that her home was both these things. Perhaps it was her fault; she had not brought the youthful gaiety and vigour that Fergus had expected and wanted in a wife. She did not yet ask *herself* what she had expected or wanted in a husband.

She slipped the car key into the lock. "Let's have a look, then."

Simon had waited. She flushed with pleasure —or was it embarrassment?

She *was* a married woman, after all.

Nevertheless, Sandra turned her head this way and that, posing in a way that was quite foreign to her, smiling happily. It was quite nice to be admired, she discovered.

"What do you think of mine, then?" the young man asked." "I don't know what my mam's going to say – she'll probably throw me out."

Without a thought, the retort bounced back.

"Well, you can come and stop with me if she does."

Sandra coloured a deeper pink. What had come over her? She hardly knew the lad. Simon took it in his stride. He looked her in the eye.

"I'll remember that. If Fergus can bring his tarts home,

then I guess you're entitled to have a visitor of your own now and then."

Sharply, he turned on his heel and walked away.

Sandra was dumbfounded. His tarts? There had only been Marianne, an old school friend. Fergus had been trying to please his wife. The boy was crazy and that's all he was, she reminded herself, a boy. He must have some mad idea about Fergus – or Marianne – or about them both. Maybe Simon had a crush on Marianne (and who could blame him?). Perhaps he'd been jealous when she was mentioned in the same breath as Fergus, earlier. Yes, that was it; the silly boy. She breathed more easily, determined not to let this misunderstanding spoil the pleasure she'd felt at her new look … and at Simon's admiration. Driving home, she tried not to dwell on the boy's choice of vocabulary: tarts?

Mum and Dad had occasionally used a similar expression to show disapproval of some young woman's mode of dress: "Ooh, she looked very tarty, with all that makeup and a skirt nearly showing her backside."

So was a tart someone who wore short skirts and lots of makeup?

Her last Christmas at school, some of the prefects had wanted to put decorations up in the Common Room, "Just to tart it up; a bit," someone had said. Makeup and Christmas trimmings were both forms of decoration, and there was no doubt that Marianne was very decorative. But at the bread shop they'd sold a whole variety of tarts: apple, blackcurrant, and strawberry … lots of different sorts. She couldn't quite see the connection there.

She had even, once, heard Uncle Archie us the word in yet another way when he'd bitten into an apple picked straight from the tree at Mulberry Avenue, when Uncle was still well and before her marriage – although she felt certain that Fergus was there at the time. Uncle had bitten into the fruit and pulled a face.

"Ugh! It's a bit tart!"

Fergus had laughed.

"It'd suit me then. Nothing I like better than a bit of tart." Isn't that what he'd said?

Uncle Archie had shaken with suppressed giggles and whispered something like,

"You'd better not say anything like that in this house."

Nodding towards Sandra, he'd added, "More likely to get a wholemeal loaf."

"Better for my health but not as tasty."

Isn't that what Fergus had said as he turned away?

She hadn't understood at the time, nor cared much. She still didn't understand, but was beginning to care. It was her duty to please her husband, but would he prefer a tart or that wholemeal loaf he'd mentioned? The fruit in the garden was ready for picking – she'd choose the sharp-tasting Bramley apples – and make a tart. Her mother would have called it a pie. Sandra planned to miss out most of the sugar so the sour taste remained. Fergus would be pleased with her. Next time, she'd look up how to make a wholemeal loaf. That would be better for Fergus's health and he was bound to be grateful.

She smiled to herself as she steered the car towards Mulberry Avenue.

Visiting home had become a weekly ritual. She enjoyed it with only a little reserve. Deep within her, questions waited to be asked. Why had Mum been so keen to see her married to Fergus? Why hadn't Dad made more of a fuss? She was sure, now, that he had been a reluctant party to the marriage. Did her parents ever wonder if she was happy? Why did she have no friends?

She could not see herself asking these questions outright. The relationship between parents and child, though fond, did not allow examination of motives or emotional need, being based more on practical realities, with Dad willingly acting as a taxi-service when Sandra needed it, or fixing anything that needed fixing. Mum cleaned the house relentlessly, baked expertly for every school gala, Christmas party and any other function requiring buns. Every necessary study guide, thesaurus, cookery apron and art folder was provided as soon as asked for, with apologies for not having thought of it sooner. There was no need for outsiders. No need for swimming clubs or Brownies, or the intense girly closeness of Best Friends. No sharing of secrets and confidences on experimental trips to shopping malls or theme parks.

For Sandra, fun had been a nice drive in the country with her parents and Uncle Archie; a game of Scrabble to improve her spelling or playing with next door's kittens – of which there had been many. She'd enjoyed the hockey matches but never lingered in the changing rooms after the game.

The classroom chatter did not include her. No one wanted to hear about Uncle Archie's in-growing toe-nail and how he had moaned all the way to Whitby. If they'd thought about it at all, her classmates would have told Sandra: "Get a life!"

Malcolm and Pamela's watchfulness had kept their daughter safe, protected and intact. Then, suddenly, Miss Mousy herself had vaulted over the heads of her peers and landed in the pit of matrimony ahead of them all. Her peers stood back aghast, not knowing how to approach her or respond. Sandra had never been in anyone else's league; now she was playing a different game altogether, one whose rules they knew only from observation.

Marianne Reed was playing a different game still, Sandra thought to herself pulling on to her parents' drive, but there was no time to worry about that now.

The back door opened as Pamela appeared, wiping floury hands on her apron. Her mouth dropped open. Her hand lifted to her forehead, tears leapt to her eyes.

"Sandra! What on earth have you done?"

Her daughter's mood swung from ebullient to defensive.

"Don't you like it? They said at Justine's that it looks really good."

The discouragement floored her. She had always needed Mum's approval. Her crumpling face struggled to conceal the disappointment.

"I think Fergus wants me to get a new image."

Maybe, just maybe, she could talk to her mother about Saturday night, get another perspective on things. She looked at her mother expectantly, wanting Pamela to take up the baton of dialogue and run with it, but was disappointed.

"Nonsense, Sandra," her mother insisted. "Fergus chose you because you were unspoilt, not like the other girls with their false eyelashes and forward ways, always thinking about how they look and what they can spend their money on. Has he seen it yet?"

"No. I've only just had it done."

Crestfallen, eyes overflowing now with held-back tears, Sandra felt like the naughty child she had never been.

"Well, if we get down to the chemist's quickly they might be able to sell us something to change the colour back again before he sees it," she twittered on. "I can't imagine what your father will say, but it's taking advantage of Fergus's good nature to expect him to put up with hair like that!"

She wanted to say that Fergus's good nature was not always apparent, but she must be loyal; knew Mum would not countenance disloyalty, yet she tried once more.

""Fergus said I ought to try to make the best of myself," she murmured, eyes downcast. "I was trying to please him."

"Huh! Getting yourself up like a tart won't do that." That word again: tart.

"What do you mean?" Sandra was bewildered.

"You know perfectly well what I mean, my girl. Don't pretend to be all innocence. *You* weren't brought up to doll yourself up and go parading the streets like a clown!"

Like a clown? All she'd done was have her hair tinted and cut short.

"But you have your hair coloured, Mum!"

"That's different. *I* have highlights, to cover up any grey hairs. And they're very subtle, not bright orange … and what about the length? People will think you're … you know…

"People will think I'm what?"

"You know," Pamela whispered the final words through tight lips, "a lesbian."

Sandra was shocked that Mum even knew the word. Were all short-haired women gay? She didn't remember learning that in Sex Education. And why should anyone give a thought to her own sexual orientation? She was a married woman, after all, and it was no one else's business anyway!

For Sandra, this was a revolutionary idea. "What must people think?" had been a regular question in the Pogson household when the failings of other people's children were being discussed. People's opinions mattered and the Pogsons liked to think they were well thought-of

"People can say what they like. It's *my* hair and *I* like it … and other people like it too," Sandra's retort was her boldest yet.

"Like who?"

"Well, Cheryl, who did it, and the other people in the salon at the time."

"They're having you on, let me tell you. You look dreadful," her mother insisted. "You've let yourself down … and me and your father … and Fergus."

This was too much. Even Sandra, compliant as she was, knew that no haircut was *that* important. Puzzlement battled with defiance. Rarely, if ever, had she exchanged harsh words with Mum. Now, when she really needed an understanding ear, she was met with incomprehensible censure. Hurt made her continue when tact might have suggested silence.

"I met Simon Fownhope and he said it looks great."

Pamela's eyebrows shot up.

"Met him? How do you mean, *met* him?"

"I bumped into him in the street." She felt the blood rush to her cheeks.

"That boy's been dragged up." Pamela's tone was scornful. "His mother and father work all hours, and when they're not at work they're at the Working Men's Club. I wouldn't take any notice of what *he* says. He's probably used to his mother and sisters looking like that."

"How do you know?"

Pamela hesitated, as if selecting her response from a range of options.

"Josie told me. She and Ralph go there quite often, and she says the Fownhopes often have quite a lot to drink."

"So it's alright for Josie to go to the Working Men's Club but not for Mr and Mrs Fownhope, is that it?" What had got into Sandra?

"Josie has to go, because Ralph's secretary of the Pigeon Club and they have the committee meetings there. So don't go classing them with people like the Fownhopes."

She was on her high horse now, a position never before adopted in front of her daughter. Why all this fuss all of a sudden? What had got into Mum?

"Well I think Simon's a nice lad. He's always pleasant to me."

It was time for a diversion. Sandra reached into the kitchen cupboard and busied herself with teapot and tea-bags, the milk and the sugar, trying to bring everything back to normal. It was difficult to believe that a visit to the hairdresser could be met with such disapproval.

She did not like ill-feeling; would do anything to avoid it. The fault was her own, for sure. Of course the hair was ridiculous. It was pointless for her to pretend that titivating herself up would make her more attractive. Any attraction she possessed lay in her plain simplicity, her compliance and lack of adornment. She had always known it and must continue to accept it. She had been foolish and vain, trying to be something she could never be. She braced herself to apologise but, handing the cup of tea to her mother, she was alarmed to see tears in Pamela's eyes.

"You've never spoken to me like that before," Mum sniffed. "I thought we got on well together. I'm very hurt that you've shown me so little respect." She dried her eyes on a crumpled tissue.

Sandra didn't know what to say. Wasn't *she* the injured party?

"OK. I'm sorry, Mum. I was just disappointed that you don't like my hair. I thought it looked good … but I suppose you know best."

"Just you remember that, Sandra. I don't know why you need to listen to other people … your father and I know what's best for you and we know what suits you. Fergus probably meant you should learn to cook some new recipes. You know what they say about the way to a man's heart being through his stomach."

She turned away, only partly mollified, and picked up the little red-rimmed mirror. Fetching her handbag from the hall, Pamela took out her powder compact, a lipstick and some pale eye-shadow to repair the damage to her blotchy face. She ran a comb through her hair, replaced the mirror on the tiled window ledge and smiled fixedly.

Ignoring the cup of tea, she announced that she had to pop out to see Josie, calling,

'Drop the catch on your way out!" as she left.

Sandra was left in no doubt that her mother expected her to be gone when she returned. Dully, she poured her tea down the sink, left the house (remembering to drop the catch) and went into the back garden. She examined the windfall apples on the lawn, selecting four that weren't too worm-eaten, and was soon driving away from Mulberry Avenue. If only *she* had a friend to call on. It was nice that Mum could go round to Josie's when she was upset

The only person Sandra wanted to see right now, the only person who would *really* understand, was Simon Fownhope.

*

Josie Maycock lived in an almost identical house just round the corner from the Pogsons, although their gardens adjoined at one point and inside they were very different. The Maycock home was full of untidy youngsters, dogs, cats, gerbils and un-ironed laundry. The two women shared a friendship that denied logic: as if each valued the faults or weaknesses of the other. Josie admired the organised efficiency of Pamela, although not aspiring to it herself. Pamela enjoyed the busy chaos of the Maycock household while never failing to tell Josie how she could do things better. Although they rarely agreed, they bounced off one another and back to their own realms feeling renewed and refreshed. There was no happiness they did not share. When the chips were down, they were there for one another, but not today.

Pamela's knock went unanswered. The dogs barked in their kennels. The doors were locked, the gate fastened. The visitor did not know that a sudden bereavement had called the family away to Leeds.

Pamela's heart sank. This was an occasion when she could *really* do with a chat. The signs of rebellion in Sandra had unnerved her. Josie had told her many times that young people need to rebel.

"Not my Sandra," had been Pamela's self-satisfied reply. Now, it looked as if it *was* happening after all, and she needed listening ear. Swallowing her disappointment, she returned home, disconsolate and aware that she must seek some other kind of remedy.

Hard labour was the next best therapy to talking to Josie. Pamela's kitchen was normally spotless and today was no exception, although the scones she'd been in the process of making on Sandra's arrival remained unfinished. She squeezed together the gobbets of dough and pressing it out on a floured board before cutting it into rounds. These, she placed on a greased tray in a medium oven, which had been heating up for too long. Having set the timer to twenty minutes, Pamela set about clearing up the mess, wiping the worktops and washing utensils. The floor needed cleaning again: she'd spilt flour and dough in her fluster. She would sweep it by hand and give it a good scrub, to relieve her stress.

Pamela was not used to emotional upset; so ordered was her life that it was not given house-room. Taken by this surprise hurt she was thrown, unable to cope. It wasn't just Sandra's hair, although that was bad enough, but her daughter was showing signs of thinking for herself – and her mother did not like that idea. Following Fergus's wishes – that was OK, because Fergus was of the same generation as Pam and Malcolm and would have similar morals and expectations, she assumed. The Pogsons had not spent the best part of twenty years protecting Sandra from modern corruption to have it all undone by some slip of a girl in a hairdressing salon.

And Simon Fownhope! This really stuck in her craw. He was the youngest of a big and boisterous family, known about the town for all sorts of reasons. They were hearty, cheery, disorganised and loud, yet well-liked by many.

The many did not include Pamela Pogson, though she would never have admitted to *disliking* anyone.

The floor was soon clean but Pamela had still not worked out her temper. A strong smell of burning told her the scones were overdone. Although they were removed from the oven in time to prevent total incineration, the quality was not up to her usual standard and she was annoyed with herself. The crumbs that had fallen to the floor of the oven were burnt to black dots, making the cooker itself smelly and gritty. It must be cleaned thoroughly.

Half an hour later, the oven had cooled enough for this to be possible. She gathered together the pink rubber gloves to protect her hands; old cloths, a bucket of water, newspaper spread on the floor to protect the vinyl and a new can of spray-on oven cleaner. The sink was filled with a solution of washing soda and water as hot as could be tolerated. Into this, Pamela tipped the wire shelves from the oven. She sprayed the inside thickly and left it for the chemicals to take effect while she scrubbed away at the shelves, intent on returning them to the pristine brightness she enjoyed. As she scrubbed, she fretted and fumed about the Fownhopes. How was it that they could be so popular, when it was obviously they'd let their kids run wild? How could they seem so cheerful, when everyone knew that money must be tight and the youngsters spent it like water?

Bob Fownhope would have had a much easier carry-on if he'd married *her*. She would have said yes, even though they'd only been eighteen at the time. Only Josie knew that

Bob was the only person Pamela had ever been in love with. She loved Malcolm, sure, but she had never been *in love* with him, never experienced that thrill of pleasure when he touched her, never laid awake at night at night re-living private moments of passion. Not like she had with Bob, all those years ago.

But he never asked her. They'd had a few dates, some Sunday afternoon walks, and then he'd gone away, into the army for his Basic Training. He was soon back – army discipline and Bob did not get on – but not back to Pamela. She had waited and hoped for a while, but soon the rumours reached her that he was going out with Doreen Hogarth; then that she was pregnant; then that they were married. Hurt and disappointed, Pamela got on with her life, but she had never forgotten and she had never fallen for anyone else in that way.

In a small town like Wraith it is possible to follow the details of another person's life from a short distance, rarely impinging on their space or awareness, following mostly through gossip and observation. Thus it was with Pamela and the Fownhopes. She knew that there were five young ones, four girls and, after a gap of eight or nine years, Simon, who was allowed to do pretty much as he liked. The girls dressed like God-knows-what, had hair like birds' nests, skirts revealing all they'd got. They were pretty girls though, slim and shapely, with long legs and slender waists. They'd all left school as soon as they could. Got jobs in shops or offices locally; took their mum shopping when they had a day off.

Some of the clothes Doreen Hogarth wore looked shoddy. Pamela was sure they came from charity shops, and they were usually styled for a much younger woman. The girls all had partners now, to use the modern parlance, and children with names like Makayla and Cassia, Bryce and Tanner.

Pamela had never been able to see the attraction for Bob. There was nothing classy about Doreen and her family. As the years passed, he had sunk to his wife's level, in her opinion. Pamela had never spoken to him since they were both eighteen and had been taken aback to see him driving the limousine at Sandra's wedding. Fergus had taken care of the arrangements.

If Bob had been the father of *her* daughter, the girl would have been beautiful. She would have inherited Pamela's neat frame and regular features, Bob's thick blond hair and disarming smile. Pamela would have kept her on the straight and narrow, passed on all the housewifely skills and basked in the reflected glory of her loveliness. Instead of that, she had spent most of Sandra's life pretending that looks don't matter and that Sandra was all she had ever hoped for in a daughter … which of course, she was. But it would have been nicer to have a pretty girl. Why should that Fownhope woman have four?

Pamela didn't like the idea that Sandra knew Simon. She had a vague recollection that, years ago, there'd been some talk of her daughter seeing off a couple of bullies who'd been harassing the lad but she hadn't taken much notice, not wanting to get involved. She knew him by sight, she thought, but couldn't remember when she'd seen him last. A gangly, spotty youth a couple of years younger than Sandra, she seemed to think. No sophistication or style; would never have been suitable for Sandra; not at all. Thank goodness the marriage to Fergus meant no more worrying about all that.

These thoughts filled her mind as she sprayed, scrubbed and wiped off the detritus inside the oven. She worked with vigour and thoroughness into each corner – it was bound to be a dirty job. She squirted more caustic foam into crevices where stubborn black dots lurked, and scrubbed even harder with the scouring pad. The pink gloves were covered in chemical foam and her head well inside the oven when the phone rang.

She straightened up sharply, cracking her head on the keen edge of the oven rim. Momentarily stunned, she stumbled to her feet, across the wet, slippery floor of the kitchen to pick up the receiver.

It was her friend, sobbing, needing to relay the sad news to Pamela. Josie's father had suffered a stroke, been taken to hospital, where he immediately suffered a second, bigger stroke and died within the hour.

.Josie was in shock.Would Pamela feed cats, walk the dog, see to things for a few hours?

Pamela wept in sympathy. Coming on top of her own upset, tears flowed freely. She fumbled in her pocket for a tissue, found one and used it to wipe her foamy gloves and dry her tears.

The pain was searing. Her head flamed. She screamed, rubbed harder, unable to connect cause and effect. She dropped the receiver, stooped to retrieve it, knocked her temple on the corner of the table; was stunned again and fell to the floor, writhing and rubbing, the agony intensifying with each moment.

Josie's voice rang down the line. "Pam! What's the matter? Answer me please!"

All she heard was a low whine that went on and on, rising to a scream. Eventually, Josie hung up, her mind, used to coping with emergencies, already planning her next course of action.

Returning to Snellington hurt and upset, Sandra sought refuge in the sewing room, the only place in the house that felt like her own. She knelt in front of her what-not, trying to calm herself. This was her first ever real row with Mum. To be dismissed in that way was heart-breaking but it must be her own fault, for Mum was always right. Sandra must make amends. And she would, just as soon as she felt calmer.

She ignored the ringing telephone; another unsolicited sales call, no doubt. It rang insistently. Just as insistently, she refused to answer.

Mum had said she looked like a tart. Simon had called Marianne Fergus's tart. She knew she would never look like Marianne, and she knew that, deep down, she *did* understand. Deep down, she knew the several meanings of the word; deep down, she knew she'd been deluding herself. There *was* no innocent explanation for Marianne's performance on Fergus's knee; she knew that Simon's description was accurate. Deep down, it hurt like hell to admit it. Sandra didn't think she could; would rather not; would turn a blind eye and pretend everything was normal – or as normal as her life had become, because there was no remedy. She had made her bed and so she must lie on it.

Perhaps Fergus wouldn't hate her hair. She was past hoping he might like it. Maybe she should buy something to tone the colour down, as Mum suggested,

Unable to reach a decision and weary from all that had happened, hurt by the contrast between the warm busyness of the salon and the sharp frigidity of her mother, she stretched out on the sofa and fell into a doze.

She dreamt of her wedding day, only it was not her wedding day, it was Simon Fownhope's, and he was marrying a girl who looked like Sandra but wasn't, and the wedding was not in a church but in a field, and Fergus was there, but he wasn't part of it, and yet she knew it was her wedding day, and that it was glorious.

8

In Leeds, Josie Maycock's only viable course of action was to dial 999, tell the operator of the abrupt end to her conversation with Pamela, and return to her grieving.

By the time the message reached police HQ and a patrol vehicle despatched to Mulberry Avenue, twenty minutes had elapsed. It took a further five for the car to reach the house.

The young police constable peered through the kitchen window, saw Pamela curled up on the floor and affected a forced entry. Though conscious, the middle-aged female victim was traumatised, unable to tell what had happened. With difficulty, he pried her hands from her eyes and removed the ball of tissue she grasped so tightly. Its pungent smell gave a hint of what might be wrong.

His First Aid training told him to irrigate the eyes, their livid hue giving more clues as to the nature of the accident. He took a cup from the draining board, filled it with water and poured it in the woman's eyes before summoning an ambulance. He kept on pouring the water, not knowing what else to do. The injured woman kept up a low, constant moan.

They had difficulty in contacting the husband or anyone else connected with the injured woman until, at last, a female receptionists explained that Mr Pogson had been in earlier and would be back later, but right now she did not know his whereabouts and no, she wasn't able to get a message to him.

The patient was incoherent, then sedated. Further efforts must be made to contact her. Phone calls went unanswered A home visit was required.

Soaking in a warm scented bath, Sandra was coming to terms with the loss of her juvenile innocence. It seemed that she had moved from child- to woman-hood, which saddened her at the same time as she recognised its inevitability. Her childlike trust had been lanced like a boil. She would miss that trust in others, would let the poison seep out in an effort to survive.

The phone rang again, and again was ignored. Uncharacteristically, she would put herself first, never mind making the caller feel better about his lousy job. Luxuriating had been foreign to Sandra's nature; now, she resolved to be self-indulgent. Perfumed oils in the bath lured her hidden femininity from the shadows; heightening her understanding of its prospects; leading to exploration of what might lie ahead, of what Sandra might have in common with Marianne Reid and those other women she'd been taught to avoid.

Heat from the water reddened her flesh, swelled it to even greater fullness. Inhaling the aromatic vapour caused a heady, joyous relaxation which encompassed her mind and body as one; made her, for the first time, glad to be a woman. It was not something she had ever thought of before. Somewhere close, she could not tell where, was the secret that eluded her. The secret of what Marianne had but she, Sandra, lacked.

Perhaps it had something to do with her name, for in her

reverie, as she lay there in the cooling water, she was not Sandra but *Cassandra*. This was a true woman, a woman built to the same dimensions as Sandra but who was comfortable, even exultant about her curves and bulges. In her dreams that woman was she; elevated from the primness of her upbringing, she soared into realms of exploration she had not yet dared to imagine

Unconsciously she allowed her hands to explore her body. The guilty embarrassment which swam on the edge of Sandra's awareness was firmly submerged by Cassandra and held under until it drowned. Firm stroked of her hands on her thighs, her belly, her breasts, brought a comfort she had not found in physical contact with another, yet she knew it was not enough. Better than nothing, but not enough. Even as that thought formed, another image filled and overwhelmed it; long, slender, masculine and blond. As yet, a youth, but Cassandra knew that with her, the boy would become a man; that they would grow and explore together, finding possibilities and dimensions as yet unknown. Her head swam, surfaced, gasped for air, dived again and swerved delightedly amongst reefs of golden prospects, glittering bubbles highlighting the rays of sunshine from a world she knew was waiting for her, if only she could find the entrance, the tunnel through from the world she had inhabited until now.

*

The police officer had to ring the bell several times before he heard movement in the house. Seeing the car in the drive, the engine with still a trace of warmth, he was sure there was someone at home

At first, Sandra didn't recognise the sound. Cassandra would not let go, had to be forcibly removed, cast aside to a place of safe-keeping until the time was right for her re-appearance. Sandra climbed from the bath, pulled on the candlewick dressing gown and went downstairs to answer the door. By the time her fingers twisted the lock, Sandra's old self had returned. Her face dropped on seeing the young man in uniform on the doorstep.

He asked to come in; told Sandra of her mother's accident; that her presence was needed; that they had, as yet, not located her father.

Until now, there had been few crises in Sandra's life. The Pogsons had everything so well-ordered that accidents didn't happen, until now. It was all Sandra's fault, of course. That was plain to see. She was surprised the constable didn't arrest her there and then for causing grievous bodily harm by means of coiffure. A daughter had a duty to live up to her parents' expectations and standards. By adopting this ridiculous hairstyle, she had caused her mother irreparable distress and physical harm. The young PC was explaining that the chances of saving Pamela's sight were slim. That was his own opinion, of course; she would have to speak to the doctors at the hospital. Was she able to contact her father?

Why was it that the images she'd seen on the video flashed before her mind's eye? Not just the youth. The boat, the curving bunks, the table covered in maritime charts, the ladder leading up on deck.

The best she could do was to ring Fergus's number. It *was* possible that the two men were together for business purposes. Mentally, she put inverted commas around the word 'business,' but why was it that images seen on the video flashed before her mind's eye? The curving bunk, the maritime charts, the youth, the ladder... all seemed indelibly linked to her husband's 'business affairs' and, by extension, to her father.

His phone was turned off. She left a message, stating the

facts clinically, brief and curt, with instructions to pass on the news to Malcolm and join them at the hospital. That done, she allowed herself to be driven there in the police car.

Somehow, it was not distress she felt, but guilt. She was to blame: definitely and unequivocally. All her actions had led to this catastrophe for her mother: trying to pretend she was something she wasn't. Then, for the first time in her life, Sandra had found the temerity to answer her mother back. She should have known that no good would come of it.

Her perceptions had dimmed again; she was once more the simple, gullible, compliant and lumpen Sandra, with the burden of her body to carry, a perpetual reminder that she must not expect all that came to other women; that she would have to make do with what she was offered, however flawed that might be. So she put away disloyal thoughts about Fergus, turned the key firmly and tucked it away in the recesses of her mind.

At the hospital, she went through the formalities in a daze before, eventually, being taken to see her mother. Behind large eye-patches, the face glowed with an eerie pallor. The brown hair highlighted in gold, usually so neat, was in disarray. A washed-out hospital gown emphasised the deathly, bloodless face. Smudged and stained clothes, worn when cleaning the oven, protruded from a plastic bag by the bed, exuding a smell of chemicals.

It took several seconds to approach her mother with bated breath. No words came from mother or daughter. Sandra reached out to touch Pamela's hand and pressed it gently; spoke quietly. There was no response, save a deep, guttural sigh, a sob that seemed to come from the depths of Pamela's being.

This alone brought tears to Sandra's eyes, for Pamela was not an emotional woman. In truth, she had operated at a superficial level throughout her adulthood, not allowing herself to become involved in the tragedies and crises which afflicted those around her. Even family deaths had been prepared for, expected and efficiently mourned. She was unprepared, now, for this. Most women, by observing and aiding others in their trouble, had rehearsed their own reactions, gone over them in their minds, recognised that each of us copes differently with tragedy and pain. They learn that no way is the right way, no way is the wrong way. We just have to get through it or go under.

Pamela did not believe she could get through this, and nor did Sandra. The distance that had gulfed between them earlier was there still, only now, where before there had been bumpy ground, a chasm yawned. How could the divide ever be crossed? The silence spread like a fog, mystifying the nurse who came to explain the situation to the patient's family. There was no response from mother or daughter, who just sat, not knowing what else to do.

It seemed a long time before they heard the sound of footsteps and the drawing back of a curtain, as Sandra's father and husband drew around the bed. Hushed words, a brief, explanatory visit from a doctor – a young man with a harassed expressions and bags under his eyes – and it was decided that Pamela could go home for the night, to return first thing in the morning when she would be seen by an ophthalmologist. The prospects for her sight were not good. The delay in irrigating the eyes had been too long; the damage caused by the caustic foam so severe that Pamela was unlikely ever to see again. The patient's husband was handed a small bottle of medication that should keep her calm through the night.

In silence, they wheeled her to the parked car. They travelled in Fergus's Mercedes. Brief exchanges established that he and Malcolm had been at a business meeting in the city when Sandra left the message. It was another two hours before he heard the dreadful news and had driven at speed to the hospital. There was a bluff manner about Fergus that made his wife uneasy. Malcolm was silent. She put this down to shock and fear for Pamela. At the back of her mind the thought swam, "What business?" but now was not the time to delve. She had enough to face up to, just now. The patient sat in the front passenger seat, silent except for the intermittent long, low groans and sighs.

Sandra had to face up to her own responsibility for what had happened; how it was that the meticulous, careful Pamela, for the first time in her life, had been careless. Sandra knew nothing of the phone call from Josie.

Although Pamela had been conscious at the hospital, her grasp of events, recalled through a haze of medication, was vague. Even so, she was sufficiently aware to be resentful, even vengeful. Sandra should suffer for what had happened, to teach her a lesson.

And suffer Sandra did. Her hair did not raise a comment from Fergus, although her father said something about not being surprised at her mother's reaction. She knew better than to challenge him … look how answering her mother back had turned out.

Numbly, she endured the journey, almost sorry when it ended and the trappings of normality encompassed them again. They dropped Malcolm and Pamela off first, calling in to survey the scene of the accident, help tidy up, help Pamela into bed and reassure themselves that things would work out. They'd be in touch first thing in the morning.

It was well into the early hours by the time Sandra reached the house in Snellington, exhausted, sad and in need of some comfort to assuage the guilt. She was touched when Fergus poured something into a glass and offered it, quietly.

"You need this to steady your nerves and help you sleep."

His tone was kind and gentle. How she craved a father's comfort. She took the glass and swallowed the contents in one gulp. Her face screwed up, her eyes watered, her throat burnt. She expected a 'Good girl!' and a sweet to take away the taste. Gradually, the sensation turned to warmth, a glow which suffused her blood, warmed her chilled soul and enlivened her deadened mind. She climbed the stairs, debated whether to have another bath, sat on the edge of the bed, undecided. Her mind would not focus on the decision. Overwhelmed by weariness yet not sleepy, Sandra yearned for comfort.

Fergus followed her up. For the first time, he noticed Sandra's hair, sleek and glowing. His wife looked very different from the staid, plain young woman he'd married a year ago. Moving over to the bed, without speaking he stroked her hair gently, as if to soothe. For the first time Sandra did not stiffen at his touch, did not move away or erect defences he could not penetrate. Instead, she inclined her head and leaned it against him as he stood, allowing her emotions to surface, exhaustion and alcohol to mingle and bring tears to the surface. They flowed freely down her face, dampening his trousers. Still he stroked her hair, gradually moving his fingers around her ears, the lobes, her neck, inside her collar, gently, subtly, yet with increasing compulsion and gentle murmuring. Exhausted, Sandra relaxed into the motion, not associating the tenderness with the brusque claiming of marital rights she had come to expect.

Her inhibitions relaxed, an unrecognised sensation crept through her body as Cassandra surfaced and replaced Sandra in her husband's hands. She buried her face in his trousers, felt a reaction, held his buttocks through the fabric, allowing her grief and yearning to surge over her in sobs and howls. She offered no resistance as he pushed her back on the bed, unfastened her blouse, undressed her firmly, even deftly. She had the impression he'd done this many times before. The image of Francine, his daughter, came to her mind. Sandra imagined Fergus the doting father undressing his sleeping child ready for bed. She let herself imagine she was his little girl; be manhandled, unresisting, as he took her to bed.

Sandra and Cassandra were both there, battling for control, Sandra unaware that a battle was in progress; that she was defenceless against the predatory, the voluptuous Cassandra. As Fergus joined her under the sheets, she was empowered by urges that swamped her natural modesty and moved her body sinuously in ways it had never moved before.

"At last!" thought Fergus. "I knew she had it in her." Maybe this was the moment to start her initiation, begin to groom her to satisfy his baser needs and desires in a way that, so far, she could not dream of. Not in her worst nightmares.

As Cassandra gained supremacy, as she surrendered herself to the stirrings of passion, even as she abandoned the fear and the guilt and the worry she knew she ought to be feeling ... as Cassandra was winning, the meek voice of Sandra spoke into the real world,

"It's my fault. My fault that Mum's going blind."

Her body shook as it responded to his caresses. He tried to soothe her, hiding his impatience.

"You're being silly," he whispered. "How could it be your fault? Accidents happen all the time ... can happen to anyone."

He sounded calm, reassuring – fond, even. She could really trust him. He would look after her, help her cope. In his arms, now, she felt safe and secure – maybe *really* loved. Fergus would understand. She had no need to fear him, to spend her days in anxiety lest she displeased him. For here they were, warm and loving, a proper marriage. Her body snuggled closer; her limbs wrapped themselves round his. Fergus would help her. He would know what to do.

He nuzzled her neck, her ears, tried to silence her mouth with his tongue, more urgent in his demands, but the meek voice prevailed even as Cassandra's body yielded.

But the video ... I didn't want her to see the video! I wished it on her."

With one ice-cold movement he pushed himself back, upright and away from her.

"What video?" The voice was iron.

"The one in your study ... with Dad on it ... with that boy," she whispered, gushing with relief.

A smack with the back of his hand lacerated her cheek. His feet touched the floor. He grabbed her arm, lifted her, pushing her back against the bed-head. Already aroused physically, now his temper flared, violence surged to dominate, to reign supreme. As his left hand held her still, his right slapped back and forth across her face, round her head. The left hand began to yank her forward then slam her back. Her head banged against the mahogany surround of the headboard.

Cassandra's spirit had fled at the first sign of trouble. For Sandra, it seemed that a thunderbolt had descended from the sky. Never before struck in anger, she had no instinctive reaction in defence. Passively she allowed her head to rock back and forth with the blows, her upper body to fall whichever way he thrust it. The brandy had befuddled her mind. She could find no reason for what was happening. Seconds passed before it dawned that Fergus was doing this. That she must get away.

She writhed and struggled in horror. The fight or flight instinct at last aroused, she pushed with all her might against the hand that pinned her back. She had never fought or wrestled in play and her husband was in the dominant position. Desperately, she reached out in search of some weapon, anything that might come into her grasp. Her fingers found a bedside glass, still holding some water. The liquid flew into his eyes, caused a momentary hiccup in his assault, but not enough. She rammed the glass at his face.

It caused enough pain to stop the onslaught, enough to take his breath away and allow Sandra to wrench herself free. She struggled to her feet; ran to the bathroom; locked the door behind her.

Shaking violently, gasping horrendously, she fell to the floor, curling up in a ball of terror that blinded her brain. Moments passed. She became aware that her head hurt; felt a trickle of blood down her cheek, eyes closing as they swelled, lips thickening as with a bee sting. What had happened? She did not know. What must she do next? She did not know.

*

Fergus was annoyed with himself. He was not averse to using violence on a woman – in fact it was what he'd hoped to train Sandra to enjoy – but he did like to adhere to certain standards.

For one, he did not like to leave a mark, not where it would show, at any rate. Secondly, he liked his women spirited enough to fight back, not run away and lock themselves in the bathroom. Thirdly, he liked to be sure they wouldn't talk. Fergus had let himself down on all counts.

He had seen blood as Sandra dashed the glass into his face, blood on her face. He had not groomed her for this. She had first been passive, then terrified. He had hoped for a spirited resistance culminating in submission. Nor had he had time to instil in her the need for secrecy. He had an image to maintain; a Mr Clean image. Fergus had a hold over many people in East Yorkshire but, always careful never to be seen as anything other than a *bona fide* business-man: no-one could touch him. His acquisition of Sandra had been part of this image. Her wholesomeness would rub off on him in the minds of any who cared; in the minds of any who had more than a passing interest in the doings of Fergus Hardisty.

This was why the likes of Marianne Reid would not have fitted the bill; not at all. He was titillated by what he termed 'scrubbers', but had not seriously considered taking a woman of that ilk up the aisle. He liked his domestic life to be dully normal, as far as others could tell. He would liven up the bedroom with his little idiosyncrasies just as soon as Sandra had loosened up enough … and as soon as she could be trusted to keep quiet.

Now, he might have blown it, and must decide which tack to take with her. Should he be harsh and domineering to frighten her into submission? Or wheedle himself into her good books by pretending it was the drink, the shock, pressure of work and so on that had caused an uncharacter-istic outburst of which he was abjectly ashamed?

Deciding on the latter course, he crossed the landing, calling her name softly.

"Sandra, forgive me. I've never hit a woman before. I don't know what came over me … I'm so ashamed." He allowed a little sob to break his voice here, squeezed a few tears onto his cheeks for good measure for when she opened the door. "Please, my dear. You mean so much to me. Can't we talk about this face to face?"

The ball of terror on the bathroom floor heard, but did not respond. It seemed to have lost the ability to move.

"It was when I thought of you witnessing that dreadful

stuff on that footage, my mind just snapped. I imagined it was Malcolm, your father, I was hitting, punishing him for the hurt … and the shame … and the insult to you and your mother."

It was plausible, she thought … just about. But Cassandra, peering cautiously out from her hiding place, whispered, "Bollocks."

It would be easy to let Sandra give in, to believe his lies, to go with the flow and pretend it was all a misunderstanding, another dreadful accident. It would be so much easier than facing the truth.

Cassandra knew that she was worth more than that; knew that her life was just beginning and that now was the moment when its true course would be decided. And this time, this time it was Cassandra that screamed through the door.

"Bollocks!"

On the landing, Fergus was stunned; amazed that Sandra even knew the expression; was perplexed that his submissive young wife spurned his apology. He tried once more, struggling to keep his temper in check.

"You're upset, Sandra. Understandably so, after all that's happened. Open the door and let me comfort you, to show that everything will be alright."

She knew she would have to leave the bathroom at some stage without more violence. How was it going to happen?

Her mind was clearing, considering her options. She had to get out of the bathroom, had to get out of the house, but could not return to Mulberry Crescent. Her thoughts raced. What could explain the bruises and thick lips? How could she ever face anyone again?

She grasped the bath-rim, pulled herself up and rinsed her face with cool water. Steadying her breath and voice, she called through the door.

"I'm alright, Fergus. Please don't come near me. I understand that these things happen at times of stress. Just let me go downstairs on my own to pull myself together."

Her voice was measured, reasonable, he thought. Best to humour her … he didn't want the boat rocking any more.

"Very well then, love. I'll just go to bed and you can join me when you're ready." He couldn't resist adding, "We'll carry on as if nothing happened. Don't worry about me being upset … I'll get over it, then we'll carry on from where we left off."

Best to act as though nothing out-of-the-ordinary had occurred.

At the other side of the door, her anger surged. *Him* upset? *She* shouldn't worry? But she must let it ride for now. Hearing him move away down the landing, she waited a while, brushed back her hair, lifted her chin and unlocked the door. She ran down the stairs lightly, silently took her anorak and shoes from under the stairs, took them into the kitchen and closed the door behind her. She made a noise filling the kettle, opening drawers, chinking crockery, making things sound normal.

Ten minutes later, she judged that Fergus would have relaxed his vigilance; perhaps he'd be asleep. Wearing the coat and shoes, she sneaked out of the back door, pulling it to behind her. She walked on the grass, leaping pathways where necessary so as not to make a sound. Soon, she was outside the gate with no clear idea of where she should go, aware only that she could not stay in the house.

She began to walk towards Wraith, only a couple of miles away. Although it was dark there was a bright moon to light her way. She was on edge, but not afraid of the dark. Such simple fears were easy to handle.

9

The air was pleasantly cool, the rain from earlier having left slight moisture on the grass verges without turning them to mud. Mostly she walked on the metalled surface of the lane, only stepping onto grass when a vehicle passed. Quite a few overtook her: several taxis carrying people home to the outlying villages from pubs and restaurants in the bigger towns; shift workers from the power station looming over miles of countryside in every direction.

She had walked about a mile when a sleek white limousine drove by; travelling in the same direction. It pulled up a hundred yards ahead of her. Deep in thought, Sandra did not notice.

Bob Fownhope had been collecting VIP guests from a charity dinner in Helsington, one of the smaller, better-off towns in the county. His work as a limousine chauffeur meant he kept odd hours and had plenty of spare time. It also meant he had a pretty good idea of who should and should not be wandering the by-ways of Yorkshire at midnight. It was unusual to see a female figure, alone, at that time of night, on an unlit road a mile from habitation.

Conscience battled with self-preservation. He ought to offer assistance but was afraid of frightening the woman or being accused of harassment. He pulled up well ahead of her and watched through his rear-view mirror as she drew nearer. It was difficult to be certain in the dark, but he thought … yes, it looked like … it *was*, young Sandra Pogson … Hardisty, as she was now.

He had never spoken properly to the girl, as far as he could remember, though he'd watched her grow up and had probably exchanged a word or two when he'd driven her wedding car. He had faint memories of a brief dalliance with her mother when he was a teenager. An uptight, busy little madam she'd been, he recalled, over-keen to get him to conform and settle down to a life of Saturday nights at the pictures and Sunday tea with her family. So when he went away to the army, he'd made a clean break of it and rarely given her another thought. He still knew her by sight, though, and wouldn't like to think of any harm befalling anyone's daughter. No. He'd better do the chivalrous thing and check that the girl was alright.

Head down, hands in her pockets, Sandra was unconsciously moving out to pass the car when he wound the window down. His steady voice barely penetrated the fog of her mind.

"Are you alright, love? Do you need a lift?"

The girl looked up from the road surface, still not associating the voice with the vehicle.

"It's Sandra Pogson, isn't it? I mean Hardisty. I think you know my son Simon."

He was anxious to reassure her, aware that she could easily be terrified. But something, or someone, had already done that to her. Her face turned towards him. Even in the dark, he could discern the thickened lip and nose, the closed, swollen eye. That didn't look like accidental damage, to him.

Sandra's feet stopped in a reflex action. She was almost relieved, for neither they nor Sandra herself knew where they were going. In a daze, she peered at the face which showed pale in the darkness of the car's interior. It was vaguely familiar. She knew it was someone local, but there was something even more familiar. The certainty increased when the man smiled. It was a wide, open, honest smile that inspired trust, and in her present state she was desperate to believe in it.

"I'm lost," she whispered.

The father in Bob came to the fore. He had four lasses of his own and had seen them in many a predicament. He knew it was best not to ask questions at this stage. Reassurance and a place of safety were the first priorities. He stepped out of the car and gently led Sandra round to the passenger side. As she settled in the luxurious leather seat he leant over, fastened the seatbelt across her and made sure her coat would not get trapped in the door. The memory of doing the same with her wedding gown flitted across the back of his mind.

He decided to take her to his home. Doreen would look after the girl. With any luck, one or other of their own girls would still be there, and Simon would certainly be in soon. There was usually a houseful, even though the four eldest had nominally left home. If it wasn't one who'd had a tiff with her partner, it was another's children who needed babysitting and were spending the night with Gran and Grandad. Bob loved it … never wanted his kids to grow away from him, to leave the area. So what if other kids did well in exams and went away to university? As far as Bob could tell, sending a kid to university was the surest way to fragment the family unit. They rarely came back to live round the corner or down the street from their mams and dads like his girls did. And there was love enough for however many partners and grandchildren they cared to present him and Doreen with. They might live in a scruffy house, their garden more noted for rusty bike frames than prize blooms, but there were few houses in Wraith that echoed more with laughter and tears, affectionate cuffs and warm cuddles, than the Fownhopes'.

The door was always open to passing waifs and strays, too, and it never failed to amaze Bob just how many came and how reluctant they seemed to leave, despite the bedlam. He was utterly confident that Sandra would be made welcome. Some folk might call Doreen common, but she would not bear a grudge.

She'd always known that Bob had been out with Pamela in his youth but, she reasoned, he'd been a handsome lad and most of the girls in town had had their eyes on him. She was proud of her husband and children – loved them avidly and unconditionally; would fight their corner come what may. Nothing and nobody would come between them, and the best way to ensure that was to welcome everyone with open arms, make them all friends of the entire family. That way, no one could injure any family member without hurting and incurring the wrath of the whole lot. Very few took the risk.

By the time Bob's limousine reached his street in the centre of Wraith, it was almost 1am, but lights still shone through the curtains of number seventeen. Sandra was silent, barely aware of where she was or with whom. She sat there while the man bounded up the path and let himself in. He stayed in the hall, keeping his eye on the girl through the open door.

"Doreen!" he called. "I've brought someone home. Can you come here, love?"

A door opened. A woman in her fifties appeared.

"What's up love? Who is it?" She didn't seem particularly curious

"I've just picked up young Sandra Pogson down Long Lane. Looks as if there's been a spot of bother, like, but I haven't asked. I thought she'd be safer here than wandering the lanes."

"Poor lass."

Doreen set off down the narrow path to help the new arrival from the limousine, not saying a word beyond

"Here you are, love. Just come in the living room for a cup of tea and we'll see what's to do." Her words conveyed a certainty that nothing was as bad as it seemed, that it would all come out in the wash, that there was no problem she couldn't get sorted.

Sandra allowed herself to be led up the path into the small, concrete-rendered home. She barked her shins on a baby buggy in the hallway as she was pushed gently forward into the living room.

Living room: yes, this room was to be lived in, there was no doubt of that. She edged in, past a settee covered in worn, red velour on which lay an ancient, black Labrador. The dog's head rested on the lap of a woman in her twenties., her other knee occupied by a chubby infant, wearing only a disposable nappy in need of changing.

The baby's mother sat in an armchair opposite, deftly shuffling a pack of Tarot cards. A third young woman stood behind, absentmindedly brushing her sister's long, blonde hair. Hairdressing magazines lay on a shabby coffee table made of black fibreboard where the carpet had worn thin in front of the gas fire. A budgie hopped list-lessly from perch to cage-floor and back again, occasion-ally tucking its head beneath its wing as if to remind the family it was bed-time. Ignored, a television flickered in the corner. The warm fug of the room smelt of old dog, young women, and wet nappy. The air was exhausted, the occupants almost somnolent.

Sandra's arrival caused barely a flutter. The girl on the settee hutched up a little and woke the dog in a vain attempt to shift it. Doreen steered Sandra to the seat next to the dog. Making no reference to her unexpected arrival, she called out,

"Make an extra cup of tea will you, son?"

Sandra noticed the door leading from the back of the room. It stood ajar. Sounds of crockery and kettles came from the next room. She was shaken out of her stupor when the cropped, blond head of Simon Fownhope appeared round the door jamb.

No one noticed that both Simon and Sandra blushed. Their eyes met fleetingly before he disappeared into the kitchen again. A moment or two later, he re-appeared carrying a plastic tray of steaming mugs, a single teaspoon and a basin encrusted with tea-stained sugar.

"Sugar, Sandra?"

She shook her head. He passed over the mug, delivered the rest of the cups to his family and returned to the kitchen. This was enough to tell his mother that the boy had some kind of feeling for Sandra. She didn't yet know what kind of feeling, but she would find out, or her name wasn't Doreen Fownhope.

Doreen didn't invite Sandra to remove her coat, having noticed that the legs were bare and the heavy breasts untrammelled beneath the anorak. Using her eyes, she signalled to her daughters that they should act casually and eventually, leave for their own homes.

"We've been having a bit of a psychic evening," she smiled. "We sometimes do the cards or hold a séance, for a bit of fun. Bob thinks it's a load of rubbish but that's men for you!"

She laughed lightly in her husband's direction.

"Mum's psychic," said Tracey, the infant's mother. "She doesn't need the cards really, but we generally use them because it helps people believe in what she tells them."

The sister with the hairbrush smiled as she continued the strokes.

"We had a few women round earlier on, for an underwear party. Laugh! You should have seen some of the stuff they were selling. Didn't know whether to wear it or go fishing with it! Have a look what I bought!"

Setting down the brush, she rummaged in a second-hand carrier bag that was stuffed under the chair and brought out an unidentifiable garment of red nylon lace. It seemed to have no purpose that Sandra could think of and looked excruciatingly uncomfortable. She felt herself reddening as she examined the split crotch bound in satin ribbon. What on earth was the purpose of that? Did it mean you didn't need to take your knickers down when you needed a wee? She didn't think so, somehow. But how could this woman … Carly, she thought it was … flaunt such a thing in front of her mother … or even contemplate wearing it? But Mrs Fownhope was laughing like a drain, eyes twinkling with youthful naughtiness. Scarcely befitting a woman of her years, Sandra thought. No wonder Mum thought the Fownhopes were common … although she'd never said so, not exactly. She reminded herself that her mother always knew best.

As this thought sped through her mind, it brought a flashback of earlier that day … probably yesterday by now. Images crowded in upon her: Justine's salon, the little pile of hair upon the floor; the rain; Simon outside the car; her mother baking and raging at the sight of her hair. Then the hospital, and her mother's pain and anguish; Fergus tender; Fergus violent; the blackness of Long Lane and the sumptuous comfort of the limousine. It was too much to take in. Too much for one life, let alone one day.

Her head began to swim. Doreen subtly gestured that her daughters should leave. There was a muddle of coats, of wrapping the baby in blankets and strapping him into the buggy, of Bob and Simon ushering the daughters into the night.

"We'll just walk 'lasses 'ome, love." Bob turned to Sandra. "Our Carly and Tracey both live just along 'street, like, and Hayley lives on one of them flats over the shops on High Street. They've not far to go, but we'll just see they're alright. Doreen will look after you, love, don't you worry."

Doreen stood at the door to wave them off before going upstairs. Sandra heard the sounds of movement, of drawers opening and closing, but gave them no thought.

She had no strength left to worry about anything, though she supposed she ought to be worrying about Fergus. He must surely have noticed her absence by now. Her mind refused to consider what might happen next. She could only go with the flow.

Doreen returned carrying purple velour dressing gown and a pair of pink socks. Without speaking, she laid her hand gently on Sandra's cropped head, letting its weight and energy flow through it into the drained, defeated girl. A flow of great comfort emanated from the gesture, more than Sandra had gained from another individual. In the wake of comfort came reassurance and finally, a wisp of strength. Not enough to use, as yet, but enough to be a faint trace of hope for a different future.

They stood in silence for a few minutes. As the tranquillity seeped into her soul, a trace of the old Sandra cast a look at the incongruous situation, fading as Cassandra began to re-emerge, Warmth; human contact; intimacy: these were Cassandra's virtues. She needed to receive, but was also able to give. Sandra herself had not yet learned to do that. Perhaps she needed to be shown, shown by the Fownhopes how to break through the shell of correctness she had developed. Meant as protection, that correctness had created a barrier to keep her apart from her peers. Part of her hoped that the Fownhopes would reach out to her; teach her to be one of them; show her how to believe that Cassandra within her was not a hussy, a sinner, but another facet of her own humanity.

Doreen unfastened Sandra's anorak and helped her, unresisting, into the dressing gown. Kneeling at her feet she removed the leather shoes and slid on the fluffy pink bed-socks. Taking Sandra by the hand, she led the way upstairs, whispering.

"There's always a spare bed made up. You can sleep in Simon's old room ... he moved into the girls' old one when Hayley moved out. You have a good sleep. We'll see what's to do in the morning."

Ever compliant, Sandra followed into the tiny room above the front door. Its walls were covered with posters of footballers, snow-boarders and motorcyclists doing daring stunts, except for that at the foot of the bed, which was completely taken up with a life-sized pin-up of Pamela Anderson in her red, Baywatch swimsuit. Silicon breasts erupted from a neckline not designed for serious water sports; sinewy thighs akimbo appeared to extend to the model's pelvis. The eyes invited the viewer to indulge.

Tired though she was, Sandra experienced a twinge of jealous embarrassment. If this was Simon's type of girl, there was no chance at all that he'd ever fancy her. But such a thought was unworthy of a married woman like herself ... and Simon *was* only a boy! Tiredness had made her think such thoughts. She was, and ought to be, ashamed of herself.

She was. She was already thoroughly ashamed of herself for all sorts of reasons. One more wouldn't make any difference. Maybe she would just have to accept that she was shameful. Right now, she was too tired to care much.

Doreen turned down the red and white Manchester

United duvet and helped her climb into bed. Instinctively, the mother-figure stroked the child's forehead, turned out the light and tip-toed from the room. Within seconds, Sandra was asleep.

10

It had been decided that first thing next morning, Bob Fownhope would pay a call on his old flame and her husband, Malcolm. Putting two and two together, Bob and Doreen had reached the conclusion that the damage to Sandra's face was not accidental and had been caused, most likely, by another human being. The obvious suspect was the girl's husband, but they had experience enough to be wary of easily-reached conclusions. For all *they* knew, Sandra might have been playing around (and who could blame the girl?) and been roughed up by a lover. Going direct to Fergus Hardisty might not be a good idea.

Swigging the dregs of tea from his cup, Bob winked at his wife as she brushed toast crumbs from his chest.

"She was a bit keen on me, you know, that Pamela. Are you sure you can trust me to go on my own?" He smiled, confident of the answer.

"Play it carefully," Doreen replied "Whatever happened to the poor lass, we've got to be careful not to make things worse for her. She can't stay here forever, but she can stay as long as it takes for her to be safe."

Bob grabbed his anorak and left the house on foot, making as little noise as possible. Mulberry Crescent was at the opposite end of Wraith from the Fownhopes' street, but the town, little more than a village, could be crossed in a quarter of an hour. He'd checked the address in the phone book as a precaution.

Number 43 was easy to find. The curtains were already open. Somehow, he'd expected the Pogsons to be late risers, but the outside of the house was exactly as he might have expected … finicky in its neatness.

Inside, Malcolm and his wife sat together at the dining room table, wondering when the ambulance would arrive. They barely spoke, both still in shock. Pamela was beyond tears. She felt that no blood reached her face, no thoughts made sense in her head. Blindness was all she could contemplate and with that, a corresponding blackness of emotion, the absence of hope, a future beyond comprehension.

Malcolm looked with pity at the wife he had loved, gently and patiently, for twenty years. She had never been one for breakfasting in her dressing-gown. Always well groomed, was Pamela, but today her hair was dishevelled. Broken fingernails showed beneath the cuffs of her mauve housecoat, her bare legs looking scrawny, somehow. Her face was red and puffy behind the two enormous gauze patches covering her eyes. The lines he'd never noticed before were etched to unnatural depths. Around the lips, the livid pallor reminded him of a corpse.

The running chime of the doorbell came as a shock. They were not ready for the ambulance yet, but Pamela barely noticed. Malcolm hesitated a moment before answering, but reasoned that it might be the police … or even Sandra.

The tall figure on the step was not familiar to him … although the face was a local one, he was sure.

"Mr Pogson?" Bob enquired politely. Malcolm nodded.

"My name's Bob Fownhope. You probably don't remember me." Another silent nod. "I wonder if I could have a word … it's about your daughter, Sandra."

Malcolm struggled to make sense of what the other man said but stood aside to allow the man into the hall. He gestured to another door and followed the visitor through.

The sight of a woman wearing two eye-patches was a shock. He could barely recognise her as Pamela, despite having passed her by about town over the years. The cold air of calamity in the room silenced him.

"My wife had an accident yesterday." Malcolm's tone was subdued. "We're in a bit of a mess, so I hope you'll excuse us. Now, what was it you wanted to see me about?"

Bob wrestled in his mind with words that in rehearsal had seemed tactful yet direct. Now they seemed inappropriate. How much should he add to this couple's distress? Was Sandra's plight anything to do with the accident? Had she, in fact, been in the same accident as her mother? This seemed the most likely explanation, he reasoned. That's how he would play it.

"Well … I was driving down Long Lane about one o'clock this morning and I saw a young woman walking by herself. I thought it was peculiar, like, so I kept my eye on her for a while to make sure she was alright. After a while I thought I'd better have a word, then realised it was your Sandra. I drove the wedding car for her, remember? She seemed in a right state and didn't really say anything, as if she were in shock or something."

He was running out of words now, fumbling lest he put his foot in it.

"Any road, I took her back to my house and let our Doreen look after her. She's good in a crisis, is Doreen."

The couple in front of him barely moved a muscle. What on earth was going on? Surely one of them could spare a thought for the girl, even though they were in shock? *They* were adults, after all, while Sandra was hardly more than a child.

He tried again.

"I thought someone might be worried about her ... that's why I'm here. Our Simon knows where she lives with her husband, but I didn't want to go round there in case it was some domestic that was bothering the lass. I reckoned that coming to you was ... the safest thing to do ...?" The plea in his voice went unheeded. He waited for some response.

"Sandra came to the hospital last night when they took her mother in," said Malcolm. She were perfectly OK then." Stress made him lapse into the dialect grammar they had so carefully eradicated from Sandra's speech. "They went home together, her and Fergus. Can't see what could've been the matter. Are you sure they'd not just had a breakdown?"

"It didn't look like that. I certainly didn't see no broken-down car, any road." Bob squirmed inwardly, wishing this task had not fallen to him. "Thing is, like, it looks as though Sandra's had a bit of an accident herself."

At this, Malcolm's heart somersaulted in his ribcage. No, not Sandra as well! Not his little girl, the light of his life? Somehow, he knew that whatever had happened to his daughter was *his* fault. But his blame, his *shame* must be hidden, come what may.

"What sort of accident? I thought you said she was alright."

"Her face is a bit bruised ... thick lip an' all. We haven't asked her what happened ... seems to be in shock ... just put her to bed at about two o'clock this morning and she's still fast on. We – me and Doreen – were hoping you'd know what to do for the best, but I can see now that you've enough on without sorting out your daughter." He paused before asking, "What happened to Pamela, then?"

Pamela bristled behind her eye-patches. To be spoken of as if she wasn't there!; to have her family's crisis witnessed by Bob Fownhope, of all people! To have him see her in this state, in her housecoat at the breakfast table! He probably thought of her as no better than that slatternly wife of his. And how dare he interfere in her family's affairs?

Shock and fear made her defensive. She wanted to scream and shout and cry and bawl; to kick and struggle; to stab and throw and slash and smash; to mangle and strangle, to weep… and be comforted. But she was Pamela, and could do none of those things. Her whalebone control suppressed any coping mechanisms. Fear held them back. She felt only bitterness.

"Tell him we're almost ready to go back to the hospital … waiting for the ambulance to pick me up. Tell him … tell him how I'm in this state because of our Sandra. I don't know why he thinks I should care if she's got a bit of a bruise. It's more than likely it's their lad, Simon they call him, who gave it her in the first place. Yes, I'll bet that's it."

Gathering momentum, Pamela turned towards Bob's voice.

"That's why you're here, isn't it? Pretending to be so kind and helpful, while all the time, you're just trying to protect that wayward son of yours!" She hiccupped away a sob. The flowing tears were absorbed by the eye patches.

Both men were silenced by the outburst. Both straight-forward souls, neither had ever wished harm on another, nor were they any match for Pamela in this frame of mind. They eyed one another warily. What did one know that the other didn't? Or what did both of them *ought* to know that neither of them did? A bond was forged between the two men at that moment, and tacitly they decided to take things gently. No good would come of recriminations. Matters must take their course slowly.

"He's not a bad lad, our Simon," murmured the youth's father. "Beats me how he's grown up so considerate, in a house full of women always bossing him about. I doubt he'd hurt anyone, though, and I've never known him start a fight." He pondered a moment. "There was that time when he was eight or nine, when your Sandra stopped those two other kids beating *him* up. Did she ever tell you about that?" He laughed quietly. "You don't suppose that's what happened this time, do you, but she got socked in the mouth herself?"

The attempt to lighten the atmosphere had no effect. Malcolm didn't know what to think, except that he'd get it in the neck from Pamela if there was any washing of dirty Pogson linen in public, and in front of Bob Fownhope in particular. It would be best to get the man out of the house as quickly as possible. They would return to the Fownhope's house together and have a chat on the way. Settling Pamela into an easy chair, he assured her that he would be back before the ambulance arrived. The radio would kill that dreadful silence. Pamela accepted it all without protest, her spirit of rebellion exhausted. Speedily, the two men left the house.

They walked in silence for the first hundred yards before Malcom broke the silence.

"You'll have to excuse Pamela. She had a terrible accident yesterday. Got a load of oven cleaner in her eyes and the doctors don't think there's much chance she'll be able to see again." He waited for the news to sink in. "She was in the house on her own and seems to have banged her head … knocked herself out somehow … so she didn't wash her eyes out straight away."

"That's awful. No wonder she's in a state. But what's puzzling me is what our Simon's got to do with anything? I know for a fact that he was at home most of last night. He was there when I got back with your Sandra."

Colour rose to his cheeks. He didn't want to ask the obvious. Squeezing out the words through tense jaws, he broached the subject.

"A bit of an odd couple, aren't they, your Sandra and that Fergus Hardisty? You don't think they've had a disagreement and things got out of hand?"

Bob cast a sidelong glance at his companion, waiting.

Dread and shame overwhelmed Malcolm. Please God, why could he not be obliterated from the earth? He knew Fergus Hardisty to be an evil man. Had known it for years; had known it when he'd agreed to trade his beloved daughter for the man's silence.

Now, his acquiescence had brought her physical harm. He did not doubt that the bodily scars would prove as nought when the psychological wounds were assessed. Yet still he was paralysed. Still he must pretend innocence, that all was as it appeared on the surface. What was it in him that refused to admit his sin?

Pins and needles pricked his upper lip. He gasped for breath, tried to speak, recognising the other man's concern, one father to another. If only he could confide – what a relief that would be! But he hardly knew this chap. What would Pamela say if she found out he'd been sharing secrets with someone else? Sharing them with Bob Fownhope in particular?

His agony intensified, reminding him of the brief, sinful joy he had apparently taken in that young boy's body. Never in his fifty years had Malcolm experienced a homosexual attraction for another man – had no such tendencies that he was aware of although, with the sheltered life he'd led, he wasn't sure he'd have recognised such tendencies if they *had* appeared. He was still not clear what had happened. As he walked, flashbacks of that day on Hardisty's boat filled his mind's eye, refusing to be blotted out. A still image, flashed in front of his face by Hardisty at the end of the episode, was the only certainty. Try as he might to remember, Malcolm could only imagine the secret clips his employer claimed to possess and had used as a threat ever since. Yet now, Malcolm felt comforted by Bob's proximity. Oh, God. What was happening to him? Minutes passed before he found his voice and a false bluffness.

"Well, there's nothing wrong there that I know of. Our Sandra's a good girl, and I don't think she'd get into an argument with her husband. She knows who's boss."

Bob's eyebrows rose.

"I've got four daughters and a wife, mate, and I'm telling you, as far as they're concerned no-one bosses them around except their mother, and they only take that when they know she's right. It's a different world from when we were young, y' know. The lasses today want it all, and it seems to me they're quite capable of handling it all, too. They run rings round the lads: things are done and dusted while their fellas are still thinking about it. If your Sandra's not like that, she's a rarity, and she might be finding things tougher than you think."

How desperately Malcolm wanted to confide. Dare he, just a little? He wavered.

"I was a bit uneasy when Fergus told me they were getting married, granted, but Pamela was dead set on it. Our Sandra being on the plain side, Pam thought it might be the best chance she'd get of finding a husband …"

He was ashamed of his own pathetic side-stepping of responsibility.

"She's becoming a bonny lass, I'd say. Any road, it's not looks that hold a man, is it? They might grab his attention in the first place, but any man with sense knows that looks don't last and character does." Bob looked sidelong at his companion, unable to get the measure of the man. "Was Sandra in love with him, would you say?"

Malcolm had not been prepared to dwell on the matter. He'd put all thoughts of love out of his mind. For what *was* love? He wasn't certain that he knew. Was that what he felt for Pamela? Fondness, familiarity, comfortableness, companionship ... he could say for certain that he had found these with his wife. But did he *love* her? Had he ever loved anyone? Loved with a passionate intensity that made his heart pound, his mind race and his body ache?

Yes. He had loved like that once, long ago, but he had loved in vain. It had hurt so much that he'd vowed to make do without it, to settle for the lesser feelings, and he had been content with his lot, by and large; had been content, too, for his daughter to live her life without the pain of passion. She may not thrill to Fergus's touch, but nor would she feel the anguish of rejection – or so he'd believed. But he could not tell Fownhope all this.

He stared at his hands.

"Aye, she seemed to be. I've never heard her say a word against Fergus, any road. He seemed to think the world of her. But you never can tell, can you?"

He turned to face the other man, allowing his eyes to search Bob's for some fellow-feeling, a glimmer of understanding. Instead, they found puzzlement.

They turned a corner, Bob leading the way and indicating the brown gate hanging crookedly on rusty hinges. Malcolm was unable to think straight. He had no plan, no idea what to expect or how to react to what he might find.

*

Hearing the key turn in the lock, Doreen Fownhope pushed Simon into the kitchen, took a final drag on her cigarette, hitched up her Lycra leggings and turned to face the girl's parents. She felt a twinge of insecurity at the thought that Sandra's mother had once been in love with her Bob. Would he make comparisons, she wondered? Did Malcolm Pogson know that his wife had once had the hots for the man who'd been to fetch them? And how had Bob felt when he visited the Pogson home? She'd bet it was a damn sight tidier than his own…but then he'd known she was no tidiness fanatic when he married her, so she wouldn't feel guilty about that. Still, no woman likes to be compared with her husband's old flame.

No woman arrived with the two men It had been taken for granted that the girl would need her mother at such a time of crisis. Heaven knows, Doreen's girls called on her to bail them out often enough. That's what mothers are for. She cast a querying look at her husband, who compared quite favourably with the staid-looking Malcolm, despite being thin on top.

Bob spoke first, explaining Pamela's accident.

"So you see," ventured Malcolm, "I can't be away from her for long. Heaven knows how she'll manage in the house on her own. I can't think straight. And all this about Sandra – I don't understand it." He seemed to crumple, on the edge of collapse.

Without speaking, Doreen led him into the living room. From a cupboard in a mock-mahogany unit she drew a glass and a near-empty bottle of brandy, emptying the dregs into the glass. She handed it to Malcolm, who hesitated before throwing the liquid to the back of his throat. He had no energy to resist.

"We've got to get you sorted out or you'll be no use to anyone," said Doreen. "You're going to have a lot to cope with. You must look after yourself if you're to look after Pamela."

He was struck by her calm common sense. How would Pamela have reacted in the same circumstances? He knew: such a question would not have arisen, for no stranger would be taken into their home at dead of night. No fortifying swig of brandy provided; no quiet understanding, unless maybe for immediate family. Even then, there would have been some tut-tutting, some blame allotted, some effort to stop the mischance or misdemeanour reaching the wider community; but non-judgemental sympathy? No, Malcolm couldn't imagine that.

Simon, who struck Malcolm as a pleasant-looking, ordinary sort of youth, brewed tea as Doreen suggested that someone should wake Sandra.

*

In the little room above the front door, snuggled under the Man U duvet Sandra had slept her soundest sleep since her marriage. Despite the soreness of her face, possessing the ability of the young to lie on a bed like a sleeping policeman across a busy street she had been unconscious within moments of her head touching the pillow. Although her face was red and puffy, the comings and goings downstairs did not stir her, nor penetrate those dreams in which she was once more the stolid but secure virgin child. Cassandra had been put away, for now.

The door creaked irritatingly on its hinges as Malcom pushed it ajar. Sandra didn't stir. His head appeared first, as if anticipating the need to beat a hasty retreat. Seeing the girl, her head facing the wall, his first impression was that he'd entered the wrong room. This bright, cropped, golden-chestnut head did not belong to his Sandra, until he remembered. The hair made the situation worse, somehow. Nothing was as it should be. He shook his spinning head, but what he saw stayed the same.

The body beneath the duvet moved; the head turned to face him. Even now he doubted. One eye was swollen and purple, the upper lip bruised, protruding at twice its normal size above the other, a cut gleaming red and moist where pierced by a tooth. Still she slept, allowing him time to recognise that yes, this *was* his girl, his darling child, whom for so long he had sheltered from harm.

In the end, he had not only failed her: he had delivered her up as a sacrificial victim. There was no doubt in his mind that Fergus Hardisty had done this. The reason didn't matter.

The marriage was over. Sandra would return home. Damn the shame. He knew Pamela would be concerned about that.

Pamela. For a few minutes he'd forgotten her tragedy. How could his carefully-regulated life have fallen apart so quickly? He knew without thinking: Fergus Hardisty. Now it was time for him, Malcolm Pogson, to show what he was made of. Now it was time to make Fergus Hardisty pay.

He reached down to touch the pallid forehead, a gesture of protection, offered too late. One eye opened; the other flickered beneath the swelling.

It took a few moments for Sandra to collect her thoughts. She'd been asleep for eight hours. The events of the previous night flashed through her mind, out of order, jumbled up with the hairdressers' and the row with her mother. Slowly it registered that, standing beside the bed, in this strange room, was the man who had caused her suffering: her father.

She sat up sharply, gasping, almost screaming.

"Get out! Get out! It's your fault. You're evil! Take him away! Help me!"

Three pairs of footsteps sounded on the stairs.

What had they done? Had Malcolm attacked Sandra himself?

Doreen reached the landing to see him backing, horrified, onto the landing. He looked at her, bewildered. All three Fownhopes turned suspicious eyes on him.

"I don't understand," he whimpered. "I saw her at the hospital last night, her and Fergus, and they dropped me off at home. She was alright then." He paused, uncomprehending. "Why is she saying it's my fault? She says I'm evil! Why?" His eyes searched theirs. "God help me!"

The man who had tried all his life to do no harm dropped to his knees on the fraying carpet, weeping prayerful tears.

Bob and Doreen recognised that the tears and anguish were genuine. They knew true grief when they saw it, but there was an explanation somewhere that needed to be found. Bob helped Malcolm downstairs, gesturing to Simon to make himself scarce, but Simon had other ideas.

The three men settled in the comfy chairs, unsure what to say until the youngest tentatively voiced an opinion.

"You know, Sandra has to spend an awful lot of time on her own up at that big house. It must be awful for her."

Malcolm looked up, surprised.

"Surely Fergus is there most of the time?"

"Don't think so. I often see him driving through Wraith at night … she's never in the car with him. I know his work takes him out at night, like, but whenever I go up there cleaning windows in the daytime, she's on her own. Usually, she's just sat staring into space."

Malcolm had never let himself wonder how his daughter spent her time, in case he had to face some uncomfortable truths.

Soft treads on the stairs signalled that Doreen was on her way down. She had comforted the girl in the bed, trying to piece the fragments into some discernible picture. What she'd composed, though close to the truth, seemed fanciful. Her expression was perplexed as she turned to face Malcolm.

"She's saying something about a video … something she saw that had you on it."

"Well … I know that Fergus has a video camera and takes footage of the family …"

Malcolm was puzzled. Thousands of people did the same. Nothing wrong with that, surely?

Doreen hesitated. There was no easy way to say this.

"It was something on a boat, something that shocked her. She wouldn't tell me more than that and when she mentioned it to Fergus, he went wild, hitting her and banging her head against the bed-head. She managed to lock herself in the bathroom. After a while she escaped from the house. That's when Bob spotted her on Long Lane."

The bombshell hit Malcolm in the midriff. His mind's voice repeated,

"Cannon to the right of them, cannon to the left of them, cannon in front of them

Volleyed and thundered…"

Just about the only lines of poetry he knew. They seemed to describe his situation perfectly.

That bastard, Hardisty! He must have fixed up the camera in advance, hidden it somewhere in the cabin before inviting him for a sail on the Humber. Flattered, Malcolm had accepted; had accepted with alacrity. Pleased, truth be known, for the chance to spend an afternoon away from Pamela, doing men's things.

Fergus had been making the boat ready when the youth turned up as if expected, although he was a stranger to Malcolm. They'd had too much to drink; it was hot; they'd stripped off, joking about taking a dip in the estuary, jocular bravado. There'd been some horse-play. The lad was beautiful – like a sculpture from ancient Greece, slender and willowy – reminding him of that girl from long ago. It was all hazy, but somehow the picture in Malcolm's mind always went black at the same point. He had lost himself in admiration for a few, rare moments… but what happened after that? He had no idea.

Now, shame fought with fury in his heart, surging in his breast like a rip-tide. Rising, he pushed his way out of the house and onto the street. He knew not where he was going. He only knew the passionate need for revenge, the exultation of having just cause to commit a murder.

At number 17, Doreen soothed Sandra back to sleep, to blot out the truth until some distance had grown between what was true and what could be borne. Oblivion would be the girl's best friend for now. When the dust had settled, the Fownhopes would have to seek another way forward.

At 43 Mulberry Avenue, Pamela sat in blackness both real and metaphorical. Like her brain, the pain was dulled by medication, but not enough to block out the piercing horror of reality. She had always been concerned with how things look…aesthetically, and mroally. What cruel irony, that she would never again be able to see how things looked. Her fastidious neatness –once her pride and joy– would soon become a necessity if she was ever again to function in her own home or take an independent step outdoors. That was for the future. For now, she sat in a void of time and space, emotionless yet ravaged, calm yet inwardly hysterical. She sat waiting. She did not respond to the doorbell when the ambulance transport arrived and went away again.

Malcolm found her there when he returned around midnight. If asked, he could not have given his whereabouts during his absence, though his feet ached, hunger gnawed his belly and his head pounded. Rage had subsided to simmering shame and the unrequited need for revenge.

Gently, he roused his wife from her stupor and led her up to a bed already warmed by the electric blanket. He drew her to him and soothed with bland reassurances until she slept. He slept also, a sleep bedevilled by swollen lips, black eyes, and a baby in a pram. He dreamt of wedding days, the fear of waking and boats tossing on cold grey waves.

Jolting awake momentarily, he remembered the ambulance, and closed his eyes again. He would deal with that in the morning. He put Sandra's predicament to the back of his mind also: she had rejected him most vehemently. Only able to cope with one thing at a time, he must put Pamela first, for now; Pamela, and then Fergus.

*

Staying with the Fownhopes, Sandra graduated from invalid status to visiting guest, growing to love the barely concealed mess, the shabbiness, the warm banter and spirited tiffs. Never had she known such freedom of expression; the spontaneous communication of thoughts and feelings, however trivial. Joining this family had been like a re-birth, she sometimes thought.

At first, Doreen and Bob were happy to care for her; she was quiet and helpful enough, although they wondered how long the situation would continue. There had been no further sign of her husband or parents, nor had she referred to them since that first morning. Yet money was not plentiful; they wondered how to broach the matter of paying for her board. Times were hard. They couldn't keep feeding an extra mouth. As for Sandra... her brain was unable to cope with this reality. She spoke as if she would always be, one of the family.

Sandra's husband was a wealthy man, everyone knew. He must pay for her keep. Bob would have a think about how best to approach Fergus Hardisty and the matter of money.

11

Over recent years, Francine Hope (nee Hardisty) had seen as little of her father as possible. At thirty, and since her mother's death, Francine could now see her parents through unclouded eyes. This clear view left her in no doubt as to who was to blame for her mother's death. Nothing she could prove; nothing tangible; just a fuller understanding she would have preferred to do without.

Memories of her childhood were good, but things had changed. Dad became distant, mostly absent in spirit though often present in body. Mum had always blamed the money. Once Dad no longer had to worry about paying the mortgage or toeing the line at work, he'd taken on a different persona. Aiming for debonair, in his daughter's opinion he'd hit the target on sleazy. The ridiculous, velvet-collared camel over-coat said it all. He looked like a bookies' runner, whereas in fact he was the owner of several successful racehorses. He knew nothing about horses. It was all about image.

One-by-one, Mum's friends had dropped away after he'd purchased, as a surprise, the big house in Snellington, a couple of miles from Wraith. A couple of miles from every-one they knew. On her infrequent visits to the little town, Enid's former acquaintances would say hello quickly and scurry on, their eyes failing to meet hers in friendship.

Francine's brother, Irwin, had chosen to migrate to Canada with his wife and children at the same time as Francine went away to college. Instead of rallying round to spend more time with his wife, Dad had splashed out on horses, bingo halls and a couple of small casinos. Then there were flash cars and boats. True, he'd hung on to the small motor-sailer on the Humber, hung onto it for old times' sake, he'd claimed, although Enid never went near it. She hated the sea – only had to look at it to start feeling queasy.

After the big win, Dad had money to burn and *he* loved the sea, so in addition to the motor-sailer, he'd picked up a couple of luxury cruisers, berthing one on the Mediterranean coast of France and the other on the Isle of Wight. 'For business purpose', he always claimed vaguely. Checking up on these vessels gave him plenty of excuse to absent himself on a frequent but irregular basis.

When Marianne Reid first telephoned to say her father had not been into the office for some time, Francine was unconcerned.

"That's typical," she told Marianne. "He could be in Saint Tropez or Bembridge. When Mum was alive he'd just disappear for days on end without warning, then pop up again saying he'd been called away on urgent business. Have you asked his new wife?"

That was another thing: why the child bride? He'd made himself look absurd, in Francine's eyes. Gav, Francine's husband, called him a dirty old man.

Gav's mate's daughter played hockey for the school in Wraith, and for a while had been on the same team as Francine's so-called stepmother. Hardisty had been a regular spectator at interschool matches, even *after* his second marriage. Gav's mate's daughter said so.

Francine was not happy to have a stepmother eleven years

her junior. There must be something wrong with Sandra Pogson, she thought.

She and Gav had attended the wedding and stayed just long enough to get on a couple of the group photos. The thought of her father in bed with this girl made Francine heave. She hoped there was no afterlife; no chance that her mother was looking down from heaven at her father's goings-on. Francine missed her mother, especially now, this week, when she'd missed two periods and been full of hope, but this morning the pregnancy test had come back negative.

Marianne's call made Francine even more depressed. When she was small, Dad had been the one she'd turn to after a nightmare or a bad day at school. He'd always had love to give, comforting cuddles and reassurance. She needed his comfort and reassurance today of all days. Maybe she would try to build bridges; give him another chance. Francine was so upset she'd taken a day off, but no one from work would check up on her.

She decided to take a drive east and see if her father was taking a break on the *Young Enid*. At least he'd not renamed the boat *Young Sandra*, as far as she knew. Mum had never been keen on the name. Said it was a bit insulting, as if Dad had stopped caring for her when she reached middle age…

…which he had, actually.

Young Enid was still moored at the same pontoon as always. Francine felt uneasy; this was her first visit for several years and would be the first time she'd seen Dad since the wedding. She hesitated; chose to go for a coffee and maybe a look round the shops. She'd seen his car parked in the usual spot; she knew he was there, so must be on the boat or nearby. Did she *really* want to see him?

What if she *had* been pregnant this time? What if she one day had to explain to her child why its grandmother was younger than its mother? She hadn't thought of that before and couldn't imagine ever doing it.

Bored by the shopping mall, she returned to the marina more angry than depressed. His car was still there. She walked onto pontoon number 4. The *Young Enid* seemed to be bobbing up and down more than the other craft. There was obviously someone on board. The hatch cover was closed but un-padlocked. She drew closer. Saw the open padlock on the cabin roof.

She could hear a grunting sound: regular and strenuous. Flames of fury swept over her. He'd got a woman in there! Having sex! Flames of shame swept over her; flame after flame of shame, of pity for her mother; none for his new wife.

Later, Francine could recall neither getting back to her car nor the drive home. She never told Gav about the trip: he assumed her quietness was due to there being no baby. They were both disappointed. Francine blamed her father.

*

The marina sat in a reclaimed fish dock, approached down cobbled streets of smart, red-brick mews houses which overlooked the water and the rows of leisure craft. Pedestrians approached through a gate with electronic access, installed to keep out the riff-raff.

The Marina Master was a busy man who liked to keep a watchful eye on the moored boats. Some were visited each weekend, like caravans on water, but never went to sea. Others made mysterious trips at peculiar hours ... perhaps for rendezvous at sea for the transfer of illicit cargo. Who could tell? The six-berth motor-sailer *Young Enid* was moored on the fourth pontoon and visited only occasionally, taken to sea rarely. The Marina Master had the idea that she was used to entertain business clients by its owner, who was something in the gambling industry.

Due to a 'flu epidemic, the marina was functioning with a skeleton staff and daily checks on the moored craft were, for a spell, at best perfunctory, and so it was that by the time Young Enid was seen to be listing, her rear deck and cockpit were inundated. Both fore-and aft-cabins and access to the pump were securely padlocked, so an external pump was brought to begin the procedure of emptying the oily sea-water from the hull. It was a slow process and in truth the responsibility of the craft's owner, not the Marina Master. Efforts were made to contact the registered owner at his home address by numerous phone calls and later, by letter. All efforts failed to elicit a response.

Eventually the boat was re-floated, but it was soon obvious there was a problem below the waterline. The vessel must be lifted from the water by crane. Normally this would only be done on the owner's instructions, especially as the crane was booked up weeks in advance, but on this occasion a decision was made to get the job done the following week. Meanwhile, efforts to contact Mr Hardisty would continue.

Six days later the huge, yellow, four-legged crane manoeuvred itself into position over the slipway. *Young Enid* was towed round from pontoon number 4 to be nudged and floated over the massive straps which would cradle it out of the water. Slowly, the straps tautened, taking the strain; lifting, creaking and groaning as the briny water cascaded from the decks in snot-brown gushes. Once lifted, it was carried bizarrely aloft along the street for fifty yards and into the boatyard. Again, the driver positioned his vehicle to perfection before lowering the fibreglass vessel onto the wooden cradling blocks. The straps were removed, the boat left to dry, and the men who had effected the rescue went for a pie and a pint at the pub across the road.

*

Marianne had been elevated to the role of general facto-
tum and P.A. at Uncle Fergus's office, and was quite used to
making small, day-to-day decisions on her own initiative.
Now, members of staff were asking questions. There had
never been a period of five days without him either showing
his face or bombarding each of them with faxes, texts and
phone calls. He didn't like to employ a trained secretary
because they were nosey and, being usually women, could
be guaranteed to gossip. He felt safe with Marianne because
she needed him more than he needed her. Her affection
for him was genuine but had been, at first, a fondness of
convenience. *He* could supply what she needed … and her
requirements became more complex as their involvement
deepened. From Fergus Hardisty's perspective, his niece-of-
some-sort had the virtue of simple efficiency without trou-
blesome initiative.

On the fourth day of silence she'd done her duty and
gone through the motions of tracking him down, first by
phoning his home, then the Bingo Hall near the M62 managed by Malcolm Pogson.

There was no reply at the first and the cashier at the
second had seen neither the owner nor the manager for
four days. More time passed, with no word. When con-
tacted, Hardisty's daughter Francine admitted not having
heard from her father for weeks. To quieten the employees'
concerns, Marianne made an executive decision. She had
Malcolm Pogson's number on file, so would seek out Sandra
via her parents.

She was taken aback by the apathetic response from
Sandra's father, who briefly explained that his wife was ill,
hence his absence from work. No effort to justify his failure
to phone in sick, no apology for inconvenience caused. That

was not like Malcolm Pogson at all! When she asked about his employer's whereabouts, the reply was non-committal. He felt sure that Sandra would be unable to help either, as she was staying with friends for a few days. He hung up, almost rudely, Marianne thought. She didn't like being snubbed.

On the eighth day, Marianne decided it would be appropriate to call the police and report Fergus missing. They were not particularly helpful, since a man is entitled to disappear if he wants to and she had no evidence that he'd come to any harm. She was persuaded to run through the possibilities with them, in the hope of jogging her memory for any clue Fergus might have given.

In listing her employer's assets and interests (with which she was more *au fait* than he'd supposed) she came eventually to the *Young Enid* and acknowledged that, yes, she supposed he could be having a few days on his boat for a break. Odd that he hadn't mentioned it, but it was a lead worth following up.

Marianne decided to give herself some time off and take a trip to the marina. Most of her previous visits had been at night, with Fergus. Under the present circumstances she felt insecure; exposed. Her bravado shrank from sight.

On arrival, she went straight to the office to explain her quest. The woman at the desk recognised the name of Hardisty immediately, having spent many fruitless hours trying to contact the *Young Enid's* owner since the craft's condition had been spotted.

The two women, so very different from one another, looked deeply into each other's eyes. Marianne saw dread and fear in the receptionist's. The receptionist couldn't decide what to deduce from the PA's expression.

The Marina Master was summoned and given the facts. It was his decision to climb aboard the boat, high on its cradle, and affect an entry. A ladder was fetched, a crowbar found, and all interested parties followed him to the boat-yard, where all but he stood around in attitudes of bewilderment. A stout man, short and balding, he climbed the ladder with an air of authority, the crowbar jammed down his belt.

Straddling the step down into the cockpit he drew a deep breath, before applying the tool to the lock. It was barely needed, for the hasp was rusty and the padlock flimsy. He slid back the hatch cover and peered inside.

The stench that mushroomed out knocked him back, paled his face and repelled his stomach. He looked again. Green slime coated bunks, cushions, cooker and floor. Equipment and personal possessions that had floated off shelves lodged damply in incongruous places. Something large and dark occupied the floor-space beside the galley.

It was the body of Fergus Hardisty.

"Call the police. There's a body in there." He sat shaking, on the side seats of the open cockpit. His breath came deep and rumbling.

The small crowd on the ground whimpered in distress, Marianne most visibly moved. The administrator from the office ran to summon the authorities while the rest helped the trembling Marina Master down the ladder. The September sun, which had gently stewed the corpse in its broth of slime, warmed their backs as they huddled away from the stench that swirled in the sea breeze whipping through the boatyard.

The victim was known to have a young wife, who proved difficult to trace. Marianne suggested the police try Mulberry Avenue and, eventually, Sandra's whereabouts were discovered from her parents.

In the early evening, the young constable knocked on the Fownhope's door. Doreen's open face clouded when she saw the uniform. Fear brought her gorge to her mouth. Images of her entire family flashed before her mind's eye. In subdued tones, the constable explained his need to speak to Mrs Hardisty and was ushered into the living room.

Sandra was up and dressed in one of Doreen's jogging suits. It pulled a bit across the chest and was short in the leg, but Sandra was beyond caring what she looked like. She barely raised her eyes when the new arrival came in, until he addressed her.

"Mrs Hardisty?"

Despite having been married for over a year, Sandra had rarely been called by her married name. It seemed alien. When he had caught her attention, the P.C. delivered the sad news in a hushed, nervous voice.

There was no response from the widow. No tears, real or crocodile, ran down her cheeks. No emotion registered on the pale features. Then the officer noticed the bruises on her face ... the lip, the half-closed eye. There seemed to be more to this story than a straightforward sudden death.

Doreen moved forward and took Sandra's hand. At the back of her mind, a still, small voice was asking how the hell she'd got mixed up in this business. She pressed the girl's hand, moved round to look her straight in the eyes before repeating the news. The constable looked at her questioningly. In response, she attempted to explain Sandra's battered appearance.

"Sandra and her husband had a tiff the other night and she came here for a bit of space."

That sounded reasonable enough, although the idea of finding space in this cramped little room struck the constable as ironic. Someone was needed to identify the body. Was Mrs Hardisty up to it?

Doreen didn't think so. Maybe he could ask Fergus's daughter, Francine, who lived in the next town?

"That could be a problem," the officer opined. It would mean involving the North Yorkshire force, whereas the death had occurred in the jurisdiction of East Yorks. Much unnecessary duplication of paperwork would be involved.

With a sigh, the constable took down the necessary details, asked Sandra to keep the station informed of her movements for the time being, and took his relieved leave of the stupefied widow. He tried to put his mind to pleasanter things: his girlfriend, his mates and his tea. By the time he reached the station, he was back in control.

Sandra sat still. She stared ahead, expressionless. Doreen was at a loss. Before this latest twist Sandra had been quiet enough, giving hardly anything away about what had led her to this pass. Only when Simon was about did the girl show any spark of life and, even then, it was more a glint in the eye than anything definable. What must the poor child be feeling now? And where were her parents? The policeman had explained that he'd first called at Mulberry Crescent, so even if Malcolm and Pamela weren't aware of the full extent of the situation, they must realise something bad had happened.

Why didn't the girl scream, or weep, or even laugh? Anything would be better than this blankness. There was nothing to react to, nothing to soothe or get cross with. Doreen had never, in all her experience with youngsters, come across a reaction like this.

"I killed him." The voice, when it came, was quiet but firm.

Doreen gasped; gaped, steadied herself. This must be handled calmly. It was nonsense, of course. "How do you mean, love?" She tried to sound understanding; not over-concerned.

"I killed him."

Nothing more. No movement, no change of expression, still no tears.

"Try to explain what you mean, Sandra. I don't think it's possible that you killed him."

"I killed him." Steadily, insistently, the girl repeated the claim.

After half an hour, she was persuaded to take a nap. Doreen took the opportunity to phone the police station.

It was not possible that Mrs Hardisty had killed her husband, she explained, because Sandra had been at the Fownhope's house since the night of the argument. There had been barely a moment when she was in the house alone. Certainly, someone would have known if Mrs Hardisty taken herself forty miles to the marina.

The officer on the other end of the line took down some notes and agreed to pass the information on. As he did this, someone pointed out that no cause of death had been established, as yet. There were no visible injuries on the corpse, which had been in a rather bloated state, so any speculation was pointless before the post mortem.

A WPC working away at a computer, half-listening to the conversation, floated the idea of poison.

"Nah," scoffed her colleague. She's in fairyland. From what I heard she's round the twist. She'll be making it up!"

"It's a confession. We've got to take it seriously." The WPC resolved to look further into the matter.

When discovered, the body had been laying face-down in a foot of water; the sea had filled half the cabin before the boat was winched out of the marina. There were signs that the body had, in fact, floated around before settling on the bottom.

Marina Master Alec Jessop was certain that the cabin had been securely locked from the outside when he boarded her. Indeed, there were several witnesses who had seen him use the crowbar to break the lock. Here was a puzzle. Jessop sifted his memory. Had he absent-mindedly boarded the craft and made her secure without first checking if anyone was aboard? He knew in his heart of hearts that he hadn't been near the *Young Enid*. In fact, he had of late been somewhat dilatory in his surveillance of all the craft due to money worries and overwork, but he dared not admit to it. The last thing Jessop needed was more stress provoked by inquiries into his work habits. The Ports and Harbour Authority left him to get on with the job, by and large, and that was how he wanted it to stay. He could just about keep his head above water financially, but any meddling with his earnings would ruin him. He stuck to his story about visually inspecting the boats on a daily basis, but not boarding unless he found cause for concern.

The police had no alternative but to interview the widow again. Her 'confession' was put to her verbally. Again, her only comment was,

"I killed him."

A middle-aged DS was on the case. He had little truck with those who sympathised with trauma victims. He believed in straight talking.

"Now listen here, Mrs Hardisty. You say you killed your husband. I say you didn't. And do you want to know why I say that?"

He waited for her to nod.

"Because your husband had a heart attack and drowned. What do you say to that?"

For the first time, as if wrenched from their blankness by his brusqueness, Sandra's eyes lifted and met his.

"I wished him dead."

DS Sykes guffawed. "By God, if every woman who wished her old man dead confessed as soon as he snuffed it, there'd be a queue a mile long outside every cop-shop in the country!"

This was one to tell the lads about.

"I made it happen." Evenly, she maintained her gaze.

He hadn't got the patience for this. There were real crimes out there waiting to be solved. He couldn't waste his time on some nutty lass who just wanted attention. Deciding to take no further action for the time being, he took a hasty leave and sped off back to the station and something more interesting. At the back of his mind remained the puzzle about the padlock on the cabin hatch; he knew he really ought to be following that up.

Ten days after the body was discovered, the post mortem established that Fergus Hardisty had drowned. The deceased had been suffering from an undiagnosed heart condition, and it was likely that he had suffered a heart attack which, although not fatal, had rendered him unconscious. The partial sinking of the *Young Enid* must have occurred soon afterwards, hence his death by drowning.

*

When asked to identify her father's body, Francine Hope refused; couldn't bear the thought. Didn't want to listen to a load of suppositions about how he died. When the police-man said something about exertion bringing on a heart attack, shame flared afresh. She would not let him finish and refused point blank to see the body. Why couldn't her step-mother do it? Gav showed the copper the door hoping the task would not fall to him, which in the end, it did.

Francine was not interested in the results of the post mortem. He was dead. Good riddance to him. At least when Francine and Gav *did* have a child, there would be no need for awkward explanations.

Down at the police station it was noted that both the deceased's wife and his daughter had refused to identify the body. Odd, that, especially with the mystery of the padlock, but the force was understaffed and had more important conundrums to solve.

There had been no murder, so DS Sykes was not interested any more. Probably just the Marina Master finding a boat left unlocked and securing it without checking for persons aboard. It wasn't up to him, Alan Sykes, to get the poor bugger sacked.

Nevertheless, it preyed on Jessop's mind. Bit of a funny coincidence, Hardisty having the heart attack at the same time as the boat sank. Nothing like this had ever happened in his marina before, although the police were no strangers to the place. He like to think he knew what was going on, which berths were occupied and which empty, which faces belonged to which vessel, but he had to admit he'd let things slide. Something shifty could have been happening and he would not, necessarily, have noticed.

Re-playing events in his mind, he stood at last beneath the slowly-drying hull of the *Young Enid*. His expert eyes scanned her fibreglass bottom. Reaching up, he let his fingers slide along the anti-fouling paint which had been applied only months before. All seemed intact.

Eyes flicking from left to right, he moved, head tilted back, towards the stern end of the craft, until he reached the point where the propeller shaft passed through the hull. His fingers prodded, probed and came away tacky. He had found the cause: the stern gland, whose job was to seal the orifice between shaft and hull, had perished. Over a period of days or even weeks, water had been seeping into the bilges. The Hardisty chap often went for a month or more without visiting the boat – ample time for tonnes of water to enter the craft – until it lay low in the water, undetected.

Alec Jessop pondered the scenario. It seemed likely that Hardisty had gone aboard, seen that the craft had taken on water and begun pumping out the bilges. If he was not a fit man (and at fifty, who is?) the exertion could have prompted the heart attack.

Jessop felt happier having found a plausible scenario and chose not to dwell on the padlocked hatch for the time being. There were things on his mind that he ought to have reported. He knew that, sometimes, he'd turned a blind eye which could be construed as dereliction of duty. Until recently, he'd prided himself that few things escaped his notice; that he knew the comings and goings of his marina. He still noticed, but did not, now, always follow up the questions which puzzled him. It had become so hectic. Sometimes, you'd have thought it was some Caribbean holiday island rather than the east coast of England, folk were that keen to get on the water. Not that he'd ever been to the Caribbean, but it *sounded* hot, and a damned sight more inviting than the grey concrete and cold grey estuary that greeted him each day.

There had been that occasion, one busy weekend, when a surprising number of passengers had disembarked from a small motor-sailer. Although it had registered in his mind as an oddity, he had been comfortable with his own unspoken explanation: some folk loved showing off their boats and would glibly invite family and friends aboard for a blow up to the Humber Bridge without caring too much whether the craft was overloaded or not.

Now he *did* dwell on it. He thought there'd been more than one occasion. He had dim memories of six or seven young men being led out through the gates to a waiting white transit van. He screwed up his eyes as he tried to recall the scene. Could he remember which boat they'd disembarked from? Or who let them through the security gate?

No, Jessop couldn't, and to be honest, he didn't want to. Illegal immigration was in the news all the time nowadays, but ... nah! They wouldn't come in via Yorkshire ports, surely? And he wouldn't want to be the one to grass them up either. He had a certain grudging respect for anyone who was prepared to risk life and limb, endure God knows what hardships and awful conditions in search of a better life. He had never known his maternal great-grandfather, but had heard his grandma tell of Jewish migration to the suburbs of Leeds and Manchester in the early years of the twentieth century, fleeing persecution and hardship ... just the same as the poor beggars who were at it nowadays. At least his great-granddad had had family and friends to go to. Even though times were hard, everyone had mucked in. Alec Jessop hoped that any poor sod who had come through his patch without benefit of passport would find support and prosperity, as Great-granddad had done eventually, and not the constant racist harping that seemed so fashionable at the moment.

So he kept quiet, whilst admitting to himself that it was a dirty trade. Those who transported the migrants weren't in it for altruistic reasons, for sure. If the papers were to be believed, the racketeers didn't give a damn who lived or died, just as long as they got paid up front. There were bound to be some grudges built up along the way. A sur-reptitiously-closed padlock could have been pay-back. Alec Jessop would never know, for sure as hell he was not going to start investigating.

Wiping his hands on the seat of his pants, he walked away. He tossed his bald head as if his youthful auburn locks were still in place, took a deep breath, paused and moved on. His eyes focussed on the horizon and allowed the vast, bleak expanse of the incoming Humber tide to wash such thoughts from his mind.

12

The house on Mulberry Crescent was in mourning. The very bricks seemed to weep. For twenty years, no great drama had been acted out within its walls. Like the little family which dwelt within, the building had existed in a state of calm satisfaction, its needs competently catered and cared for. No great swathes of black or red, no chaotic swirls or horrid clashes to set its nerves on edge. Number 43 had enjoyed the peace, seemingly set apart from its neighbours by its own predictability. There had been a small flurry of excitement at Sandra's marriage and her absence was noted, but she'd visited regularly and the house had not felt too bereft.

With the accident, everything changed. In a way, the house had been to blame for Pamela's fall, in that its kitchen floor had taken a long time to dry. Without that disastrous slip, perhaps none of the rest would have followed.

Malcolm perched on a stool in the kitchen. Three weeks had passed since the accident, but he had not yet restored the room to its former neatness. Baked bean cans peered from beneath the lid of the pedal bin; laminate worktops were smeared with gobbets of margarine, marmalade and bacon grease, and pellets of dried carbon from the oven, crushed underfoot and traipsed across the lino-tiled floor, were gradually being transferred to the hall carpet. He felt the mess dragging him down, but was beyond doing anything about it.

During the first week after the discovery of the body, Malcolm used checking up on things at work as an excuse for leaving his wife's bedside from time to time. There were bound to be jobs that needed doing, such as checking the mousetraps or clearing the gutters. He would change into some old clothes he found in the caretaker's room and do his best to keep the place in good order, the former caretaker himself having, as soon as the boss's death was announced, snapped up another position advertised on a card in a newsagent's window.

Marianne, the boss's PA, took it upon herself to close all aspects of the business until further notice, so by the second week, with no work to go to, Malcolm's time was spent tending Pamela with decreasing levels of sympathy or in numbly staring into space. Until now it had been too soon to start processing the upheaval, to understand what had happened: the why, the when and the how. A little earlier he had helped his wife to bath, and dried her hair with the new Murphy-Richards in an effort to restore her dignity. A new satin nightdress with matching negligee – he really had tried to comfort and lighten her mood – and after a soothing

draught of medicine she'd gone back to bed. Now, she slept deeply and noisily for the first time since the accident.

Malcolm missed his daughter. If ever he'd needed her love it was now, but she had rejected him with force, without hesitation or explanation. He was afraid to delve too deeply into her reasons. Knowledge of Hardisty's hold over him was always present, deep in the recesses of his mind, even though he had tried to layer it over with purer things, like a stained sheet shoved under clean linen in an airing cupboard.

Perhaps he ought to try again, to go round to the Fownhope house now. He hadn't thanked them for their kindness to his daughter, nor offered any support, just left them to get on with it. Regretfully, he acknowledged to himself that, had the positions been reversed, he and Pamela would not have given house-room to some stray picked off the street: to do so would have un-tidied the house, disordered their routine, even introduced dissent, heaven forbid! The idea would not have been entertained. That would have been that, but the Pogsons were getting their comeuppance now.

Even Josie had only called round once since the accident. Granted, she was wrapped up in her own loss, had her own family to haul through the turmoil of bereavement and relocation. Malcolm and Pamela had no other friends, no one to offer assistance un-asked for. Even now, in her desperation, Pamela insisted that no outside help should be sought.

Malcolm knew he could not cope alone. Quietly making himself a cup of coffee, he took a handful of biscuits from the barrel-shaped tin, noting that it was now empty. He carried the cup through to the sitting room. No saucer, no coaster on the dusty coffee table to protect the polished surface. His wife's rules were ignored with gentle determination. Squashed sofa cushions, not plumped up in three weeks, blew a fine drift of motes into the sun-warmed air as he sat down. Slowly, he relaxed back, allowed his eyes to close and at last, replayed the melodrama from the moment he'd been told of Pamela's accident. He knew the problem went further back, but he was not yet ready for that.

Fergus had invited him to the boat again. There was some overseas business venture he was involved in, to do with imports, he'd said. Even at the time, Malcolm had been perplexed by the possibilities. His boss claimed to have a variety of businesses but only the bingo parlours were known to Malcolm. He did not want to know more. As far as he was aware, the bingo and gambling business was run on legitimate lines and that was all he cared about. There was no reason for him to poke his nose in any deeper, father-in-law or not.

They had eaten a meal at the boat club, joined by the business acquaintance Fergus wanted him to meet, a foreign chap, East European, perhaps, who gave the impression of having done business with Hardisty before. There had been references to live cargo, minimising red tape, ports of embarkation and entry, but nothing specific that Malcolm could remember. Then Fergus had gone to the Gents and come back looking flustered. It seemed he'd checked the messages on his mobile and read the news of Pamela's accident.

Fergus had ended the meeting immediately, making a separate arrangement to see the foreigner again at the boat next day. He drove Malcolm straight to the hospital, learned what little was known of the circumstances and, eventually, dropped him off at Mulberry Crescent. There was nothing inexplicable there. No light shed on Sandra's outburst against her father.

Malcolm fell into a doze. Flaccid lips purred with each expelled breath. His limbs flopped sideways, twitching from time to time like a dog which dreams of chasing rabbits, then a bigger twitch, a lurch, which woke him in panic and horror. He remembered the words of the Fownhope woman, telling what Sandra had seen: "Something on a boat; something shocking."

His mouth was sour as curdled milk.

It had only happened once. One brief slip, hazy in his

memory, and Hardisty claimed to have it on camera. But how and why had Sandra found out? He, Malcolm, had submitted to all his son-in-law's shady suggestions, had never rocked the boat – literally or metaphorically. Protecting his wife and daughter had been the point of his existence. There could have been no reason for Hardisty to betray his weakness, but betray him he had.

What happened after he'd heard of Sandra's response? He could not remember. Why were there long gaps in his memory? He recalled storming out of the house intent on revenge, but where had he gone? He'd left the Fownhopes' no later than 10am, yet returned to Mulberry Crescent after midnight. His car had not left the garage. What he'd done during those fourteen hours was a mystery.

Rousing himself, he moved back to the kitchen and swilled his face under the cold tap. The towel he found to dry himself smelt rancid. Domestic chores were now his responsibility. It was time to read the instructions on the washing machine. They must be near end of their supply of clean clothes. He'd been wearing pretty much the same things for the past three weeks. Malcolm sniffed his underarms cagily and acknowledged that now was indeed the time to come clean.

With a sense of purpose he went upstairs, quietly emptied the contents of the dirty linen basket onto the bathroom floor and surveyed the pile. Under Pamela's rule it had been regulated with such efficiency that he'd never questioned her methods. He did, however, recall that she would separate the laundry into piles. Based on what? A pair of maroon boxer shorts, turned inside out, rested like a fallen flag at the top of the pile. He noticed a white, satiny label with lots of writing on it, which he read. The numbers and symbols were foreign to him, except for the instruction: Wash dark colours separately.

That was a start. He would make a pile of the dark clothes. Smells of stale body odour, dirty socks, whiffs of deodorant and hairspray alternately repelled and pleased him. What happened to his discarded clothes each night had never been his concern. They'd always just re-appeared, clean and ironed, in his drawers and wardrobe. Now he must take charge of this domestic world. He had let the side down in a big way, but there was no need for the world to know. He, Malcolm, must set about restoring order.

It was not a huge pile: some cotton underpants in autumn fruit colours, his gardening corduroys, Pam's navy blouse and skirt, a deep green dress, and the smart grey trousers he'd worn to the meeting beside the Humber. He thought back. When had he changed them? The beige cords he was wearing looked grubby. They'd certainly been in use for weeks. One by one, he picked up the soiled items, looking for pockets, and was surprised how few there were in Pamela's clothes. He checked his trousers. In those he wore for gardening: a length of hairy green string, a few grains of earth and a handkerchief. The grey ones were next. In the first pocket he found two ten pence pieces; in the second, an unused handkerchief, grimy along its folds. He almost forgot the zipped back pocket. He tugged at the pull, which resisted a little, then slid open. He could feel something papery inside. Fore- and middle-fingers reached in, closed on the slip of paper and drew it out.

Green, with orange bands, each half bearing a single puncture, it was a rail ticket from Wraith station to one near the city on the estuary. A return ticket which, although still joined at the perforations, had clearly been used. Malcolm wanted to be puzzled, wanted not to recognise what it was or why it was in his pocket. He had no recollection of such a journey, but as he held the ticket between two fingers he sensed a return of the murderous anger he felt towards

Hardisty. His memory came up with nothing. He could feel nothing. He dare not examine the print. If the date on the ticket should to be the day after the accident, then it must be assumed that *he* was responsible for the death of his loathsome son-in-law; must be assumed that he, Malcolm Pogson, had clicked the padlock shut. He would have to confess to the murder of Fergus Hardisty or, at the very best, his involuntary manslaughter.

It was best not to know for sure.

The ticket tore easily into tiny fragments. Softly, he carried them downstairs, found matches in a kitchen drawer, a saucer. He ignited the shreds and watched them smoulder. When all was turned to ash, he held the saucer under the fierce cold tap and washed it clean. Now, he would never know; nor would anyone else.

Lighter now, he leapt back upstairs, scooped up the pile of dark colours and returned to the kitchen. They fitted easily into the machine. Detergent, he found in a cupboard, together with something called fabric conditioner. He ignored that, poured blue-speckled powder straight on top of the clothes, slammed shut the door and studied the symbols on the dial. Choosing one, he pressed START. As the machine slurped into life he stood up from the floor, feeling a much happier man.

This rejuvenation sent him once again up to the bedroom, to seek out clean garments. Pamela stirred at the slide of the wardrobe door. He bent close, stroking her hair reassuringly.

"It's only me. I'll be five minutes in the shower and then I think I'll go for a walk. You'll be fine for an hour." He didn't ask. He told her. A new departure, that.

Feeling fresh and like a prisoner on release, he strode down the path onto Mulberry Crescent. The gate clicked shut behind him. He felt his throat tighten with something akin to gladness. A fresh breeze chilled his cheeks and brought a sparkle to his eyes with its hint of an early autumn. He thrust back his shoulders, raised his chin and prepared to face the world.

*

Doreen was just drawing back the curtains when he reached the Fownhope home. Although the family had been up for some time, it was their habit to spend the breakfast hours around the kitchen table, winding themselves up slowly to the business of the day. Doreen had been expecting Malcolm, not today, necessarily, but soon, and had been trying to prepare Sandra for the moment. The girl had given little away, but Doreen had pieced together a story that was something like the truth.

Not much shocked her, except perhaps restraint. This she found difficult to deal with…would rather any day sort things out with an argument than with polite hedging, but she recognised that her ways were not the Pogsons' ways. When she opened the door to Sandra's father, she bit back the accusations that inevitably rose to her tongue and invited him to sit down. Sandra was stroking the cat in the kitchen when Doreen announced,

"Your dad's come."

Sandra's hand stopped mid-stroke, her breath halting momentarily. She looked at Doreen with trepidation. The older woman laid her hand on the girl's head in a calming, gesture

"I think you ought to see him," she said softly. "Just listen to what he has to say. I'm here. Nothing bad will happen."

Wordlessly, Sandra rose from the table, tightened the cord of her borrowed dressing gown around her waist, and walked through to the other room.

Malcolm half-rose from the sofa, but held back from crossing the room to embrace his daughter. She looked different; older – haggard, even, if that was possible in one so young. They sought each other's eyes across the room, each seeking a glimmer of the lifetime's love between them. It was Sandra who spoke.

"How's Mum? Can she see?"

"No love, she can't. She's in a bad way. She's so down. It's just her eyes, the doctors say. There's not much chance they'll work again. But your mum doesn't seem to have the fight to handle it. Just stays in bed and cries."

"Can't Josie help?"

"Not really. She's been around once or twice, but what with her dad dying and her own mam to take care of, she's enough troubles of her own without taking on more."

"So who's looking after Mum now?"

Sandra was once more the concerned daughter. In the few moments that her mother's plight had crossed her mind, she'd reassured herself that it was OK to push any concerns away because Josie could handle anything. Sandra had met the grandparents in Leeds once or twice. Both had seemed quite young and hearty – surely not of an age to die, not without anyone wishing them dead. How would Mum manage without Josie's chaotic laughter and disorganisation to spur her on? Something like a sense of responsibility sent tiny bubbles rising around Sandra's heart, like water round an egg set in a pan to boil

Malcolm fumbled with words to find a way to plead, to beg an explanation of her rejection. He knew. He *really* knew, but had reached the point where truth was the only thing left. There could be nothing worse than the loss of his daughter's love. Even to hear her spell out the reason for its withdrawal could not be worse. At least then he might be offered the chance of penitence.

Doreen left them alone. Malcolm moved silently across the room, raised his hand slowly to lie on Sandra's shoulder. She swayed a little, went to step back, but her shoulders slumped, a moist sparkle sprang to her eyes. Her face crumpled into a waterfall for her tears. Gaining strength and reminding himself that *he*, not Bob Fownhope, was this girl's father, he folded both arms around his daughter and held her close until her sobbing was done.

"I'll come round to see Mum, but I won't see you. I never want to see you again."

His hopes were dashed. He wished he hadn't come, couldn't bear this awfulness. What was going on inside her head?

Sandra hated herself now, even more than ever. She had caved in, shown her weakness, even tenderness, for this abomination who called himself her father. She began to retch, rushing upstairs to heave over the toilet. Malcolm floundered alone in this strange house, until Doreen sat him down and offered tea.

"I don't know what to do. My world has fallen apart," he said quietly. My wife is blind, my daughter abhors me, my job doesn't exist anymore – yet I am not a bad man, Mrs Fownhope. Why has all this happened to me?

"Have you really no idea what's the matter? Why Sandra's behaving like this?"

. "Not that I dare admit, even to myself." He forced the words out, his cheeks burning…

"Well, Malcolm, *I* know. You don't need to be embarrassed with' me. Go ahead."

"What do you mean, *you* know?" He was horrified at the thought. "What has Sandra said?"

"Nothing much. You might think it's all baloney, but I can see what's happened in the past and what might happen in the future. Take my hand."

Reaching forward, she took his hand in hers before he had time to protest.

"Let me hear your voice."

"Saying what?"

"Say anything. It doesn't matter. If you can't bear to unburden yourself, shall I tell you what I sense?"

"I don't understand what you're talking about but go ahead if you want to."

He was beginning to think Sandra had been living with a freak.

"This has something to do with Sandra's husband, I believe." She paused. "Just answer yes or no, nothing more."

"Yes," he muttered.

"I sense trickery and betrayal. Something shameful happened that you don't know how to handle. I can feel confusion and terror around you."

"Yes." His voice was a whisper.

"He was a violent man, a bad man. You were afraid of him."

"Yes. Oh yes."

"You allowed him to lead you astray. I see bottles. Cards. Was there a boy? I don't know this boy, but he was beautiful. Like a young Greek god. Sandra's husband was manipulating *him*, destroying *him*, too."

"I don't know about that."

"You were both out of control…that is, your own control. Hardisty had you under *his*. Does it help you to know that the boy feels as badly as you do? It was out of character for him, too"

"I never even knew his name. He just appeared and … I don't know exactly what happened … I can only recall being on the boat and this lad arriving. He reminded me of someone I once loved."

Malcolm's voice broke. Until the boy, he had barely thought of Susannah since he got married. The similarity had been so striking that he could have been her son. Malcolm had not been unhappy with Pam, but there had never been that toe-curling ecstasy he'd felt that other time. Then, at fifty, there had occasionally been a fleeting yearning for something more, but he had refused to give it headroom, too fond of his safe situation ever to put it in peril. Had Hardisty been able to detect his suppressed yearnings?

"You don't need to tell me what happened," Doreen went on. "I can see enough to know, to know why you're ashamed, but also to know that that man wasn't the complete you. He was one tiny part of you … like we all have a tiny part of us that's … not bad, exactly but, shall I say… inquisitive … or perhaps weak?"

"As far as I can remember, no one forced me to do anything. I can't blame anyone else."

If only he could, he thought, maybe there would be some way out of this pit of desperation.

Doreen sat of the sofa next to him, still holding his hand.

"Let's sit quiet," she whispered "Let all the hurt and fear and shame inside you flow down your arm and into your fingers."

That seemed impossible to Malcolm, yet he made a mental effort to imagine his trapped feelings moving down his arm. Strangely, after a while the arm began to feel slightly different: heavy and hot, aching dully.

"Imagine you're pouring water out of a kettle or a teapot," she went on. "Your fingertips are the spout. Pretend you're a little kid again, doing that 'I'm a little teapot' rhyme. Remember how you used to tip over to one side at the end as you sang, 'Tip me up and pour me out'?

With closed eyes, he smiled. Involuntarily, his left shoulder dipped.

"Now, as you tip, allow the water in the teapot to pour out of your fingertips."

Loosening her grip on Malcolm's hand, Doreen cupped her own, allowing his fingers to rest in her palm.

"Your arm is full of all your worries. It's feeling heavy and the water is gushing down it, carrying all the pain out through your fingertips." She paused for a moment.

"Now, the teapot's emptying and your arm is feeling lighter. The weight that was inside has poured out into my hand. You've given it all to me now, but I can deal with it. I can put it aside somewhere until you decide what *you* need to do with it."

"How *can* I deal with it?"

"Well, we'll have to think about that, but for a start, we could put it away for a while. You could pour it down the plug-hole if you wanted to, but it's early days for that. We could use it to wash things clean or to bring something back to life. Think of all the things you can do with water … maybe swilling it straight down the drain would be a waste."

"Pamela might think she's common as muck," thought Malcolm, "but Doreen's a clever woman."

Already the cleansing image was working. How long had it been since the last time he smiled? Now, sitting in this grubby, smelly room with a near-stranger holding his hand, he found himself grinning at the childish simplicity of what had occurred. Pamela would have a fit at the very idea … but Pamela need never know, would never know that he was grinning unless he chose to tell her. He need never explain, unless he chose to. He was shocked by his own glee … for his mood was quickly becoming just that. Like a helium balloon firmly tethered to the ground and suddenly cut free, his spirit soared without restraint, seeming to toss and fly amongst the clouds, glad to leave the earth behind.

"How did you learn to do that? I feel loads better, even though nothing's really changed"

"*You* have changed," was the simple answer. "I don't think it's something I learned," she went on. "I just said what came out of my mouth – didn't really think about it. It's instinct, maybe. But I *can* see or sense other people's troubles. It's a bit of a bind sometimes ... I feel sort of responsible, even when it's nothing to do with me."

"I suppose my problems – our problems – are nothing to do with you." Malcolm smoothed his hair with his free hand. "I'm sorry that you've got caught up in them. Normally, we never tell other people our business. This feels like it's happening to someone else, but Sandra's ended up here and I'm grateful to you and your husband for taking her in. Heaven knows what may have happened if you hadn't done that. But I want her to come home. I love her so much ... and we both need her."

"I think she needs you, too, but she's too afraid, and she's had a rough time since she married that Hardisty." Doreen glanced at Malcolm obliquely. "You did know what her life was like, didn't you?"

His eyes took on a defensive look. "We thought she'd be set up for life and want for nothing. There weren't many young folk knocking on the door for our Sandra, either."

It was the reasoning of the old Pogson, spoken without conviction.

"Sandra needs you to admit you were wrong. I think you always knew it. I think you always knew that living your life for appearances was a mistake. You let that ruin Sandra's life, and now you've got to find a way of making it better."

This plain speaking was taking its toll on the elation

which had lightened the gloom yet, like that balloon in the sky, he could now see the problem from a different angle.

"Don't do anything just yet," Doreen went on. "At least you've seen Sandra. That's a start. Come again tomorrow… even if she won't talk, keep coming for just a few minutes each day and see what happens. She's still young. With love, she has time to heal."

He stood, straightened, stretched out his hand.

"I will. Thank you. I … I wish Sandra would give me a message for her mum … something to give Pamela a bit of a lift, like."

The door creaked open a little

"Give her my love," said the girl crouching on the bottom stair.

How much had she heard? Malcolm had no idea. Somehow, it didn't seem to matter.

13

She hadn't meant to do it. Not the first time, nor the second.

It had been necessary to set her mind on other things during that terrible act, which still made her shudder to contemplate. She had to imagine it was not Fergus who caressed her with skilful, manipulative hands, but someone younger, someone lithe and tender. Shame stopped her naming him, even to herself. The man in her mind's eye was not yet even a man. His chest and cheeks were smooth, his legs softly, silkily downed with palest gold. His eyes sought hers. No words were needed, but in her imaginings he held her with warm and tender looks, soothed her soul, set urges in her body and satisfied them tenderly. These things were only in her imaginings, but she knew that she had sinned in her heart. Her thoughts were sinful, and for that she was, and would be punished.

"Harlot! What words are there to describe me?" she wondered. Tart, strumpet, floozy – one of granddad's that. Loose woman. No better than she should be. Fergus had been her husband. She owed him everything. It had been her duty to learn to satisfy his appetites and needs, not to switch off and think of someone else, to think of Si…

If only her mother had prepared her, maybe then she would not have been so appalled; might have responded as he expected her to.

"I will make a real woman of you."

Isn't that what Fergus had promised that day in his car? She had not understood, but was enticed by the rich note of promise. That the future could be anything but wholesome had not occurred to her but, as time wore on, he had demanded more and more. Had demanded, with icy coldness, responses which made her retch even now at the thought.

Why had he not been kind?

She recalled his instructions. "Turn around. Get down. Not like that, you fool."

It made Sandra weep to think how she had displeased him while trying so hard to do things right. She did not have the words, even in her head, to convey the depths to which he had driven her, dared not, even now, admit that he had exceeded his rights, that his desires had been depraved. It had been her place to comply and show him love. She hadn't meant to kill him.

The frigid horror of her father's betrayal remained with her, would remain for evermore. What had become of them all? Where was the link that joined Malcolm's dreadful act to her revulsion at the marriage bed? That it had anything to do with Fergus was out of the question, even though it had been his boat in the video. The episode with Marianne had, surely, been acted out for her own benefit, to lead her to true, wifely fulfilment. He had never physically forced her to do any of those things and Sandra clung to the certainty that he had known nothing of her father's conduct with the boy. And yet...and yet...before Fergus had asked for her hand, they had all been so ... *nice*.

She wanted them to stay nice, or rather, to be nice again. For this, it was imperative that her mother remained ignorant of her father's transgression, essential that she did not see the evidence. But Sandra had never wished her blind, not blinded in that agonising way. Not changed into a help-less, mewling wretch.

In her pain she cried out for her mother's love. "Mum! I never wanted that to happen. Forgive me. I meant no harm."

Her thoughts, arrows aimed in defence, had in their flight from daughter to mother taken on barbs of evil to decimate their lives. She *must* be evil, yet she had never meant to be.

She had just wanted him not to be there. She had never wanted him *dead*. Once, she'd let herself wonder at what age she could look forward to being widowed, wondered if she would have chance to rebuild her life, maybe find another husband, perhaps even have babies. Even had Fergus lived to seventy-five with her to tend him in his dotage, there might still have been time for her to have a child. Lots of women became mothers in their forties. So she hadn't wished him dead. Not in so many words.

Fergus had made it clear that there would be no babies. "You will make sure of that," he'd said.

Sandra might not have used the words, but the wish was there, and she knew it. In fear of giving that truth light and air, she tried to close her mind tightly against all thought. It had taken so much courage to admit her guilt to the policeman, yet she had not been believed. They had thought she was crazy. She knew she was not. Not crazy. She was wicked. She was evil.

This was to be her punishment. Her soul would be oppressed until death with the truth of what she had caused to happen. There was to be no retribution, no penance, no relief, because she would not be believed. They would try to comfort, to soothe and calm her, while she alone would know the depth of her wickedness.

What of the future? Could she live a life without thought? Was that possible? Yet she must, for even now in the acknowledgement of her wickedness, she wanted it to stop. If she could not obliterate that which was done, at least she must cause no harm in the future.

She had read about those who spread evil and murder with their thoughts. Now, *she* was such a one. How this had come about, she had no idea, had never considered that there existed people with harmful powers, really existed outside fairy tales. Where had those stories come from? Were they based in truth, wrapped up in fiction to fool the innocent?

Her mind flashed back to childhood days, of rare walks home from primary school along Duck Lane, past the rickety wooden bungalow inhabited by a solitary old woman. Sometimes, this troubled soul would hobble to her gate, shake a wizened fist and hurl words at the children as they skipped and ran past, words that Sandra hadn't understood. The other children had called out names: Witch Big-nose; Loony-Lottie, names that meant little to Sandra. Had the other children understood more? Had they already made that superstitious link between madness and evil, or was it imagined? In Witch Big-nose, had they recognised more than a crazed and lonely old woman? Sandra had chosen to be driven to school by her father lest she should be harmed.

She recalled, now, how in later school years books and plays had, from time to time, brought up the word; the idea. Macbeth, the witches' prophesies. She had always assumed that Shakespeare had invented them as entertainment, but maybe not. Maybe *he* had suffered at the mercies of those who wished him harm. What if spells and incantations were not needed? What if the thought is enough, the thought of an evil person, one with malign powers to make those thoughts become real, to damage all those who cross her mind?

In her mind's vault, malevolent voices chanted rhythms of dark rounds over which faintly, tinnily, Sandra's own voice struggled to be heard.

"I do not want to be a witch."

But could one choose? Are witches chosen by the devil to be *his* angels, spreading blackness and sin as holy angels spread light and love? With vacant horror, she believed she had been chosen by the devil, the Dark One, to be his servant.

Determined to fight him, using words dredged up from who knew where, she called to heaven:

"Lord, Lord, come to this your child and drive the demon away!"

She heard no reply.

"He has deafened his ears to my calling," she told herself. "He has cast me into darkness. I am alone."

So alone she must deal with it. No thought was possible. In fact, she forbade it. She would resist the devil slave master; passive resistance. Empty your mind. In its place, let there be a void. Concentrate on the void. Allow no light or dark, no sound or sight or touch or smell, Push them out. OUT!

See the void. Feel the void. Let it remain. Let none be harmed.

An hour later, Doreen found her asleep behind the coats, back to the painted wall, drool on her chin. Touching the girl's hand and finding it chilled, she gently roused Sandra with soft strokes on her brow. Doreen was tired. Although she'd grown fond of Sandra and would never show her the door, it would have been a relief had Malcolm persuaded her to go home. Still, a little progress had been made.

It took Sandra some seconds to remember where she was. Her dreams had not been troubled by the realisation of her own evil, and for a few soaring moments she smiled at the oddness of her position. Catching and holding her gaze for a few moments, Doreen glimpsed a glint of something like mirth or pleasure flash between them until, like shutters unrolling down a shop front, an impenetrable stare obliterated Sandra's spirit.

Doreen had thought they were becoming close; had chosen to hope that her father's visit would help Sandra turn the corner back to normality, but the signs suggested the opposite. The hand Doreen offered as Sandra rose to her feet was ignored. The girl climbed the stairs to the tiny bedroom and closed the door decisively.

Inside the room, Sandra must concentrate on not thinking. Really, she wanted to think about Mum, but she dare not. Look what damage she'd done already! She must allow herself to think only bland thoughts, with no minor diversions round the by-ways of what-ifs or maybes. But it was *so* hard. How to arrive at a neutral thought without visiting other possibilities was like trying to skate on crazed ice, so best not to try. Only harm could come of it. It was difficult to keep her mind a blank. She couldn't relax for a second, lest thoughts about real people crept in unbidden and sealed their doom.

She would have liked to think about Simon, but must not. What would she do if harm should befall him? There! She'd thought it. He was as good as dead. A flash of recall told her that Simon had filled her dreams, that in them he had been very much alive and warm to the touch. Her soul longed to be back in the dream, yet logic told her that Simon could have no place in her thoughts or fantasies. His presence in her thoughts could kill him.

She spoke severely to herself in her head.

"Loved him? That's ridiculous. Love is what Mum feels for Dad and vice versa. Wipe the image of Simon from your mind." Her closed eyes saw only black as they focussed on the void.

*

Sometime later, Sandra was aware of the front door slamming and of muffled, troubled sounds below. She tried not to listen, but became aware of a discordant note, a muffled sob and voices raised in exasperation.

Bob's day had been a bad one. There was talk of lay-offs at his firm. The decimation of the coal industry in Yorkshire meant that there was less money for people to throw around on weddings and formal occasions, so the luxury limousine business had hit a rocky patch. No decisions had yet been made, but the boss had made it clear he would not stand in the way of anyone who found work elsewhere.

Bob liked his job. He liked people and he liked to see them enjoying themselves, which they generally were when he had dealings with them. The money wasn't great, but the family had most of what they needed: hand-me-down clothes shared by the grandkids, the girls all earning and Doreen not bothered about expensive stuff. They rated the value of love and companionship above all else, but he did need a job and, in all honesty, having Sandra to feed had begun to pall just a little, even before today. Now, worry about his job caused a slight ripple of resentment to cloud his placid features. The girl was loaded, for God's sake. At least she could make some contribution for her keep. Or her dad could. Had he even offered?

Doreen, too, was feeling dejected after absorbing Malcolm's transferred troubles. It was all too much. She'd noticed that, as he'd left her house with a lighter tread, her own legs felt leaden, her spirit like stone. Like her husband, Doreen normally sailed lightly across life's pond, but today the slimy duckweed was pulling her down.

Sandra heard the door slam a second time; a lighter voice, questioning; murmurs and dull-sounding responses. Was that a sob again?

It was nothing to do with her. Concentrate on the void.

The creak of stair treads and the opening swing of the door failed to penetrate the void. Her eyes stared ahead, not registering Pamela Anderson's amplified bosom on the wall. Then Simon stood before her, and the fixed stare wavered.

Her mind raced. Ought she to look at him? The word *basilisk* flashed through her mind; it had cropped up once in a Scrabble game in those far-off days with Uncle Archie, Mum and Dad. Someone had challenged the word – Mum, she thought – but Uncle Archie had been certain it existed. Sure enough, it did, some sort of mythical creature which could kill by looking at you. What if Sandra herself was a basilisk? She kept her gaze on Pamela Anderson to be sure.

Simon was having none of it. Fazed by the depressed state of his parents, he needed to talk. He *wanted* to talk to Sandra. Not anything heavy, just to chat like they used to do before whatever it was that happened.

"Oh, for God's sake, Sandra, pull yourself together!" he snapped, infuriated by the blank eyes. "You're not the only one in this house, you know. We need you to start pulling your weight a bit instead of locking yourself away like the mad woman in the attic!"

Sandra's gasp was audible. Tears flooded her eyes, overflowed and streamed down her nose and cheeks. The shattered glass of her cold reserve fell in shards around her. She felt nakedly exposed to the stones of Simon's exasperation, yet she dare not risk that basilisk gaze, dare not let her eyes dwell on his form.

He grabbed her shoulder and shook her roughly.

"Look at me. I'm not going to hurt you. Please, you need to start acting like a grown-up, whatever's happened. People are willing to help you, but you've got to let them help…and help yourself, too. I used to think you were great … I even fancied you a bit … but now I think you're just selfish. If you'd stop wallowing in self-pity you might get a bit more out of life."

He stopped suddenly, ashamed of his outburst although not regretting it. Things had to be said and his mother was too kind to do it. The time had come for him to be a man, to be the voice of his family while his parents tried to handle their own concerns. He had known Sandra for a long time, though not well, and was prepared to risk her anger. The unchecked tears, the mute heartbreak, the deathly agony in her eyes shook but did not deter him. Yet still she refused to look at him, turning her face away.

He bent his knees and peered into her face, adjusting his position until his eyes met hers. They snapped shut.

"Am I so awful that you can't bear to look at me?" he asked. "I thought we were friends."

"We are." It was barely a whisper. "That's why I can't look at you." Her breast heaved.

He sat on the bed.

"Well I'll just sit here until you tell me what's going on. Mum's in a right state down there. I've never seen her cry before, except when our Shannon was born, and that was just happiness and relief. Whatever's happened, it doesn't only affect you, Sandra. Now come on. Tell me what's up."

A small kitchen chair faced the chest of drawers which doubled as a dressing table. Sandra lowered herself onto it and adjusted the angle of the mirror. Now, she could only see the red cotton curtains through the looking glass. Taking deep breaths to staunch her sobs, she struggled to find words to convey her fear.

"I can't look at you in case I kill you."

"What?"

"I'm a witch, or a basilisk ... oh, something evil, anyway!" Her voice rose, tinged with hysteria. "If I look at you, or breathe on you, or even think about you, something terrible will happen." She fought to regain her composure.

"So – you never think about me? Well, thanks a lot!"

"Yes I do ... I did ... but I mustn't in case you die." She fiddled with the bits and pieces in front of her, absentmindedly breaking teeth from the plastic comb which had been in her pocket the night she fled.

"You're nuts, Sandra. I can't believe you're being so selfish. Refusing to look at people is just one way not of not getting involved, and not getting involved is just another way of being selfish. I never thought you were like that."

He stood up, took the two paces the small space allowed, turned and leant against the door. The sole of his trainer left scuff-marks on the yellowing paintwork.

"What if Dad had refused to look at you the night you ran away? Where would you be now? Dead at 'bottom o' dyke, I shouldn't wonder. And what the hell's a basilic or whatever you call it?"

"Basilisk," she corrected. "It's a mythical creature that can kill just by looking at you."

"Oh, so you've just turned into one, have you? Why aren't we all dead already then? You looked at me this morning when I handed you that piece of toast, and I'm still here. You're talking through the top of your head, Sandra."

"A witch then," she whined. "Every time I think about someone they die or get hurt. I don't mean to do it ... I can't help it! The only thing I can do is make sure I don't think about anyone."

"OK. I'll do the same, shall I? And I'll make sure no one else bothers with you, so no one's in any danger. I'll make sure Mum doesn't cook you any tea or put your clothes in 'wash. It'll be a relief to her ... she's worn out fetching and carrying for you all these weeks without a word of thanks. And I'll tell Dad he's not to worry about making ends meet if he loses his job. You'll not be eating anything in case you have to sit at 'table and look at folk."

His anger rising, Simon suddenly grabbed a pillow from the bed and flung it at the side of Sandra's head. As her arm shot up to ward it off, he grabbed it and swung her round to face him.

"And don't you dare shut your eyes," he muttered through gritted teeth.

Mesmerised by the power of his glare, Sandra's eyelids fought to close. Her pupils dilated and drank in his strength. His fingers relaxed gently, drawing her face closer to his.

Involuntarily, it seemed, their lips touched. The lips parted. Two sharp intakes of breath, a closing of the eyes, lips touching again, longingly, light as gossamer, before a turning away, an opening of the eyes. A re-opening, re-opening on a world changed for both of them.

He was angry. Once, he wouldn't have minded something like this with Sandra; he'd always been a bit sweet on her since that time when he was a kid, but the way she was carrying on now ... well, it just wasn't normal. Or if this was normal for her, she was just a selfish cow.

He'd never have believed it if he hadn't heard such whining self-pity for himself.

He pushed her face away, embarrassed; sat on the bed, tracing Pamela Anderson's calves with his fingertips, forcing his hand down when the thighs got close. Blushing, he thrust both hands into his pockets and stared at the floor. He wanted to storm out of the room, for the last five minutes never to have happened. He wanted to kiss her again, but right now he couldn't stand the sight of her.

Sandra hadn't moved since their lips touched. Her mind blanked, torn between wanting more and dread of the consequences. She was stunned by his reproach, so unexpectedly harsh and unforgiving. The passive Sandra kept her still, dominating the foetal heartbeat of Cassandra pumping heat into her loins.

Her eyes found their way to the mirror. Knocked to an altered angle by the flying pillow, it now reflected Simon's troubled expression and angry eyes. She let herself look, without thought, still rigid with shame at his censure.

Minutes passed. The voices from downstairs altered in tone. A note of urgency, the sound of a door yanked open, two-at-a-time bounds up the stairs accompanied by,

"Simon! Simon? Where are you, son?"

The door flew back.

"Simon, it's your mum. Come quick. I think you'd best call an ambulance. She's taken bad."

As Simon leapt down the stairs in response, guilt engulfed Sandra once more. She had brought this upon Doreen. She'd been right all along.

She shut the bedroom door quietly, crept under the duvet and emptied her mind.

14

It was several hours before Bob and Simon Fownhope returned from the hospital. Doreen was being kept in overnight as a precaution; doctors thought she'd suffered an ITA – an intermittent ischemic attack. She would probably make a full recovery but would need looking after for a few days.

Between them, father and son were agreed: it was time for Sandra to move out. Bob felt to blame. He should never have tried to help the girl in the first place. None of them ever dreamed she'd instal herself in the spare room and still be there six weeks later. Sandra would have to go. End of.

Father and son both knew, however, that sending the girl packing would be easier said than done. No good asking her father for help; that was obvious. Her mother neither. Bob was wary. *He'd* messed things up in the first place, so in one way it was his responsibility to sort them out. On the other hand, the girls said he was a pushover for a weeping woman. Best leave it to Simon.

Having decided to postpone the task until morning, the young man lay awake half the night choosing his words, but when the time came, he could remember none of them.

Balancing a plate of toast on the rim of a coffee mug, he knocked hard on the door of his old bedroom.

"Sandra! Are you awake?"

He heard a muffled sound and knocked again.

"Wake up! I need to talk to you."

He pressed the handle and walked in. Sandra's chestnut-gold crop, a little faded now, was just visible.

"Come on! Shape up."

Simon was feeling masterful. She opened her eyes, raised her head and edged higher up the pillow, silently reaching out for the breakfast.

"No. Sit up properly. Stop being lazy and stop feeling sorry for yourself." His tone was stern.

Sandra sat up, looking blankly at him as she took the drink.

"Now listen to me. This has got to stop. Mum is in hospital. She's had a mini-stroke – an ITA, they call it. She's been under too much strain and looking after you has made things worse." He ignored the tears that had filled her eyes but hesitated, unsure how forthright it was wise to be. "There's nothing wrong with you, Sandra, and it's time you pulled yourself together. You can't stay here any longer."

He set the plate of toast on the bedside table and walked out.

It took a while for his words to sink in. She sipped the coffee and chewed the toast slowly, her mind still blank. That was how she liked it. Blank didn't make her cry. Blank didn't hurt her; didn't hurt anyone else. Blank was the void. The void was blank. That was all she wanted – couldn't cope with more. She continued to sip and chew as slowly as possible, clinging on to the blank; clinging to the void.

The door flew back.

"Get up! I told you. You've got to go!"

Simon shocked himself. This wasn't him! Where was this forcefulness coming from? He took the plate and mug from her hands. She protested, helplessly.

He pulled off the duvet, threw it out of the room, revealing her vulnerability. She gasped, looking at him pleadingly.

"Get up now!" He avoided her eyes and her body. "Go to the bathroom. Have a shower. Wash your hair. Put some clean clothes on. Then I'm taking you home."

He swept downstairs, shaking.

Sandra looked along the landing to where the duvet had landed. She needed its warmth. She needed its protection. She set her feet to the floor; tiptoed out of the room, intent on retrieval, but as she reached out her hand another, Simon's, reached up between the spindles and whisked it away.

"Shower! Hair!" He paused for a moment. "Now!"

She was left with no option.

*

Simon had thought it through. As far as he knew, the house in Snellington had gone unvisited for weeks – presumably since Fergus set off for the coast some time before his death. The lad had taken the liberty of searching the pockets of Sandra's coat, which had been hanging on a hook in the hall since the night she arrived. No keys.

He'd given thought to how to gain entry to what must, surely, be Sandra's own property. One or two lads he'd been at school with might have been able to help, but on reflection, asking them for advice might be risky.

"How will we get in? Do your Mum and Dad have a key?"

Sandra didn't think so. Fergus had taken charge of all keys.

"Did you bring a handbag with you? Your own key?"

"Only my anorak. I didn't think."

"Well think now. Come on, Sandra. Shape yourself. How are we going to get in?"

"Break a window? Or bash the front door in? It doesn't matter. It's my house."

"I suppose so. Are you sure that's what we should do?"

"Hmm."

She didn't really care how they got in; didn't want to go inside. She dreaded it. The house held no good memories.

Simon had made a few preparations: he'd borrowed the window-cleaning ladder, grabbed a hammer and chisel and a few screwdrivers from his dad's shed and trusted to luck for the rest.

*

Albertina Hedge had only been working at Mr Hardisty's house for two months but for most of that time, the boss and his young wife had been away. On holiday, she presumed, although there'd been nothing said. Inconsiderate, she'd call it. She was owed over a month's pay, apart from anything else.

The wife hadn't put in much of an appearance on the cleaner's first few visits – she'd caught merely a glimpse of her going into an upstairs room. Mr Hardisty had told Albertina to leave her be – she liked to spend time alone in her sewing room – meditating, he'd said. Not to be disturbed. Albertina was given her own back-door key, so had been letting herself in and out twice a week. It would have been nice to get to know the wife, to break the mornings up with a cup of tea and a chat, maybe share some gossip – but Mr Hardisty had implied there was something a bit delicate about his bride. Made out he'd married her out of pity. For protection, he'd said. Still, she'd thought, it takes all sorts…

To be honest, the work wasn't to her taste, but since Snellington Post Office, the pub and the tea shop had closed down, the only other jobs available locally were at Poulters Ready to Roast Chicken factory, and Albertina just didn't have the stomach for gutting fowls. She needed to work, for company as well as for the money, which was why working for Mr Hardisty wasn't turning out as she'd hoped.

This day, she strode purposefully along Long Lane, hoping to find the Mercedes in the drive and some sign of life in the house. A week ago she'd had to flush a dead goldfish down the toilet. Turning in between the stone gateposts, Albertina stopped. A ladder leaned against the front of the house, angled over the bay window of the sitting room, its upper rungs reaching just below a smaller window above – that of the sewing room, she thought.

A crop-headed young man stood balanced at the top of the ladder, hammer in one hand and a chisel in the other. More tools protruded from the back pockets of his jeans.

Gripping the lower end of the ladder was a young woman, tall and well-built with short golden hair; quite attractive. Didn't look like a burglar's accomplice, but you never can tell.

Albertina wasn't one to hang back. 'Act first, ask questions later' had long been her motto. A strapping woman, she could wield a weighty handbag with gusto.

Four heavy bounds and Albertina was upon the ladder-holder, handbag swinging, knocking the girl's head from side to side and bashing her hands to loosen their grip. Tossing the bag aside, she launched a more hands-on attack, augmented by a vocal assault of equal weight.

"Dirty, thievin' bassads! Get 'way! Why you do this? Yo' Mama she will cry to her grave wid shame. Pray to God she forgive you. Pray to God that de Lord 'imself forgive you!"

The ladder shook. Sandra was dazed. From above, Simon's voice cried,

"Hold it still, Sandra! I nearly fell then."

The ladder continued to shake. He carefully put the chisel in his back pocket, tucked the hammer down his belt and looked down.

A large black woman in a felt hat was beating up Sandra!

Seconds passed before he was stirred into action and slid down the ladder in trepidation.

"What's going on? Stop hitting her please. What's the matter?"

"What's de matta? You a burgla, thass whassa matta. Dirty, thievin' burgla'. Who your motha? Who dis gal? She your accomplice?"

"What?"

"Your accomplice. Han'some gal. You leadin' her into sin?"

Sandra tried to tune in to reality. Now her ears pricked up. "Han'some gal?" Did this crazy woman mean *her*?

"This is my home," she said. "Please stop hitting me. I've lost my keys and this young man is helping me to get in."

Albertina stopped swinging her handbag and set her hat more firmly on her head.

Standing up straight she was taller than the girl, on whom she looked down imperiously.

"You have proof?"

"I'm Sandra Hardisty. Mrs Sandra Hardisty."

"You have proof?"

"Well, no. That's because I've been staying away from home for a few weeks."

"You bin on holiday with Mista Hardisty?"

"No. No. But who are you? Did you know my husband?"

"I am de cleanin' lady. Mr Hardisty – his wife not well he tell me. Not to be disturbed."

"Mr Hardisty is dead." That was Simon.

Albertina grabbed the ladder to steady herself.

"Dead! No. On holiday wid 'is wife. Bin away four, five weeks. Owes me wages. Forgot to tell me he was goin'…" Her words tailed off.

The couple's long absence was beginning to make sense. She looked at them carefully. Maybe the girl looked slightly familiar, though they'd never actually been introduced. Her only sighting of Mrs Hardisty had been that fleeting rear view across the dimly-lit landing.

"Dead?" her hands rose to cover her face. "How?"

"He … he…drowned." Simon didn't want to go into detail.

"He drown on holiday?"

"Not exactly. He was on his boat."

"Poor, poor man." The woman held her forehead. "You his wife?"

Sandra nodded.

"You only a chile. How come you marry a ole man?"

Sandra pressed her lips together, shaking her head. She had no need to explain herself to this woman; she had no way of explaining it to herself. Real tears filled her eyes at the loss of her youth.

Albertina was quiet for a moment before slapping herself on the forehead with the palm of her hand.

"Key to dis 'ouse ' ere in my 'andbag! No need for burgla!" She shook her head in Simon's direction. "You wanna end up in jail?"

"No."

"Good. You lucky Albertina a Christian woman, believin' everyone deserve a second chance. I turn de other cheek; I forgive those who trespass agains' me."

Simon was anxious to point out that he was neither trespasser nor burglar and that this woman would not have been the victim in any case, but a pious glare in his direction stilled his tongue.

The cleaning lady led the way round to the kitchen door, opened it and paced quickly across to a small cupboard in the hall, punched in some numbers and disabled the burglar alarm.

Sandra stood on the doorstep, trembling. Albertina looked at her, wondering.

"This is the first time Sandra's been home since her husband died," Simon explained. "It's going to be very upsetting for her.

"Where you bin sleepin', honey?" The older woman eyed the young widow with more sympathy, but was met with silence.

"She's been staying with my family. Her own mother had a nasty accident around the same time." The look in Simon's eyes made it clear that the discussion was closed.

"Poor, poor man," Albertina commiserated, reaching into her capacious bag to extract a bottle of milk. "Poor, poor gal." She filled the kettle and set it to boil.

Sandra still stood trembling on the doorstep, her face white, fists clenched in her coat pockets. Dread chilled her, body and soul. The horror of that night seeped up from the step, through her toes, legs and torso until her brain was swamped by terror.

"I got chocolate digestives here." Albertina delved into her bag once more. "Very comfortin', choc'late digestives." She tore open the wrapper and offered the pack in Sandra's direction.

By some reflex reaction, Sandra took one step over the threshold towards the scent of chocolate. She picked up a biscuit between forefinger and thumb.

"Good gal. Take more – take four, five ... Very comfortin'...."

Another step forward and Sandra heard the door close behind her. Albertina's arm reached gently round her shoulders, gently edging, gently edging her forward in baby steps, accompanied at every inch by soft, matter-of-fact reassurances.

"Nice cup o' tea an' a choc'late digestive: whatever de

problem, dey 'elp. You gonna be OK, honey. You be a fine, handsome gal. I can see you'll be jus' fine. But for now, you got Albertina lookin' after you."

Having laid the ladder safely along the side of the house, Simon returned to the kitchen. He sat close to Sandra at the Formica-topped table while the cleaning lady made the tea.

There was a tacit understanding that, for Sandra, getting this far was an achievement. Some R-&-R was necessary before facing the rest of the house, although neither the woman nor the young man knew the reason for Sandra's terror.

The packet of biscuits was soon empty. Soggy crumbs floated in rapidly-cooling mugs. There was little conversation, until Albertina went through the motions of gathering her energy, cleaning equipment and spray polish to start the assault on cobwebs and dust. Spotless already, the house was nevertheless full of a dead man's possessions, she thought. Who was going to deal with those, and would she get paid for the hours she was owed?

Simon had lost his nerve and wasn't sure what to do next. It might be best to leave now. He stood up, purposefully.

"Ah, well. You'll be alright with this lady here. I'll leave you for a while."

Sandra's heart pounded. Her eyes searched for his, her hand reached out but by now he was at the door, pulling it to behind him.

"A bit o' dustin' need doin', thass all," Albertina began, "Mz Hardisty, you 'elp me for a while. What's your name, honey?" Her hands touched Sandra's shoulders, prompting movement.

"Sandra." The voice sounded blaeak

She rose from the table, staring at the staircase visible through the open door to the hall. She would have to climb those stairs, to re-enter that room, the scene of her subjection, her humiliation. Revulsion stopped her feet.

A whimper escaped from her throat. She edged through the door and stepped into the hall. A heaving gasp raised her shoulders. Its exhalation sounded as a groan, yet still she edged forward, Albertina's hand at the small of her back, gently encouraging. Sandra saw nothing, though her eyes stared ahead. Instinctively, her hand reached to touch the stair-foot newel post, its ball of mahogany polished by twenty years of beeswax and human hands. Her fingers, for a moment, stroked its smoothness, yet her feet stopped short of the first step.

Pressure from the hand at her back turned Sandra gradually. The women lowered themselves onto the second stair. So far so good.

"Somethin' bad 'appen upstairs, honey?" Sandra nodded in silence.

"Mr Hardisty … you love him? He like a daddy to you?"

"No." A whisper. "Sandra shook her head.

"Mr Hardisty … he hurt you up dere one time?

The girl's brimming eyes lifted to meet hers. Another whisper: "Yes."

A nod, repeated. Her chin dropped to her chest and the tears overflowed.

They sat for a while longer until Albertina stood up, clutching her hips with her hands.

"Albertina too big an' ol' to sit on de stairs nowadays. Mi hips too stiff. You need to 'elp me. Take mi right arm an' d' banister will take de other."

Without thinking, Sandra did as she was told and before she realised it, they were both on the landing. Albertina's stiffness seemed to have faded away. She bore left, into the bedroom that had once belonged to Enid and Fergus. Sandra could not bear to recall that it had ever been her own.

Unseeing, unfeeling, she balked at that door to the left

and steered towards the so-called sewing room, spray polish and duster now, somehow, in her hands. The staleness of the air made her cough. Simultaneous with the cough, she spotted the empty fish globe.

"Where's Fish?"

The other woman followed her in. "He with his maker, Ms Hardisty. I guess someone forgot to feed 'im for too long." Her voice was matter-of-fact.

Sandra's tears, so long restrained, now flowed unchecked.

"That was me. How could I have forgotten him? I ran away – never gave him a thought." Her sobs heaved. "I let Fish die … because I was too scared to stay. That's not what a proper grown-up does!"

"Now listen he-a, Missy. If forgettin' to feed a gol' fish be the worst thing you do in yo' life, you will be a *good* woman. Let's 'ear no more o' dat nonsense."

"But I blinded my mother, too!"

Albertina kept quiet as she plugged in the vacuum cleaner. That *was* a more serious matter.

"Well, you tell me 'bout dat some other time. We got work to do."

She indicated that Sandra should make use of the duster in her hand as the roar of the vacuum cleaner ended conversation and blunted thought. Whenever Sandra paused in her work, a thick finger pointed to the next task, until an imagined noise downstairs provided an excuse for the cleaning lady to hand over the machine.

Attaching a long nozzle to the hose, Albertina instructed Sandra to clean under the bed and left the room decisively.

On her knees, then her belly, Sandra focussed only on dust and cobwebs. There was nothing stored under the single bed, never used during her time as Mrs Hardisty, but now she was on a mission. She had a job to do.

With difficulty she forced the nozzle into the crevice

where carpet met skirting board. No speck of dust must escape her notice. Moving her body sideways was difficult in the small space. Awkward angles prevented full use of the nozzle, but she *must* free them of remaining flecks of dirt. The exertion felt like a punishment, metaphorical flagellation, welcomed in pursuit of absolution.

Wriggling her way backwards took time and effort. There were moments when she thought about calling for help, but in a last heave she arched her back, lifting the bed from beneath by perhaps a centimetre. Something fell; something that had been wedged between bed and wall, something soft. It was something like a doll. She eased her arm round until she could trap it between outstretched fingers. Inch by inch, she began her retreat into daylight.

It was not a large doll. Hand-stitched, a creation fashioned from remnants of linen and velvet, satin and lace. Its wide eyes were brown buttons on white, with embroidered brows of silky black thread. That same thread, stitched to the scalp, hung straight in a sleek black curtain over the doll's shoulders to a waist demarcated by a belt of black velvet ribbon. The doll wore a short, fluidly flimsy dress of red satin which covered only the topmost portions of its long, slender legs. Someone had fashioned a pair of high-heeled sandals from black tape to complete the details.

Sandra shivered. A chilling familiarity repelled her, something she could not put her finger on. A call from downstairs broke her thoughts.

"Nice cup o' tea, San'ra! You comin' down?"

Sandra squeezed the doll. A sharp pain in her thumb revealed, on examination, a globule of blood. She sucked the thumb, puzzled, failing to obey the summons. Checking up on Sandra ten minutes later, the older woman found her sitting on the bed with the small rag doll in her hands.

She held it out, showing the pinprick and tiny drop of blood. "There was a pin…"

Albertina took the doll and studied it solemnly.

"You know dis gal?"

Sandra nodded.

"You make dis doll to harm di gal?"

"No. I've never seen it before. It was stuffed down the side of the bed. I've never cleaned in here before."

Albertina wiped her finger through the dust on the bed-head and believed her.

"Who is she?"

"It's someone who works for my husband. Used to work for, I mean."

"She yo' friend?"

"We were at school together but weren't really friends. I didn't really have many …" Her voice trailed off. "Mr Hardisty brought her home once to help me, but I don't know anything about the doll. It makes me scared."

Albertina had seen this sort of thing before, but not since she arrived in Yorkshire all those years ago. It gave *her* the creeps, too.

"Help you wid what? You stick a pin in to hurt de gal?"

"No. I don't think she was kind to me, but my husband… he thought I could learn something from her."

Albertina shook the doll and watched the dust cloud the air around her hand. "Dis doll bin behin' d' bed for some long time. How long you been livin' 'ere?"

"A year and a half – maybe two. Why?"

"Mr Hardisty, 'e tell me his first wife die."

"Mm." Sandra nodded.

" 'Dis d e'room where she do her sewin'?"

"Yes. I think she did a lot of it."

"Then de dead Ms Hardisty – she make de doll. Maybe dis gal not kind to *her* either?"

This was a new idea. Surely Marianne hadn't been on the scene while Enid was alive? Sandra had always tried to measure her wifely skills against Enid's as they'd been reported in the bread shop after the accident with the gas cooker, and found herself wanting.

Albertina shook her head with a sigh and took hold of the pin-pricked thumb.

"De doll made to hurt de gal'. Dead Mz Hardisty, she seekin' revenge. Albertina believe dat de gal not a good soul. Feel in mi 'eart dead, old Mis' Hardisty weepin' 'ere in dis room while she sewin' dis doll."

Sandra was silenced. Her head spun. Did she believe in this sort of thing? Her parents would have scoffed, she was sure. Yet everything seemed to fit. While her head told her it was all superstitious baloney, her inner self said otherwise. A battle raged within her. She must not wish Marianne dead. The merest thought would make it happen.

She must re-enter the void. She must allow no malign thought to cross her mind. She must think the best of people, cause them no harm. Closing her eyes, she saw the black-haired doll, the flicking skirt, the big brown eyes … it was only a doll, she told herself.

Yet her lids remained closed, as if glued shut, the image slowly becoming human, alive, with a strong, confident stride. The brown eyes looked at her in direct, blatant challenge, their gaze somehow exuding the message, "You fool."

Trembling once again, she stuffed the doll back where she'd found it. Enid's spirit would help her, perhaps.

Albertina's voice intervened

"Now Mz Hardisty, gal, don' you go worryin' 'bout dis doll. 'It was only a game, maybe.

I believe in de Lord Jesus. I do not believe in de witchcraf'. You pray wid Albertina now and we send d'evil spirits away."

She took Sandra's hands and looked into her eyes.

"Ignorant people – uneducated people – dey believe in d'evil spirits. But Mz Hardisty gal, she educated; she too clever for witchcraft or voodoo."

Sandra smiled wanly.

"I'm not very well educated. I didn't pass all my exams, though I wish I had." What relief she felt; what easing of pressure in her chest, but could Albertina be trusted with the knowledge of Sandra's own wickedness? The smile disappeared. The mention of witchcraft had hit home. Her voice dropped.

"I believe that *I* am an evil spirit," she whispered, relieved to have said the words out loud. Her voice rose to a higher pitch. "If this is witchcraft, Enid Hardisty must have been a witch! Enid Hardisty left this for me. Maybe I *am* a witch. That must be why Fergus chose me."

She ended with a hysterical howl.

"But I don't want to be a witch!"

Distraught at the returning thought, she stared this way and that, looking for escape.

Albertina was silent, assessing the authenticity of Sandra's confession. She had known of such possession before, but long ago, in a different world, in a different life. She prayed silently to Jesus her Lord, asking that the evil spirit might be driven from this gal.

15

Uncle Fergus had underestimated his niece-of-some-sort-by-marriage. He'd never mapped out the familial line between himself and young Marianne – Enid had many siblings, all of whom produced a multitude of offspring and most of whose names Fergus had never bothered to remember. Had his conscience ever pricked him, there being no blood tie with the best-looking of the bunch would have absolved him of any wrong-doing.

Hardisty's eye had landed on Marianne when she was twelve or thirteen, at one of the interminable family celebrations or funerals that were always cropping up amongst his in-laws. The girl had seemed to be on the verge of puberty and, even then, had a come-hither look about her. Her own father had gone AWOL, and the mother had turned up at the do with a good-looking and very attentive new boyfriend. Marianne looked as if her nose had been put out of joint and pouted sulkily throughout. She'd hugged her Uncle Fergus and various male cousins repeatedly to attract the attention of her mother's escort. In this she failed, but her uncle by marriage began to have ideas.

As soon as she was old enough, Uncle Fergus would find jobs for her in the school holidays so that, by the time Marianne left school, she was well tuned-in to the functioning of the Hardisty empire. It made perfect sense for Fergus to make her his Personal Assistant on a permanent basis. The other nephews and nieces had mostly left home and established their own careers by the time their Aunty Enid died. None of them gave a thought to the arrangement.

Marianne would be a safe bet: bright enough to be compliant and efficient and to know which side her bread was buttered; not bright enough to want to innovate, investigate or negotiate terms. She was also very attractive, although a little bit too forward in public for more serious consideration. Always up for a bit of fun, but not a deep thinker: all in all, a desirable set of attributes in a Personal Assistant, as long as she knew her place.

Fergus had not noticed much change in Marianne since she was twelve but, by seventeen, she was not as daft as her uncle imagined. By eighteen, she had expectations. By nineteen, she realised she'd been duped. By twenty, she was determined to get what she was owed.

Marianne had never gone in for smoking behind the bike sheds at school – in fact they'd been dismantled when she was in Year 9 due to concerns about road safety. Uncle Fergus had, however, once glimpsed his niece taking a drag after one of the school hockey matches he liked to watch. Next time their paths crossed, he'd made a point of catching her alone and offering her something special, something better than anything available in the local shops. It wasn't long before she was hooked. Nothing too dangerous; nothing heavy: just something to tie her to him.

He'd started watching the hockey when his daughter Francine was in the school's Second Eleven some years earlier. It got him out of the house on a Saturday morning, and he liked to eye up the other young girls for their potential. Being in a position to offer a range of job opportunities, Mr

Hardisty was keen to have first choice when school-leaving time came. He found hockey players to be active and lively types who didn't need to be cajoled into accepting new experiences when they occurred. They weren't scared of a bit of pain, either.

Fergus Hardisty had employed Malcolm for just three years, but in that time had gained a detailed overview of the Pogson family, plus the knowledge that the girl behind the face-guard and 'keeper's pads was Malcolm's daughter, Sandra. This knowledge gave him food for thought. She was obviously a stolid, staid sort of girl. Although not a particularly good-looker at that stage, he reckoned she'd be easy to train up to suit his requirements.

During the matches, however, Fergus had focused most of his attention on the star of the pitch, young Marianne Reid. As well as being family of some description, Marianne had flair, beauty and nerve. What's more, she was readily available. He could tell that from the toss of her silky hair, the pout of her lips and the confident, shoulders-back stride. The gaze that met his eyes directly at every opportunity confirmed his instinct.

At seventeen, Marianne thought her future was assured. She'd been a dutiful little helper in the early days, developing her secretarial and financial skills at the same time as she allowed herself to help Uncle Fergus with his more personal needs from time to time. She missed her dad. At first Fergus had been a substitute, and she'd responded to the avuncular cuddles with gratitude. He made her feel secure. Maybe she responded more enthusiastically than he'd anticipated, but 'in for a penny, in for a pound', as her dad would have said.

Once, for a treat, her boss had taken her away for a weekend in Amsterdam under the guise of a business trip. (They'd spent some time experiencing the city's night-time entertainment to see what aspects might be transferable to Wraith.) Sotto voce over dinner, he'd shared with her some of his concerns about who would take over his businesses when he retired or died. Complimenting the girl on her acumen, intelligence and efficiency won her heart more effectively than any mention of her leggy desirability might have done. He led her to believe that he saw her, not as just his PA, but as a possible successor and even, maybe, heiress to his fortune. It wasn't long since Aunty Enid had died, but she knew their Francine didn't see much of her dad so could well be excluded from his will. Her brother Irwin didn't keep in touch at all. That created a comfy little slot which Marianne would be delighted to fill.

They'd returned from Amsterdam somewhat closer, with Marianne having a firmer grasp on the ropes for handling not only Fergus's business needs, but also his more intimate proclivities. Nothing had been said explicitly, but Marianne believed she had him hooked.

Only a few weeks later, she'd been shocked by his marriage to Sandra Pogson – the dowdy goody-two-shoes – but Fergus had reassured her that this would have no impact on either his need for her services or her future prospects so she let it ride. The time after his marriage, when he'd taken her back to the house in Snellington, rested in Marianne's memory as both triumph and disaster.

She was pleased that, at last, he had revealed their relationship to Sandra. The triumph was in the unspoken acknowledgement that Marianne was her uncle's mistress, and his new wife was on the way out because she couldn't please her man.

The disaster had come next morning, when Fergus peremptorily dumped her outside the office with the words,

"Tidy yourself up before you start work. You look like a drunken whore – which of course, you are.

Bad for business."

He'd driven off sharply to avoid being seen by other members of his staff. When she looked at her own reflection in the mirror of the office toilets, she realised the accuracy of her uncle's statement and her self-image was shattered.

Who was to blame? That was the question to be wrestled with.

16

Examining his soul got Malcolm Pogson nowhere. Did he feel like a murderer? How *does* a murderer feel? Surely, he would remember killing a man, even such a one as Fergus Hardisty, who deserved to die if anyone did.

No peace of mind had come with the flushing away of the train ticket. If not to commit a murder, why had he made that journey, on that day? He had no one to ask for help; thought of taking up church-going again, but Pamela wouldn't countenance the idea. All notions of a loving God had vanished with her eyesight.

Although he missed his daughter dreadfully, his shame was so deep, so overwhelming, that the possibility of reconciliation did not occur. He was dead to her. Numb, empty and emotionally destitute, Malcolm ignored the ring of the doorbell when it came.

Josie's husband Ralph kept his thumb on the button. He had his instructions: not to give up until he'd seen the whites of Malcolm Pogson's eyes.

There had never been much conversation between the two men, both being followers rather than initiators in all things domestic, but down at the club a few weeks ago Ralph had shared a game of darts with Bob Fownhope, whose wife was recovering well from her mini-stroke. Conversation had eventually touched on the Hardisty mystery and the Pogson misadventure.

After a pause, Bob had asked, "How's Malcolm managing?"

Ralph took another draught of beer and shook his head. "Dunno. Never see 'im." Taking aim, he threw his dart.

"Thought you lived next door?"

"Aye, I do. Never 'ad much to do wi' 'im. Don't want to intrude, y' know 'ow it is."

"And 'is wife?"

"She's miserable as sin, according to our lass. Won't 'elp 'ersen – an' won't let anyone else 'elp either. Must be 'ard, like, but no point blaming their Sandra like she does. They should never have let 'er marry that 'ardisty bloke in 'first place. Summat fishy there, you mark my words."

Another dart missed the bull's eye.

"Lass'd nivver bin out wi' a lad in 'er life, then gets wed to an old con-man like 'ardisty! 'E'll 'ave 'ad some 'old over 'em, you mark my words. Had an 'old over lots of folk round 'ere, There's more than one as is glad 'e's dead, but I'm sayin' nowt."

Bob was silent, his suspicions confirmed. Not knowing Ralph well, he kept guard on his response.

"Mebbe someone ought to check up on 'im – mekk sure e's copin', like." Bob could adjust his accent to suit the occasion.

Ralph didn't know about that – it was Josie who handled all the personal stuff – but grudgingly agreed to float the topic at home.

Thus it was that, as per wifely instruction, he stood on the Pogson doorstep ringing the bell. Josie had contrived to take Pamela Pogson out for a treatment administered by a trainee aromatherapist a few villages over the M62. The therapist, being friendly with one of the Fownhope daughters, had agreed to prolong the session as much as possible.

Now that Josie had cleared the decks for a chat with Malcolm, her husband stood on next door's step wondering where to begin. Eventually, he heard the sound of feet coming downstairs and the door opened. Malcolm looked grey and drawn, his expression neutral. Ralph was not encouraged.

"I were wonderin', like, if you could lend me a decent spade."

"Oh, aye?"

"Mine seems to 'ave gone missin'."

Malcolm's mind registered that, to judge by the state of Ralph's garden as seen from the Pogson back-bedroom window, it had not felt the benefit of a good spade for twenty years or more.

"Not sure where mine is either, now that you mention it." He glanced past the man to the untended borders around the front lawn.

The visitor did not take the hint but stood there, embarrassed.

"I'll have a look in 'shed. Suppose you'd better come an' all."

He shut the front door and went through the house, meeting Ralph at the side gate.

The shed was as tidy as before IT happened, although the shine was dimmed by dust. It smelt of wood and his lost contentment. There had been no new bulbs planted, no bedding plants this year. No brightness or new growth since IT happened.

Ralph was impressed by the shed and its contents, although not tempted to emulate the achievement. The loan of the best spade was swiftly transacted in near-silence but Ralph showed no sign of leaving. Malcolm tried to spur him on.

"Well … seems like you've got a job on. What y' plantin'?"

Stumped for a response, Ralph muttered something about leaving all the decisions to 'our lass' but wanting to make the ground ready to receive whatever she decided on. Still he stood, afraid to leave before extracting something he could report back to his lass.

"Best be off then." He stepped forward; paused; steeled his nerve. "How're y' managing?"

"Oh, y' know. Keep putting one foot in front of 'other. The wife needs more 'elp than I can give but she won't hear of tekkin'it from anyone but me. Still, we're copin', just about. It's nice of Josie to tekk 'er out for an hour or two."

"Aye, she tekks a lot on, our Josie, credit where it's due. She's got a good 'eart."

"Yes. Say thanks from me, will yer? I'm guessin' she'll not 'ear it from Pamela."

He looked bleak and beaten. Ralph rested the upturned spade against his shoulder and left with a silent wave, while Malcolm went back to his thoughts on murder. In a way, he hoped he *had* killed Hardisty. At least some good would have come from all the tragedy. OK, so the man had a heart attack and drowned, according to the police, but Malcolm would not have tried CPR if he'd had the chance. At the very least, Malcolm would gladly have watched Fergus Hardisty die. He was a murderer by proxy.

17

Now that Fergus Hardisty's body had been identified and the cause of death determined, Marianne could relax a bit. Having closed the businesses temporarily to get herself organised, she made it plain to all concerned that Mr Hardisty had given very clear instructions as to the procedure to be followed in the event of his unexpected demise. In fact she'd taken the trouble to create a back-dated document to that effect within hours of hearing the news. With his knowledge, she'd signed many a letter in his name when he was alive, so no suspicion was aroused now that he was dead. She'd spent some time practising Malcolm Pogson's signature, too.

Marianne had been seething for weeks about the 'drunken whore' comment, although retaliation was not her first course of action. Instead, she systematically set about taking copies of every important document relating to the businesses. Uncle Fergus had made promises. There was nothing wrong with ensuring that he lived up to them. She had soon composed plenty of evidence that could be presented in court or to a tribunal for unfair dismissal if he failed to do so. Of course, she hoped it wouldn't come to that; she'd been more or less happy the way things were. The photocopying was just for additional insurance.

When Uncle Fergus didn't turn up at the office for three days without explanation, she let it be known that he was on his boat and took a train ride to the city on the Humber herself. It was only a short walk to the shops and, after that, she would visit the marina on the pretext of papers in need of Uncle Fergus's signature. He was there but not pleased to see her, and she'd been kept on deck. No sooner had he scribbled his signature a few times than he'd returned below deck, sliding the hatch shut without comment.

Humiliated, Marianne had turned away, seen the open padlock and considered her options,

She had always believed that revenge is sweet. A return train took her back to the office to resume her composition and photocopying. Her absence had not been noticed. Wanting to keep it that way, she dumped the used ticket in the unzipped pocket of a pair of men's trousers hanging on a hook in the cloakroom. They probably belonged to one of the caretakers, she surmised.

*

Five weeks after the discovery of the Hardisty's body, Marianne approached the company's solicitor. Having made an appointment by phone, the PA explained that she'd been waiting for Mrs Hardisty to get in touch about the unpaid wages. The workforce of Hardisty Incorporated Holdings needed to know if they still had jobs to go to. Although Mr Hardisty had entrusted her with the code for the safe, she'd thought it wise to seek legal advice on how to proceed before opening it. Soberly dressed, her hair in a bun and wearing just a touch of make-up, she looked every inch the diligent, grieving secretary.

The solicitor had not previously been informed of the death, and efforts to contact Mrs Hardisty at the marital home were fruitless. As presumed executors of the will, following examination of the deceased's personal and business finances and assets, Heaval & Co would deal with all monetary matters. An Estates Practitioner visited Hardisty's office to supervise the opening of the safe and remove any paperwork. Back at Heaval & Co's Wraith office, this hefty file was put at the bottom of an overloaded in-tray for the time being.

Meanwhile, Ms Reid was authorised to re-open the businesses and keep them functioning on a low-key basis until they could be sold or wound up, depending on the instructions in the client's will.

Heaval & Co had not been made aware of the death of the first Mrs Hardisty or the client's remarriage and thus, by law, the will in their possession was automatically revoked. A new Last Will and Testament, discovered when the office safe was eventually opened and its contents removed to the solicitors' premises for safe-keeping, had been completed on a special form obtainable from a well-known High Street stationer and witnessed by two of the deceased's employees, Malcolm Pogson and Marianne Reid. One of the spaces for executors' names was blank. The other contained that of Marianne Reid (Ms).

This Will left only the motor-sailer *Young Enid* to the second Mrs Hardisty. The remaining businesses and the house in Snellington were bequeathed to her husband's niece and 'much- loved Personal Assistant, Marianne Reid'.

*

Somewhat miffed that the firm had been overlooked in the preparation of this new will, the Heaval & Co partners shrugged their shoulders and put any outstanding Hardisty Incorporated Holdings issues at the bottom of their in-trays. So it was that, by the time Ms Reid asked for a progress report on Uncle's Fergus's estate, Heaval and Co. had decided to walk away from the off-the-shelf document. The decision was conveyed in a terse written letter to Ms Reid at her place of employment and invited her to collect the document from their office. She should present it to another firm of lawyers to be acted upon.

Rumours had reached the Wraith office that late Fergus Hardisty's widow was only nineteen years old, yet some members of staff could remember Enid Hardisty as being fifty-five if she was a day. Checks were made. Local knowledge confirmed Enid's suicide, and someone at Heaval & Co trawled through the vaults to unearth the Last Will and Testament of the late Enid Hardisty, of which her husband had been unaware. Miss Reid, who had been asking the questions, had never been a client of Heaval & Co. whilst the late Mrs Hardisty had. Let some other company's paralegals struggle with the likely chaos of sorting out Fergus Hardisty's financial obligations.

Lurking almost forgotten at the back of a filing cabinet, Enid's will was dusted off and work begun on carrying out its terms. Although some of the Heaval and Co. partners had been several years retired, on hearing of Fergus Hardisty's demise the lawyers recalled with disapproval the way the man had managed his financial affairs. The Heaval partners coldly dismissed Ms Reid's demands to be told what the hell was going on.

Marianne was stumped for a while. Did she know any other solicitors who could show her the way forward without asking searching questions? She *really* wanted the house in Snellington, but news had reached her that Sandra had moved back in and, when Marianne drove past to check, the place was looking spick and span, with a well-tended hedge, sparkling windows and bright, white washing blowing on the line in the side garden.

The issue of her husband's will had not occurred to Sandra. No one had questioned the assumption that she would be the main beneficiary. Such matters were private, family stuff, not to be discussed in the pubs and shops. Sandra had never considered herself part of the Hardisty family.

18

A couple of weeks after the young widow's return to the house, Albertina made up her mind to ask about the unpaid wages. While she'd been mothering the girl, her own cash flow problems had multiplied. If she wasn't going to be paid, finding another job must be her priority. She was also concerned about the mounting pile of unopened letters for Mr Hardisty on the hall table. Sandra wouldn't countenance opening them, but made no suggestions about who else might deal with the correspondence.

The two women were about to do some housework together. It was easier to get the girl to open up when she was doing a little light dusting, so the time had come to raise the matter of wages.

"I have a big worry, San'ra. Dis pile o' letters for Mr Hardisty remin' me. Dese letters look like bills dat need payin' – an'dey remin' me dat *I* also have bills dat need payin', but I got no money!"

Sandra paused her shining of the banister.

"Bills for what?"

She had never had to think about where the money came from to keep the lights on or food in the fridge.

"You not makin' it easy for Albertina, San'ra ... I need payin' for eight weeks' workin' in dis house!"

"Who pays you?"

"*No one* since Mr Hardisty disappear. He supposed to pay me eight pound' per hour for ten hours each week. He leave mi money in his study each Friday. I is owed more dan six hundred poun', Sandra. I need money for food and to pay mi own bills."

Sandra was shaken. Why had the cleaning lady been allowed into the study when she herself was forbidden? The door had always been locked unless Fergus was in there, or so she'd believed. She began to tremble uncontrollably at the thought of her father's conduct. Once more she felt the pins and needles cramp her face, the fingers' rigid spasms, the closing of her airways, the spinning head. She reached out for something to hold before she fell. Her hand was grasped. This time, there was someone to help. This time, she did not have to face it alone. Albertina held her, speaking soothing words, helping her to sit on a stair, stroking her gently, slowing the rasping breath until the tears flowed, the pins and needles faded away and exhaustion took over.

The cleaning was forgotten, but Albertina had to press on.

"San'ra, who is payin' de bills for dis 'ouse?"

"What bills?"

"Pile o' bills I see dere on dat table."

"They're addressed to my husband. He wouldn't like me to open his private letters."

"He is *DEAD*, San'ra! He don' care *who* open his letters. Somebody has to do it, and dat somebody is *you!*"

Sandra was trembling again.

"Do it now!" The top letter was thrust into the shaking hands, a shiny steel letter-opener proffered.

She took it, looked at the point, and slid it under the flap, holding her breath in fear of repercussions.

"Why you so afraid, San'ra? Come an' sit on de stairs

while you read de letter, chile. You gotta learn to face up to life like it is. Tell me, why you so afraid?"

Silence. The cleaner was losing patience and her compassion wearing thin.

"Well, Sandra, whether you wanna talk to me or no, I need payin'. I got no money to settle mi own debts and I bin working many more hours dan Mista Hardisty engage me for, jus' to keep you comp'ny. You bin takin'me for granted an' I don't like dat."

Sandra turned, her eyes brimming. She withdrew the paper from the envelope and read the letter, a complicated grid of digits and percentages which made no sense. The tears brimmed over and she wiped them away with her sleeve.

"Dat's de 'lectric bill, San'ra. It needs to be paid. You'ave to pay it or dey will cut de 'lectric off."

Among the the pile, she found three more items bearing the same power company logo.

"You bin ignorin' de letters and dis be de final deman'. Now – you got a cheque book Sandra? A bank card?"

"No. Fergus dealt with all the money."

"You got some money of your own?"

"Fergus gave me £100 on the first day of each month for my personal needs and to pay the window-cleaner."

"What about food?"

"Fergus handled all that. He had a regular order from a shop in Wraith. They delivered the groceries in a van. He didn't like me to go to the shops. Said there was no need, and the one time I went to get my hair done he didn't even notice.

"An' who pay for de groceries? You pay de delivery man?"

"No. I've never seen him. I only pay the Window Cleaner… The food just arrives every week."

This was trickier than the cleaner had imagined. Who

was paying for the food that came every seven days? In the time she'd thought the Hardisty's were on holiday, she had herself carried several boxes full of groceries from the doorstep, to store carefully in cupboards, fridge and freezer.

"Sandra, you gotta step up an' sort dese t'ings out. You gotta start t'inking!" She tapped her own temples to demonstrate the need.

"I don't know how."

The admission came out as a wail.

The tears began to flow once more and the whining voice grew irritating. Albertina had had enough. Taking Sandra's elbow, she steered her to where several coats hung on an old-fashioned stand. The menswear was of good quality, although the velvet-collared camel coat struck the woman as an unlikely fashion option for Wraith.

"Which is yours, San'ra?"

She pointed to a school blazer and a brown anorak. "That one, and that."

"You got a better coat d'an dat, surely?"

"Fergus said I didn't need more clothes. He was happy for me to use his wife Enid's ... she died ... he said they'd been very expensive when they were bought. They're smart, but too small for me. Fergus said I looked like lamb dressed as mutton when I tried them on. I didn't really understand what he meant, so I've made do with what I already had"

In the silence that followed, each pair of eyes was downcast.

"Mr Hardisty – he was a unkin' man, I t'ink. Do you believe so, San'ra?"

Once more, the eyes brimmed.

"I don't really know what that means."

"I'm thinkin' he did not treat you well, San'ra. He unkin'. Why yo' parents let you marry 'im?"

"Fergus said they had no right to stop me. I was eighteen and could make my own decisions."

"An' you agree?"

"Mum thought it was the best chance I'd ever have to get a husband, because I'm not pretty and not particularly clever or interesting. Not like her. At least, not like she *was* …"

"You is good lookin' enough! An' you can go to Mom and Dad for 'elp now!"

"No, I can't." It was difficult to get the words out. "My mother's disowned me and doesn't want Dad to see me either."

"Why d'ey disown you?"

"Because I blinded my mother!" Her fists dug into the eye sockets as if to blind herself.

Albertina remembered hearing this before. It couldn't be true, could it? This gentle, scared child was surely incapable of a deliberately violent act.

"You do it on purpose?"

"No! I wasn't even there when it happened. But she was upset with me, and because of that she had an accident. She blames me for blinding her, as if I'd done it on purpose."

She had no sobs left now. Weariness overwhelmed them both; enough talking. They needed time to recuperate, but Albertina really *must* get some wages.

"Put de kettle on, Sandra. I's too old for all dis upset. I got my own sadness to handle."

She reached a tissue from her apron pocket.

"My husban' – he die jus' eight month ago – he no' leave me a big posh 'ouse an' a little car o' my own! He left me wid a few gamblin' debts and enough money to pay for d' fun'ral, but I need a job to keep me goin' until I get mi ol' age pension. An' *I* had loved *my* husban' for forty-four year, San'ra. He love me and give me t'ree fine chil'ren. Now '*dat* was a marriage, not 'dis cruel nonsense you be telling me 'bout. *Dat* was *no* marriage! *Dat* was *chile abuse!*"

The woman's smile had gone. No longer concealed by her buoyant, cheerful expression, lines of grief and weariness spoke of her true age. Sandra did as instructed. While the kettle came to the boil, she searched round for the chocolate digestive biscuits Albertina had described as 'very comfortin'. She laid them out on a china plate, selected a pretty cup and saucer, a neat tray, china tea-pot and milk jug which had belonged to Enid, and carried the tray into the sitting room. Sandra was aware that her own breath came more easily now.

"I'm sorry, Albertina," she called. "Please come through here."

She drew back the heavy curtains to let the sun shine in, set a disc of soothing music to play softly, set down the tray and made sure Albertina was comfy.

It seemed that the band of iron encircling Sandra's heart had been released. She could breathe deeply again. An inrush of vitality unfurled and expanded within her. As when the weight of long-lying snow thaws to reveal the green shoots of life beneath, she sensed that, sometime soon, she would see sunshine and blue skies.

Albertina's words, "'Dat was no marriage! 'Dat was chile abuse!" had cleft the constricting band in two. Once more the blood flowed freely around her body. She knelt at the woman's feet, took her hands in her own, and kissed her gently on the cheek.

"Thank you. You've been very kind. I don't know how I'd have survived without you and … Simon." She hesitated. "Simon's parents were kind to me too, but now his mother is very ill and it's my fault. I don't want you to fall sick because of me as well."

Albertina sighed.

"If I bin kin', Sandra, it because I see a lonely young woman who ain't bin treated right an' I don' understan' why. Now let me drink mi tea and calm mi-self down."

Sandra poured the tea

"Chocolate digestive?" she held out the plate. "Very comfortin'…"

She took a seat by the window. Outside, a flock of long-tailed tits swerved around the garden and disappeared into a laurel bush.

"The best thing about living here is watching the birds. Since I married Fergus, I've spent hours trying to imagine what it's like to be as free as a bird. What it's like to *be* a bird. There are the little ones, like the wrens and the long-tailed tits there, and the big bullying ones like the rooks and crows. I wonder what they're talking to each other about. Sometimes I see a heron fly over, or a skein of geese …" She tailed off, pensive.

This was a different Sandra. The thoughts she uttered came as a surprise to both herself and the listener; the softer tone came as a blessing to Albertina, who had no heart for conflict. She sipped her tea and nibbled the biscuits, letting go of her money worries for a spell, while the girl quietly spoke of her life in a world populated only by a lone goldfish in a bowl, the birds in the garden, a monthly visit and a few words from the window cleaner. She did not mention her husband. She was still in fear of what he might do, even in death, if she betrayed the full truth. The story of her mother's accident remained untold but it would come in time, Albertina knew.

"Let's leave the cleaning for now." Sandra stood up. "I don't think I'll be able to pay you everything you're owed, but I'll see how much is in my purse."

With the groceries delivered uninvited and use of her car negligible, Sandra had spent little, except of course for the disastrous visit to Justine's salon. Her purse yielded £95.

"But I have more upstairs."

In truth, since her honeymoon she'd been saving the

surplus under the mattress in Enid's sewing room – although she didn't know what for. This was *her* secret – even Simon hadn't known – and would have been very cross if he had. After the death, she'd harboured a vague notion of reimbursing the Fownhopes for their kindness, but had never followed it through. Now Albertina had to be paid. Even so, Sandra was loath to relinquish her nest-egg.

"I'll give you this £95 to start with and will try to find more for next time you come." She looked into the pained eyes. "I know you deserve to have it all now, but I need to make my mind up what to do next."

"Albertina is grateful for dis money now, San'ra, but you need to pay me d'res' next week." She set the china cup carefully on the tray and stood up slowly. "Tis 'ome-time for me. Albertina's not feelin' too good. I need mi bed."

"There's some petrol in the tank. May I drive you home?" She was excited by the prospect of having somewhere to go. "Let's see if the engine will start."

Sandra was surprising herself. This new *her* was taking the reins, reins which felt unfamiliar in her hands … and she began to believe that she *could* survive; felt a glimmer of confidence that she *would* survive. She knew that she must put things right, and that the transformation within her was not her own doing.

"Albertina…" Her face was solemn. "Thank you."

"Thank me for what, San'ra?"

"For setting me free."

Albertina perched on the arm of the sofa.

"For settin' you free?"

"Free of guilt. You told me '*That* was no marriage. *That* was child abuse.' You kind of told me it's alright to be glad that Fergus is dead. You saw what my own mother could not see: that my husband was an unkind … no … a *cruel* man. It was as if … as if I'd been kidnapped."

Another silence.

"An' what about yo' daddy, chile?"

"I don't know. He did come to see me once when I was staying at Simon's. I used to be his little girl and I loved him *so* much, but it was as if a thick pane of glass stood between us. I just couldn't bring myself to speak to him in case … in case …"

"In case what?

Sandra breathed in deeply and held her breath.

"I daren't say it."

"Say it San'ra."

"In case I killed *him* as well. You see … I think … I think…" Her voice was fading now, her eyes searching the floor.

"What you thinkin'?"

"I think my thoughts can harm people – even kill them."

Albertina stood, grabbing her hefty handbag with determination. Her expression was angry.

"Not dat nonsense again! I nevah hear such wicked ideas befo'! Take me 'ome now, please."

Albertina was not telling the truth. She *had* heard such ideas before, but thought she'd left all that mumbo-jumbo behind her. She set her feet apart and stood as if to flee. In fact, her stance was to conceal the trembling in her legs and in her heart.

"Take me home."

She bustled to the door to wait. Sandra knew she had confessed too much. Maybe she'd frightened Albertina away for good.

"I don't even know where you live," she said. The answer was a tiny hamlet two miles away down country lanes.

"You've been walking two miles each way each time you come to my house? That's much too far."

"For a woman o' my age, you mean?"

"Well yes. Give me your phone number. I'll ring you tonight to make sure you're OK. Next time, I'll pick you up in the morning. No arguments."

"What a relief," thought Albertina.

"What a relief," thought Sandra. Now she had a reason to get up in the morning. Now she had a purpose, someone who needed her help. It was time for her to help the cleaning lady. That would be a start.

That evening, she finished the housework, baked biscuits to share on Albertina's next visit and made her mind up that there would be no actual cleaning for the woman to do. Next, she lifted the mattress in the sewing room and counted her stash of notes.

*

It was bigger than she'd expected, but not enough to settle all the bills. That evening, with no-one to guide her, she set about becoming a grown-up. The bills and bank statements lay open on the table in front of her. She forced herself to open Fergus's desk in search of anything that might help; found an old calculator, pen and paper, and set about the arithmetic. The desk smelt of him. Sandra shuddered, deployed a can of air freshener and pressed on.

She could pay Albertina what she was owed. That was a relief. Her remaining funds would just about cover the fuel bills and the demands for payment from the grocer in Wraith she'd found amongst the unopened mail. Soon, she would have nothing left; nothing to live on. Turning to her father for help wasn't an option although, for the first time since her marriage, inwardly she acknowledged how she yearned for his comforting hug.

In bed, she tossed and turned. Becoming an adult overnight made her nervous but held some excitement, too. By dawn she was convinced that the house would have to be sold. At daybreak, she set off in the mini to seek out homes with For Sale signs in their gardens, noting down contact details for six different estate agents. The house would have to be valued: she visited the agents in turn. Times were hard and house owners were staying put, so arranging two prompt valuations was easy.

Back at the house, elation and trepidation took turns. Small steps at first, she told herself, but there was freedom ahead. 'With freedom comes risk', another voice whispered, but what had she to lose? The answer flashed like a beacon in her mind's eye: she had Simon to lose. But she didn't *have* Simon. That was just a dream, a dream not even admitted to herself, until today. He probably never gave her a thought or, if he did, it was to call her a selfish brat.

Albertina was taken aback by the FOR SALE sign when Sandra fetched her to work the next week. She hadn't expected that! Her mind scrabbled around thinking where else she might find employment. It would be a relief in some ways – she could do without Sandra's angst and tears – but she was growing fond of the girl. Her own grown-up children were all living in separate northern cities and, although they rang her every week, it was not the same as having them on the doorstep to fuss over from time to time.

She saw the kitchen table was neatly set for two. Without a word, Sandra gestured for her to s take a seat. Fruit juice and a full English breakfast were soon placed in front of her.

"Tea or coffee?"

"What's goin' on, Sanr'ra?"

"I'm putting the house on the market, but I want to show how much I appreciate what you've done for me. Eat up. We can talk later, but thanks to you, Albertina, I think I'm learning how to grow up."

The food was good and tasted so much better for having

been prepared especially for her. It was pleasing be appreci-
ated. She wondered if she would get her money, or was this
just a ruse to make her forget what she was owed?

19

Within a week of the FOR SALE sign going up outside the house in Snellington, Sandra was in the process of opening a bank account of her own and Albertina was enjoying the special attention and reassurance that she would get what was due to her. They were sharing a cooked breakfast in the kitchen when a ring of the front door bell broke into their chat.

Marianne Reid stood on the doorstep, sleek and glamorous as ever. Sandra, looking as unglamorous as ever, found herself tongue-tied.

"What's going on, Sandra?"

"Going on about what?"

"All these **For Sale** signs."

"I'm selling the house."

"It's not yours to sell!" Marianne waved a foolscap envelope in Sandra's face.

"Of course it is! I was Fergus's wife."

"But he's left the house to me. I *am* his niece, after all." She smirked, her eyes scanning the widow's comfy fleece top and worn jeans.

In the kitchen, Albertina crept to where she could hear the conversation properly. This young woman, whoever she was, sounded like a bully. Albertina would have no truck with bullying.

Sandra's voice wavered. "Surely the house automatically became mine when Fergus died?" She stood as if frozen, knowing she was not on firm ground. What did *she* know of the law?

Albertina edged closer to the kitchen door.

"In this envelope is Fergus's will. It was in the company safe. The solicitor came to see me open it. *Your* husband's left the house to *me*, and I am the executor! I've told the solicitor he can bugger off."

Although she had no idea what it meant to be an executor, Marianne could not suppress her glee as she waved the envelope again.

"Most of the businesses are mine, too!" Her triumph was complete.

Sandra had no response. She stood, her mouth gaping.

Albertina edged the kitchen door open an inch. Through the crack she could see a young, dark haired woman in red. Her build and clothing were reminiscent of the rag doll discovered behind the bed a week ago. Albertina's antennae sensed skulduggery.

In three bounds, the cleaning lady crossed the hall, pushed Sandra aside and snatched the envelope from the PA's hands.

"Albertina will take care o' dat. My son Tobias, he work for Mista Hardisty's lawya. I will see it get to de right people. T'ank you for callin'. I dare say Heaval and Comp'ny will be in touch."

She closed the door, setting her back against it to allow her heaving breast to subside.

Marianne stood on the step a little longer, stumped. Who was the black woman with the deep voice and how come she knew about Heaval & Co? Fergus Hardisty's Personal Assistant would not take this lying down, but she needed time to think.

Sandra still stood gaping. Humiliation swamped her. How could she ever move on now?

"We got breakfas' to finish, San'ra. I warm it up in de microwave. Come back to de kitchen. We finish our breakfas' and t'ink about what jus' 'appen."

They ate in silence, their eyes subdued.

"Does your son really work for Fergus's lawyer?"

"Well ….'dat be only a little lie, Sandra. My Tobias, he done a work placement at Heaval & Co when he was at school. Dat was at de Wraith office… mebbe fourteen, fifteen year ago."

"Where is he now?"

"He livin' in Leeds, an' workin' at de Heaval & Company Head Office dere. Doin' well. My boy doin' *very* well. My Tobias, he de firs' o' my fam'ly to attend de university. Passed a lot o' exams, and still studyin' for more. Albertina very proud."

"What about your other children?"

"Henrietta, *she* is a social worker in York, an' Nina just startin' to teach Infants in Bradfor'. All done very well. Dere daddy, he so proud of dem before he die. Me too." Her eyes brimmed with unshed tears. "Albertina jus' wish dey all live closer to Mom. But de cos' of university for t'ree chil'ren … it eat up de money. My husban'… he work and work every hour he could. 'Slow down', say de doctor. 'Mista Hedge, you gotta slow down or you will have heart attack'. But he mus' work; work 'imself to death."

"Did he have a heart attack?"

A nod of the head.

Sandra reached out a comforting hand. She wondered how Albertina could carry on after her loss, wondered at her husband's sacrifice of his life in doing his best for his children.

And what had Sandra, ever achieved? She thought of the sacrifices her own father had been forced to make when the cinema closed down. He'd loved that job. He'd once been a manager, held a position of authority, but had been willing to take on any work he could to support his family. She wondered why Mum hadn't looked for work to help out. The question had never arisen, as far as Sandra could remember. Their lives had been all about protecting their daughter, but they had not prepared her for life away from them, nor stopped her sacrificing her own youth.

"If I had a daughter," she began, "I wouldn't want her to get married until she was older."

She looked at Albertina sorrowfully.

"I didn't know what it meant. I thought it would be fun, but it was horrible. I wouldn't have believed it was possible to be married and be so lonely. Shows how much I knew. I just hope I never make that mistake again."

"Mebbe you fin' a han'some young man and fall in love, have lots of bebbies and be very 'appy for de res'o'your life. It 'appens. I hope it 'appens to you, San'ra."

She bustled about, readying herself to the housework that did not need doing, blinking away the tears that still flowed.

"You see anyt'ing of dat good-lookin' young window cleaner …?" Her voice rose inquisitively, although she kept her eyes averted.

"No." The terse response proved Sandra's disappointment.

"Honey, you tell me his mother took sick. Did you sen' a card? Or flowers? You find out if she recoverin'?"

"No. I didn't think of that."

"San'ra, you still such a spoilt chile. Dat fam'ly – dey open dere house and dere hearts to you. What yo t'inking of? Dey might need help from you dis time, and dere be no reason you cannot offer it."

It was true. She had blocked the Fownhopes from her mind, although Simon floated through her dreams in various guises. Sandra remained seated.

"Please, Albertina, come and sit down again. I don't need you to do anything at the moment, except be my friend."

She lowered her eyes. "I…I've never …" she couldn't go on.

"Never what, chile?"

"I've never really had a friend." She stared down at her hands, picking at her fingernails.

Albertina was dumbstruck. When her children were young, the house had always been open to their friends, with their shouts and laughter, the jokes and the mess, the fallings out and accidental injuries which fortunately had always been soon mended. One or two of them still called in from time to time to check that she was OK.

"No friends at school?"

"No one special. No one I really talked to. Most girls were really, really nice but I hardly ever saw them out of school … not after I was twelve or so. I used to like playing hockey – I was the goalkeeper – because it felt nice to be part of a team, but after the games I just went home. Sometimes the others asked if I wanted to go for a coffee in Wraith, but I wasn't allowed to. Sometimes Fergus would come to watch the match and take me home afterwards in his car … I didn't get much chance to walk home with the others."

Something occurred to her.

"I didn't know Fergus was related to Marianne. He never mentioned it. She was the star of the team – ever so pretty – but I never saw him give *her* a lift home. I wonder why not."

It felt good to be talking about herself. The cleaner remained silent, her perception of the late Mr Hardisty darkening with every word shared. Their eyes met.

"Go on, San'ra."

"It was one of the times after hockey …" she drew a deep breath, "that he asked me to marry him." She trembled now at the memory.

"You still at school?"

"Mmm."

"What yo' mammy an' daddy say?"

"They seemed pleased. Mum was relieved that I'd have a husband and a nice house and not have to worry about money. Not sure about Dad. He smiled, but it didn't seem real. Dad worked for Mr Hardisty, you see, so he couldn't really object."

If only her father had protested more loudly.

"He said we should wait until after my exams, but my eighteenth birthday was eight months before the A Levels so Fergus insisted we should get married quickly. I carried on going to school but didn't do well in the exams. Fergus said I would have no need of qualifications."

They sat in silence while Albertina digested this information.

"He said he would mould me into a true woman."

Albertina's eyes widened in disapproval. She said nothing.

"The strange thing is ..." Sandra went on, "I never accepted his proposal. I *never* said yes. I've gone over it in my mind, hundreds of times ... and I'm absolutely certain that I never said yes. We got back to our house in Mulberry Grove, I went upstairs to get changed and, when I came down, they were all drinking sherry and Dad proposed a toast. Then, I think, I fainted and was taken to bed. When I came down later, it was all arranged."

There was more to this than met the eye, Albertina was certain, but was it any of her business? Should she just look for another cleaning job elsewhere?

"If you don' need mi to do no cleanin' Sandra, I gotta fin' me a new job"

"Please, please – I do need you." Sandra grabbed her hand again. "I need you to help me. Just to talk to me. I'll find the money, I will. Just stay." Eyes brim full, fear in her voice, she was desperate.

"If I stayin', Sandra, you gotta start helpin' yo'self and start puttin' t'ings right."

"OK. Tell me what to do."

"Firs', you gotta go visit 'dat young window cleaner and his family, an' say, ' How are you? An' ' Get well soon and t'ank you for all you done for me'."

No response.

"Den, you mus' go to yo' mammy an' daddy, try to help dem. Talk to dem."

"I wouldn't know what to say. Mum wouldn't speak to me after her accident. I'll think about it." She averted her eyes.

"No! No time for t'inkin'. You gotta do dis, Sandra, or I go home an' not comin' back."

She left the table, lifted her heavy bag and picked up her coat.

"Albertina's tired. Needs her rest. Got her own sorrows to cry about." She pressed the door handle. "You go today. You tekk me to mi home now. Nex' you drive to Wraith and visit de poor Fownhope family. I jus' hope dey let you in after all yo' selfishness."

"Must I?"

"You mus' if you ever wanna be happy again, Sandra; if you wanna have friends and fam'ly and a normal life, yes, you mus'!" She relented just a little. "I will sit on de seat in de garden for ten minutes. You wash yo' face and mekk yo-self self tidy. Pick some flowers from de garden ...make a nice bouquet. Do somet'ing dat says, 'T'ank you for what you done. I appreciate your kin'ness."

Albertina walked slowly round the garden to the weathered seat, absorbing the birdsong and the peace, her mind dwelling on her husband Kelvin and what he would have made of all this. He would have blacked both of Mista Hardisty's eyes for even *suggestin'* he han' over his daughter for his boss's sexual pleasure! An' dat would jus' have bin de start. Her Tobias, a professional man, would have seen off anyone tryin' to tekk advantage o' one o' his sisters.

Sandra emerged looking tidy but nervous. "What if they won't let me in?"

"You jus' keep tryin'. You ax if dey need any 'elp. You write dem a letter ... lots of letters if need be. You gotta repay dere good deeds." She raised herself stiffly. "Now take mi 'ome please."

Sandra drove slowly, but within a few minutes, alone in the car, she watched as her friend opened her own front door and closed it firmly behind her. Bereft, she drove away, wondering where else she could go rather than the Fownhopes' house.

20

Two hours later she was almost out of petrol, had no money in her purse and no idea what to do next. If asked, she could not have said which roads she'd travelled, although her aim had been to drive in ever-decreasing circles until she homed in on the Fownhopes' street. The engine finally spluttered to a halt in a built-up area she knew only vaguely. There were no passers-by to ask for help. She waited a while, hoping that something or someone would turn up, but at last climbed out of the Mini and walked along the unfamiliar streets, where empty shops and full litter bins created a bleakness which drained hope.

As she passed a drab, single-storeyed building behind a three foot wall and a litter-strewn car-park, a door on her right swung open. A snatch of music carried on the air as a middle-aged man walked out and away down the street, whistling to himself. Sandra halted. She approached the building and read the words above the door:

Wraith and District Working Men's Club.

Mum would disapprove. Her daughter pushed on the door and walked in.

It took a while for her eyes to adjust to the lack of light.

A fire extinguisher hung on the wall of the grim vestibule. Through the glass panels of a pair of swing doors, a lamp glowed yellow. Every so often, she heard strange, electronic notes. A man's voice grunted and muttered to himself.

Sandra steeled herself and pushed again through swinging doors.

An old chap in work jeans stood at a fruit machine, feeding it with coins or tokens. The obscenities made it clear he was losing money fast, but he kept on feeding the machine undeterred. Another man, somewhat younger, sat at a corner table reading a folded newspaper. Behind the bar, the club manager stood with his back to her as he counted the takings in the till. Reaching a round number and sensing a female presence, he turned as she approached.

"Can I help you, love?"

"I don't know what to do. My car's run out of petrol and I've come out without any money."

Her voice was timid but the manager reckoned the face was familiar. Local, definitely, but he couldn't put a name to her family.

"Oh aye?" How many times had he heard that one? "That were a daft thing to do, weren't it?"

"Yes." It was the merest whisper.

He saw the tears waiting to fall.

"What's your name, love?"

"Sandra."

"Don't you 'ave a surname, then? Where're you from?"

"Sorry. It's Pogson … no, I mean Hardisty."

"Don't yer know?"

"Hardisty. Sandra Hardisty. Used to be Pogson."

"You're not that young lass as married that Fergus Hardasnails?"

She remained silent, puzzling for a few moments.

"No. Hardisty"

The man in the corner laid his paper on the table in front of him and tuned his ears to the conversation. The club manager polished a glass with a cloth.

"I'm sorry for your loss then, love. I heard he were dead."

Sandra gulped and nodded.

The man with the newspaper stood up and slowly made his way to the bar.

"Give me another half, will your, George? An' what you 'avin', Sandra love? I'm right glad to see yer." Ralph Maycock cupped his hand round Sandra's shoulder. "Come and sit down wi' me and tell me what's up."

She did as told. The manager brought a glass of Coke over, along with the half of mild.

"Our Josie'll be right glad I've seen yer, Sandra. We've all bin worried sick. I borrered yer dad's spade the other week. Shall I send 'im your love when I tekk it back?"

What relief! She wanted to ask if there had been any more kittens; to ask about Josie, and Sally's baby. She dare not ask about Mum, or even Dad.

Ralph was still talking.

"Our Sally had twins. Did you know? Two little boys – toddlers now – at that cute stage when you just want to cuddle and play wi' 'em. They'll soon be getting up to mischief, you mark my words."

"That's lovely. What are their names?" How she longed to hear all the family news.

"You'll not believe me if I tell you!" He suppressed a laugh. "Eric Claude and Basil Bruce! Our Sally insisted they had names no one else round 'ere would copy. They'll never use their full names though. They're Ric and Baz to everyone already."

Sandra smiled. "I'd love to see them, but I'm not allowed on Mulberry Crescent now!"

"Not allowed? Who's to stop you? You're talkin' nonsense,

Sandra. Any road, Sally and Gary live on Clipsham Terrace now. Why don't you call in? It's not far from 'ere."

Ralph supped a couple of mouthfuls from his glass and looked ahead, thinking. Sandra, too, was thoughtful.

"I … I do miss everyone." Her voice was wistful. "I do get lonely."

Would the message get back to Dad? There was no point even *thinking* about Mum. That door was well and truly bolted for ever.

"Aye, it can be tough bein' on your own, I'll grant yer that." He supped some more, still thinking. "I've just got to pop to 'Gents. We'll sort out the petrol when I get back."

Five minutes later he was back, having used the time to contact Josie.

"What should I do?" he asked.

"Find out where 'er car is, first of all. Say you need to get a container for 'petrol from 'ome before you can sort out 'er car. Anything. Say anything."

"Righto. Then what?"

"Use some gumption, Ralph. Our Sal's 'ere wi' twins. See if yer can get 'lass to come inside to say 'ello."

"Gumption. Right. Will do!"

He hung up and sauntered casually back into the bar. Sandra was where he'd left her.

"Righto, Sandra. Let's get it sorted. It's only a ten minute walk."

He didn't mention where the walk would take them.

Most of the streets they walked had never been familiar to Sandra and she took little heed of the paths they trod. Ralph prattled on about football, his grandchildren, what sort of car Sandra owned and where she'd abandoned the vehicle – anything to keep her listening politely and responding occasionally. They were through his own front gate before she recognised the house. Ralph slid a key into the lock, stepped back and ushered her indoors. Sandra registered the cat hairs on the carpet before Josie appeared, holding a large tabby and feigning surprise.

"Ee, Sandra love! Fancy *you* comin' to see us! I'm right glad you've called. Ralph, put 'kettle on, an' there's some shortbread in 'tin."

Ralph relinquished his charge with relief.

"So how've you bin, love? I were sorry to 'ear about your 'usband." Josie had no problem with hypocrisy when appropriate.

Sandra said nothing, but stroked the cat gently. It stretched its claws and purred before jumping to the ground to rub itself against her legs.

"It's Tammy, isn't it? Has she had any more kittens?"

"Not for a while, but we got a new one from 'Cats' Rescue the other day. Come in 'ere and meet 'er."

Within seconds, Sandra was swinging a twist of paper on a string while a tiny black and white creature tried to swat it with her paws. Playing with the kitten eased the tension … better than talking at the moment, Josie thought. She watched the girl laugh and smile as they played; it would do her good to relax. Later, Josie would get closer to the truth.

The sound of running feet was followed by two tiny boys in grubby pyjamas and their laughing mother.

"Hiya, Sandra! You haven't met 'twins 'ave yer?" Sally behaved as if they'd met just the other day.

"Hello Sally. Your dad told me about them." She glanced down at her feet. "I've run out of petrol," she added as an afterthought. "I didn't know what to do so I went into the club to ask for help …and… he was there! He's going to help me." Her tone was wistful.

The car seemed like a distant memory she would dismiss if she could. Sandra's attention was drawn away from the kitten as she joined in the tickling and peek-a-boo games.

Sally and Josie looked on with relief, holding a silent conversation and with their eyes suggesting mother and daughter should retire to the kitchen.

"We'll just see what that kettle's doing. You're all right looking after them for a few minutes aren't you, Sandra?"

"I'll be fine. I'm having a good time!" She laughed as one of the twins ran his tiny hands and a toy car through her hair. Sally pulled the door to as she went to check on the kettle.

Moments later, Josie was knocking on the Pogsons' door, opened by Malcolm in a grubby sweatshirt and stockinged feet.

"Your Sandra's here." Josie kept her voice low. "Why don't you come round and see 'er?"

Malcolm was shocked into silence until, hearing the circumstances, he could see a way forward.

There's a petrol can in 'shed. I can nip to 'petrol station – Pam'll be alright for ten minutes."

He smelt escape like the taste of salt on a sea breeze, grabbing his jacket and shoes, checking for his wallet and ushering Josie from the step. As the door swung shut, he called over his shoulder,

"Just got to get some petrol, love. Won't be long."

Upstairs, Pamela didn't care one way or another. She turned the radio up louder, to fill the space in her head where her life used to be. There was no need for her to be in bed. She knew that. The pain in her eyes was less agonising that it had been, but if she relinquished her pain … what else would there be to fill the void?

The keys to Sandra's car in his pocket and an empty petrol can in his hand, Malcolm waited in the street for Ralph to join him before setting off. It took half an hour to get the job done and park the Mini outside the Maycocks' home.

For Sandra, the time had sped by in delight, for Baz and 'Ric were delightful, if snotty-nosed, children. All seemed lightness and joy, a return to innocence; to unknowing. Hiding under a table while the tots searched for her, she did not hear the sound of key in lock or the quiet closing of the front door. Ralph's voice called,

"Sandra? Sandra? Are you there?"

She stuck out her head, smiling, all thought of her abandoned car gone. Her father stood in the door-frame.

He stepped forward. Paused.

Sandra froze.

He stepped forward again; held out his hand.

On her knees, she took the hand. On her knees, she edged forward. Their eyes locked, both pairs fearful.

Clear of the cavern beneath the table, she sat back on her haunches. She stretched out her other hand. The tiny twins galloped between Sandra and her father, breaking the tension. Both pairs of eyes smiled. Their hands met. Sandra stood up. In silence, they pulled each other close.

There were no words, just exhalations of relief; of release. Then, with a sob, the father took his child into his arms. The child could find no words, but only discerned the end of a nightmare somewhere in front: only the comfort of an embrace that promised neither threat nor demand; control nor expectation; an embrace with which both begged and gave forgiveness.

In those moments the cause of the rupture was forgotten. The past didn't matter. The whys had, for now, been submerged. In the silence, father and child failed to notice that now, they were alone in the room. The door clicked shut.

"I'm sorry," the father whispered into his daughter's hair.

Sandra did not reply. 'For what?' she wondered. 'For handing me over to a cruel old man? How could he?' Stepping briskly away from him, she asked,

"How's Mum?"

The magic had gone. The muscles of Malcolm's stomach

tightened once more – that familiar tension gripping the fear which never went away.

"Please don't let go," he whispered. "Please come home. Please, please forgive me."

Sandra, too, had become used to suppressing her fear. Still she wondered, 'For what does he beg forgiveness?'

She yearned for the simple trust that had once been hers. Maybe her father could make everything better, as he had when she was small. She allowed herself to step closer; took his hand and looked into his face.

"Why did you let me marry Fergus Hardisty?" She paused. "I was a *child*." Her tone lifted in distress.

He blanched, taking refuge in his wife's justification.

"We thought your future would be secure."

His eyes gave the lie to his words. For the first time, Sandra gave voice to the horror that haunted her dreams.

"Why did I find a video of you, naked, on a boat? Naked, with …with …?" She could not continue

Even now, she could not contemplate its reality.

Malcolm was silent. His arms dropped to his sides. He turned away.

"I can't answer that."

"Why not?"

"I don't know how it happened."

"You must know!"

"No, I don't, although I know it *did* happen." He moved across the room. "I honestly don't remember what happened, not clearly. There were two or three of us in the cabin … I didn't catch their names … then a young lad arrived with no clothes on. I thought mebbe he was goin' skinny dippin'. Fergus was handing out the drink … we were having laugh… like a lads' day out – and I've not had many of those – but after that it's just a blur. All I know is that afterwards, Fergus carried a photo in his pocket. Maybe he had more than one. Every now and then he'd take it from his pocket … always the breast pocket of his overcoat … and wave it in my face. Not long enough to get a good look at, but enough to put the fear of God in me."

He covered his face with his hands. Sandra waited for more.

"I've wondered since if the other blokes who were there are in the same pickle as me."

Still he covered his face. After a moment's silence, turning to Sandra he drew a deep breath and confessed.

"I didn't stop you marrying Fergus Hardisty because I was terrified of him."

Tears, held back for years, spilled over. He crouched in fear.

"He'd set his sights on you when you were about fourteen, but I didn't take him seriously. As you grew older I'd see him out and about with other young girls, even when his wife was alive – but once or twice I heard him make comments about how those flighty types were not marriage material and how, if he ever married again, he'd want a woman more homely and … and innocent, like you.

"Until the cinema closed down I didn't see much of him and anyway, I thought it was all bravado, something and nothing. Some men think they're '*The Big I Am*', and he was one of them. Enid Hardisty died suddenly. I lost my job at the cinema around the same time, and Fergus was the only employer in the area offering work. *He* approached *me* – I thought he was interested in buying up the cinema – and *I* needed a job, any job. It seemed like a stroke of luck at the time." He stared blankly out of the window. "If only I'd turned it down, we'd still be together and happy, in our own way."

"Why were you terrified of him?" Sandra didn't need to ask, but wanted confirmation,

"Because he black-mailed me. If I objected to the marriage, he'd go public with the video, starting with your mother and you."

"Did Mum know?"

"No. Of course not. She was chuffed to bits to think you'd be a wealthy woman with status and no money worries. Those Saturday nights and Trivial Pursuit ... he way he wheedled his way into our family, made himself at home, cracking jokes with your Uncle Archie ... that was all part of his game. Buttering-up your mother, playing the family friend ... she was mesmerised by his attention ... then more or less tricking me into going to his boat. I didn't even know there *was* a marina on the Humber ... he was setting it all up so he could get his hands on you."

He sought for understanding in his daughter's eyes, but Sandra was chilling by the minute. Nothing would surprise her about her late husband. She could believe the explanation. If her father's memory had been drugged or hypnotised clean – she could believe that, too. Yes, she believed the story and understood, but the horror remained.

There was no doubt, now. Her father had as good as sold her to a crooked pervert to save his own skin. Within her, Right and Wrong wrestled; were deadlocked. She had no comment to make; no comfort to offer; no forgiveness to bestow.

"If I'd never married Fergus, Mum would still be able to see. I might have passed my A Levels. Maybe I'd have gone to college or even university."

"I know." His head hung low. "Sandra, love, I know I'm to blame. I live with that knowledge every minute of every day."

She raised her head and saw his despondency. Crossing the room, she knelt in front of him, raised his chin and whispered,

"I will *try* to forgive you, Dad, but I'm not sure I can."

Turing from her, Malcolm wept.

Josie and Ralph were disappointed when Sandra went back to Snellington without saying goodbye. They found Malcolm alone in the front room, head in hands. Never quite sure of the cause of the family rift, they trod carefully.

"It were a stroke o' luck that I were in t'club this afternoon, weren't it?" Ralph ventured.

"Mm."

"Don't know how she'd have coped ..." He waited for a response.

"Suppose not," Malcolm was worrying about how much he should divulge. "It was good to see her," he continued wearily, "but I'm not sure we'll be seeing her again."

Josie and Ralph shared a look. They too had heard Sandra's closing remark, but were none the wiser about the nature of Malcolm's transgression.

*

Josie didn't drive but she'd passed the house in Snellington a few times when Pamela was showing off her daughter's upmarket abode. Maybe it was time to take a closer look and do some straight talking with Sandra herself. If she was old enough to be a wealthy widow, she was old enough to face up to her responsibilities. The softly, softly approach hadn't worked and it was time for some home truths. Ralph dropped his wife off on Snellington Lane the next morning.

She saw that the house looked well-kept, which surprised her. The brass bell on the front door gleamed in the sunlight and rang out in a triple chime when pressed. She heard movement approaching, and was taken aback when the door was opened by a large, dark-skinned woman she didn't recognise.

"Oh, I must have got the wrong house. Sorry." She turned to leave.

"Dis is Ms Hardisty's residence. Can I 'elp you?" The woman had an imperious air about her.

"Oh – I'm looking for Sandra Pogs … Sandra Hardisty."

"Who shall I say visitin'?"

"Oh … I'm an old neighbour. Tell her it's Josie."

"I will see if Ms Hardisty is available." The imperious woman turned on her heel and walked away down the hall. Josie heard a muffled conversation from the kitchen and she was soon ushered into the sitting room. Moments later, Sandra was led in by the unfamiliar woman.

There was meek politeness in Sandra's voice and timid, downcast eyes as she once again offered thanks for Ralph's help. Looking up, her eyes flicked towards the other woman as if for assistance. Josie was struggling to make out who was in charge here.

She turned to Albertina.

"Are you a relative of Mr Hardisty?"

Albertina's laugh came out more as a shudder.

"Goodness me, no! I am de cleanin' lady. Mi name is Albertina Hedge an' I am very please' to meet you." She held out her strong right hand.

Josie shook the hand warmly.

"I'm pleased to meet you, too. I'm glad to see that Sandra has some company and help. We've all been very worried about her since … since her husband died …" She ran out of words.

Sandra crossed the room to stare out of the window. Josie lowered her voice confidentially.

"In fact, we've been worried ever since she took up with Fergus Hardisty." Josie had taken to Albertina on sight and felt the truth was appropriate.

Albertina, too, felt it was fitting to share a few thoughts and opinions. While her employer peered through the glass in search of distraction, the older women conducted a private mime show conveying their opinions of Sandra, her late husband and the premises in which they sat.

"San'ra, you never really tol' me how yo' mother go blin'." Maybe the visitor could shed some light on the mystery. Sandra turned her pleading eyes on Josie, who took the hint.

"What seems to have happened is that Pamela, Sandra's mum, was cleaning the oven and got a load of the cleaner in her eyes. The pain must have been terrible. She tried to ring me for help but I was in Leeds – my father had just died suddenly. I dialled 999.The call was put through to our own police force, which sent someone round. The policeman could see Pam through the kitchen window and had to break in. He poured water into her eyes and dialled for an ambulance, but by the time they got her got her to hospital it was too late to save her eyesight."

Josie was glad of the chance to offload her own sense of guilt: she had not been in the right place at the right time.

Silence. A pause. Albertina frowned.

"Why 'dat your fault, San'ra? You tol' me dat you are to blame. How come?"

Again Sandra turned her brimming eyes to Josie for help.

"Sandra was not to blame," said Josie with a sigh. "She'd just had a little disagreement with her mother. Pam was angry and scrubbed out the oven to calm herself down. It's what we women do, isn't it?"

Albertina nodded her head. It was all making sense. It was good to talk to a woman of her own age; she was starting to feel a bond with Josie.

"It is normal for mothas an' daughtas to argue from time to time. 'T is nat'ral San'ra."

"Not for us. We never had arguments in our house."

Josie nodded.

"Being an only child, Sandra missed out on the rough and tumble that goes on in bigger families. Pamela … used to be … a very controlled woman. You'd never hear raised voices in their house. Everything was always calm, clean and tidy. That's how it *used* to be."

Sandra caught the final phrase.

"Used to be? Isn't it clean and tidy now?"

"How can it be?" Josie saw a window of opportunity. "Your dad does his best, but caring for your mother takes up most of his time and I do wonder if he's heading for a nervous breakdown. Now that Fergus is dead he's lost his job, and your mum doesn't like being left alone. He has to wash her, dress her … do the shopping, get the meals … but Pam won't hear of getting a carer in, even for a few hours a week."

"You should be helpin', San'ra. You gotta grow up and tekk de strain from yo' daddy."

Josie nodded.

"It would make such a difference. You've been through a hard time, I know, but you're old enough to face up to difficult situations and strong enough to help make things better. Like it or not, you're a grown-up now and your parents need your support."

Sandra felt chastened, but stubborn. "There are things you don't know … private things."

"We don't need to know those private things, Sandra. Your parents need you. That should be enough."

Albertina had another thought.

"Dat nice young window cleaner you so sweet on … he bin visitin' again since you called to see his fam'ly?"

"I haven't been yet. I was going there when I ran out of petrol. *I'm not sweet on him!*" The very idea embarrassed her.

"What's wrong with goin' today?"

Sandra gulped. The older women took control.

"I'll need a lift back to Wraith, so it would help if you could drive me home. And what about Albertina?

"Albertina would like to meet San'ra's parents. Mebbe together we can fin' a way o' helpin' her.'. After seein' yo' momma, you go to visit de fam'ly who were so kin' to you. You do dat, or I won't be comin' back to do yo' cleanin' no more."

Josie gathered her things together, speaking to Albertina under her breath

"Would that be Bob Fownhope's family you're talking about?" A nod.

"I didn't know anything about them looking after you until yesterday, Sandra. It was very kind of them, especially with Bob losing his job and his wife being ill. They're a nice family. I'm sure it would cheer them up to see you. They're having a hard time, too."

Change was being forced upon her. It was futile to resist. She got her coat and car keyswhile Josie and Albertina winked and smiled in collaboration.

*

Sandra had been hoping there'd be no parking space on Mulberry Avenue, but she was disappointed. Her passengers climbed out of the mini immediately, slammed their doors and waited. Still in the driver's seat, Sandra wrestled with her pride, her conscience and her fear as she searched her imagination for another excuse. The driver's door was opened from outside. Albertina stooped, swiftly removing the keys from the ignition.

"You comin' Sandra?" The question came out as an order.

By now, Josie was up the path and ringing the bell. It was soon answered. Malcolm stood there, barefoot. His eyes flicked between the three women, not understanding. He didn't speak. He looked old, tired and doubtful.

"I've brought some people to see Pamela. It will do her good." Having got this far, Josie was not going to be deterred. She moved forward, compelling Malcolm to stand aside. She turned and called back,

"Hurry up, you two."

Malcolm saw his daughter propelled up the path by a large woman he'd never met. Albertina stretched out her hand and grasped his.

" I am very please' to meet you, Mr Pogson. It is *so* good to meet San'ra's fam'ly. I hope we can be friends."

Malcolm still had nothing to say but stepped aside to admit the trio. His daughter hung back. In the hall, Josie nudged him. "Please … go and get her, Malcolm, She needs help."

Quietly, he took the six steps that would, or could, or might reunite him with his precious child. For a few moments, Pamela took a backstage position in his thinking. Opening his a arms he embraced Sandra in silence, turned her face to his and whispered,

"Even if you can't forgive me, this is your home, I am your father and I love you always."

She allowed herself to be led across the threshold of home, her real home. As the door was closed behind her, it seemed alien, yet safe. Gone was its shiny tidiness and smell of cleaning products. Subconsciously, she noticed these things. Her voice failed her. Josie took charge.

"Malcolm, you put the kettle on while I take Sandra to see Pamela. Mrs Hedge, would you take a seat in the lounge for a moment or two?"

Albertina nodded.

The noise of an electric kettle coming to the boil filled the emptiness as, step by slow step, Sandra was gently nudged

up the green-carpeted flight of stairs and into the front bedroom. Josie took the initiative.

"Pamela. Wake up. Your Sandra's here."

The sleeper woke with a jolt, panicking immediately
about the state of her hair and the rumpled bedding.

"I can't see her. I don't want to see her. She made her bed ..."

"No Pamela, *You* made her bed ... and Sandra has had to
lie on it. She's been through a terrible ordeal – *and so have
you, I know* – but it's time to pull yourself together and look
after your daughter! I'm telling you, Pam, if you don't speak
to your only child in her hour of need, you'll have to look
elsewhere for a friend."

Pamela was stunned into silence. Sandra spoke into the
musty silence.

"Mum, please can we be friends again?"

Silence. Pamela had missed that voice. Tears flooded her
eyes, a sob deep as a tuba's timbre filled the room as she
held out her arms to the child she could not see. Josie left
the room silently. Let them work things out for themselves
from now on.

Downstairs, Malcolm was drinking coffee with Albertina,
who chatted away about her own family in a determined
effort to break his icy reserve. A warm woman by nature,
she soon had Malcolm smiling and recounting titbits from
Sandra's childhood.

"Chil'ren ... dey be God's blessin' to make up for all de
bad t'ings in life," she declared. "We both be blessed wid
good-hearted, beautiful chil'ren, Malcolm, We must t'ank
de Lord and be grateful!"

Both bemused and amused, Malcolm relaxed in her company until he found himself counting the blessings which,
taken over his lifetime, outweighed his fall from grace.

Josie had quietly let herself out. No one noticed, until
Sandra reappeared, smiling a little.

"Mum's tired now, but she says I can come back tomorrow." There was relief in her voice. "Is that alright with you, Dad?" She did not approach Malcolm, but stood in the doorway.

"Of course it is." Dare he ask for more?

Albertina stood up.

"Befo' we leave, I would like to make de acquaintance of Sandra's momma. May I jus' pop upstairs for two minutes? San'ra, perhaps you will introduce me?"

Pamela didn't know how to respond to the newcomer, who barely gave her time to speak or think about what was being said. Within the two minutes, it was arranged that Albertina would return to Mulberry Close in two days' time to see what advice, company and practical help she might offer.

Moments later, Albertina was asking Malcolm for a lift home.

"You see, Malcolm, San'ra has to visit de people who were so kin' to her. I hear dey are also in need of support at de moment, an' San'ra has promise' to see what she can do to 'elp."

Abashed, Malcolm looked at his daughter's blank face. Her eyes were averted. Albertina's were on him. He took the baton of initiative from this new friend and nodded eagerly. How good it was to meet someone fresh; someone with a different perspective; someone not bowed down by his family's woes. He reached his jacket from a peg in the hall, checked for his keys and called,

"Back in half an hour, Pam!"

Albertina's instructions were delivered in a tone which, although gentle, demanded compliance. Sandra knew there was no way out. She must do as she had been told. Josie appeared at the roadside.

"Give the Fownhopes our regards, won't you Sandra? Be sure to call at my house to tell me how they are next time you come, the day after tomorrow. Off you go then, love."

With a wave, Sandra started the engine. This time there was no detour: minutes later she pulled up outside the Fownhopes' house. Her hands trembled. The mess in the front garden was perhaps no worse that it had been, but there was a dinginess, a lifelessness that Sandra hadn't noticed before. A curtain twitched at the downstairs window. Seconds later the door opened, and Bob Fownhope stepped outside for a quick cigarette He stood on the path inhaling deeply, waiting.

'About time,' he thought. 'About time the lass showed some gratitude.'

He was still waiting when he finished his cigarette. Sandra was afraid to leave the car, not knowing where to start. Her heart pounded with shame and fear. Her hands still trembled. She stared straight ahead. A loud rap sounded on the window, and the driver's door was opened roughly from the outside.

"Come on Sandra. What're you waiting for? You know the way!"

Simon Fownhope had been walking towards his home as Sandra drove past, oblivious. Unsure how he felt about her now, his tone was non-committal but polite. Bob started down the path and opened the gate, still hanging on grimly by one hinge. He patted Sandra's shoulder gently.

"It's nice to see you, lass. How're you doin'? Simon, put 'kettle on, lad."

Once inside, Sandra's trembling subsided. It felt good to be back, yet she belonged elsewhere. She could sense it. Doreen was having a lie-down, Malcolm explained, and he was just on his way out to the Working Men's Club for a swift half. It was nice to see her and she was welcome to stay and chat with Simon, he said.

"If your mum wakes up, Simon, tekk 'er a drink up, won't you? Perhaps she'll want to get up and see Sandra." He'd make it easy for the lass, he thought, by making himself scarce … and it would do both her and Simon good to spend a bit of time together. The lad hadn't been the same since the night his mam took badly.

They viewed one another uneasily through hooded eyes, afraid to break the ice. Silence stretched across the room. Sandra sat down. Simon hesitated before lowering himself next to her. The silence continued. Sandra studied her fingernails. Simon studied his. She trembled once more and drew breath.

"I really miss you, Simon."

"Do you?"

"Yes."

"I see."

The silence returned.

"How's your mum?" Their questions came simultaneously. They sniggered, embarrassed.

"A bit better." Again they spoke in unison. This time, they laughed, the ice breaking.

Their shoulders were touching. They could feel each other's breath. The sagging seat of the sofa tilted them closer. Thighs met. His chin grazed her shoulder. He twisted his torso, reached his free hand across her body and held his lips an inch away from hers.

"I've really missed you, too," he whispered. "Really, really missed you."

Her eyes closed. Seeing this, he moved closer still, flicking his tongue at her lips. They parted in submission. She pulled him close. There was no need for words. They both knew that this was real.

*

Few words were spoken for the next fifteen minutes. Simon's

experience with girls had so far not extended much beyond his sisters and the odd fumble with classmates at school and friends' parties. Sandra had been a married woman. She had experience. What did she expect of him? He wasn't ready for marriage – not by a long way – but right now, he knew he wanted her. They were good together. He knew she was damaged goods, yet still he wanted her. Knew she was trouble ... yet still...

Their lips were parted by the click-clack of the front gate. They moved apart, and by the time Bob entered the room Simon stood, staring through the window. Upstairs his mother, suspecting what was going on downstairs, had summoned her husband to call time before things went too far.

"Hey-up, Sandra, lass. You still here?" His tone was not unwelcoming. "Have you checked on your mother, Simon?"

"I was just going." He sped out of the room to hide his blushes.

Bob talked on about little of consequence until Sandra found her voice.

"I know it's a bit late, but I want to thank you for saving me that night when I ran away. I *know* I was in a state and not thinking clearly, and I *know* I gave you all a lot of worry and extra work. At the time I just took your kindness for granted, but now my mind's clearer I can see what a pain in the neck I must have been. But if you hadn't stopped to help me that night ...maybe I'd be dead by now."

Bob looked up. This was the longest speech he'd ever head from the girl. Her face looked haunted. She had told no one about the events of that night; maybe she never would, but by mentioning her state of mind she was one step closer to acknowledging what had happened.

"Aye, well, I'm glad we were able to help, but it were

Doreen who took most o' 'strain on her shoulders. It's her you should be thankin'."

"I will, when she's well enough to see me."

"Our Simon's not been himself either," he went on. "It'd do the lad good to get away for a bit, but there's no money for holidays the way things are." He stopped as his lad re-entered the room bearing hot drinks.

"Mum's awake now. When you've had your coffee, Sandra, she'd like you to pop up and say hello before you leave."

When the time came, Doreen accepted the thanks with a hug. She had aged, physically and mentally. It was nice to see the girl but, just now, she didn't want to rekindle the involvement or take on more responsibility. Doreen worried about Simon, too. He was a loving lad, a soft touch, with an even softer spot for Sandra. He needed to see something of the world before he settled down with Sandra Hardisty or anyone else.

"Be careful, Simon. Don't get too involved with Sandra." She touched his hand gently.

"How do you mean, involved?" He blushed.

"I know you're sweet on her, but whoever takes her on will have to tread carefully. She's been through a lot for a girl her age and it's bound to leave its mark. That's all I'm saying … and she's older than you. I want you to enjoy life while you're young. Don't get tied down before you've had some fun and seen the world beyond Yorkshire."

"My sisters were all settled before they were twenty – did you tell *them* the same thing?"

"Well, no, but girls are different.".

"I don't know what you're on about, anyway." The nonchalance did not fool his mother, who resigned herself to keeping her own counsel in future.

21

WPC Andrena Cooper was confined to office duties due to damaged ligaments in her knee, an injury sustained whilst apprehending a young car thief. The knee problem limited her mobility and hurt a lot so, to ease the fear that her career might be over, Andrena insisted on coming in to work to pick up whatever sedentary slack she could. Maybe she would make her name by ultra-diligently uncovering gaps in past investigations.

Ever since Fergus Hardisty's body was discovered stewing in a broth of stinking seawater, Andrena's ambition had been to solve the mystery of the closed padlock. At moments of leisure, her mind would flash back to the discovery of the corpse and that small mystery. Once the death was known to be from natural causes, no one else seemed interested, but someone had locked the chap in the cabin, presumably when he was still alive. Who knew if he'd been trying to break the hatch or shouting for help when he had the heart attack? Things had been quiet, crime-wise, and WPC Cooper wanted something to get her teeth into. Her boss was easy to persuade, agreeing that she should trawl though the marina's camera footage once more. He was irritated by the woman's mooching, and hoped this would keep her still for a while.

"Looking for what?" he wondered aloud.

"I'll know when I find it," Andrena replied darkly.

In between answering the phone and other odd jobs the boss found for her, she stared for hours at murky footage of the gated entrance to the marina. Mostly she'd be doing something else at the same time – brewing a mug of tea for others, tidying desks, making notes, but always with at least one eye on the monitor. A few other young officers thought she was making the most of her injury to get friendly with those of more elevated ranks, but Andrena said they were just being cynical.

Then she spotted her.

She rewound the tape. There she was again, that girl in the red coat, the one with long dark hair. Bitch! It wasn't fair for anyone to have hair like that! What Andrena would give for such splendid locks, not to mention the legs! Despite not being a bad-looker herself, she kept her brown hair short for work, and the best that could be said about her legs was that they filled the gap between torso and feet. The WPC's most recent boyfriend had dumped her for a beauty of similar proportions to the one on the footage, so an element of grudge strengthened her determination. The face on the video was rather grainy and blurred but, in Andrena's head, it was clear as day. Her mind's eye was filled with the visage of her ex's latest squeeze.

Of course she knew it was a different woman altogether, but the similarity was enough to add extra drive and impetus to her investigations. She took the discovery to her boss who, anxious to get her off his hands for a spell, gave permission for the WPC to cadge a lift next time a squad car was going near Wraith. There, she could track down the red-coated beauty and have a word.

When the time came she thought she'd begin at the deceased's business premises, and Andrena was in luck.

Although the reception desk was empty, a sharp ping on the desk-top bell summoned the sleek-haired one from the back office, where she'd been studying profit, loss and investment opportunities.

Taken aback by the uniform, Marianne adopted a superior tone whilst from time to time dabbing her moist eyes and sighing deeply at each mention of her former employer. At first Andrena's questions were general, concerning the nature of the business: whether the PA was aware of any pre-existing health problems Mr Hardisty suffered from; names of close associates; his habits and friends. Marianne warmed to the questioning, throwing in the odd red herring to muddy the waters.

"Did he spend a lot of time on his boat? Did he ever take you or other employees on it?"

"Not me. I can't stand water."

"But did you have to go there for work ever?"

"No! But what if I did?"

"Just wondering, trying to get a fuller picture." Andrena turned to go. "By the way, do you have the address of Mr Hardisty's solicitor?"

The PA flushed, looked away quickly and sat down. What should she say? The paperwork on her desk suddenly seemed to need her deepest attention. Had she heard?

Andrena asked again.

Marianne's look implied the question, 'Are you still here?' Her voice responded with,

"Mr Hardisty dealt with the legal side of the business himself. *I* was a very junior member of staff. I doubt if he'd have trusted *anyone* with that sort of information."

The officer was enjoying her trip away from police HQ. Not that she had anything concrete against the glossy-haired bitch, apart from her lie about the boat, but the PA was a wrong-un. Andrena could smell 'em a mile off.

"So you have no idea who will be dealing with probate and such?"

"With what?"

"Dealing with his will and financial affairs.Probate.

"I've told you already. Mr Hardisty kept his financial and family affairs to himself. And now I really must get on with this." Her tone was edgy. Andrena moved to put on her hat and leave, but turned back.

"I wouldn't have thought there was much for you to do with all the businesses closed down. Ever meet his second wife?"

"I really haven't got time for this. I'm still settling invoices from suppliers. That's what I was paid to do and I don't like to leave a job unfinished. About his wife, we went to the same school but I hardly knew her … not sure I'd be able to pick her out in a crowd."

Andrena was delighted to see her so flustered.

"Pity. I was going to ask what she looks like."

"Dowdy. Mousy hair."

"So you *would* be able to pick her out in a crowd then, or an identity parade, say?"

"Is that likely?" Marianne's heart leapt in her bosom. Was that glee in her eyes?

"I can't say. No one's under suspicion at the moment. The deceased died a natural death – but to tie up loose ends and put to bed, it would be satisfying to find the last person to see him alive." From the doorway she called back,

"Let us know if you find out who that was!"

Marianne was kicking herself. She'd missed a perfect opportunity to get Sandra or Malcolm Pogson in the frame, or even that bossy woman who'd snatched 'Fergus's' will from her own hands. She doubted it had ever even reached the offices of Heaval & Co.

*

The squad car driver had been killing time and responded swiftly to Andrena's call. Together, they went to check out the young widow in Snellington, who they found supping tea in the kitchen with an older woman answering to the name of Albertina Hedge. A fresh pot was made and poured as the officers took the spare chairs around the table.

Andrena led the way.

"How are you then, Mrs Hardisty? We don't want to intrude – just checking you're OK and wondering if you've thought of anything else we should know about."

"I don't think so."

Andrena withdrew a rectangle of paper from her pocket.

"I've been taking another look at the security footage from the marina where your husband died," she said casually. "Take a look at this picture. Do you recognise the person?"

She handed the still image to the widow. Albertina craned her neck to look and snatched the photograph from Sandra's fingers. The widow's face blanched. She remained silent.

"Dis be de gal who came 'ere wid de will, San'ra! Gal who say she own dis 'ouse."

Andrena perked up. She took out her notebook and pencil. The male officer poured himself another cup of tea and sat back.

Andrena kept her questions casual. The widow was non-committal on many things and had little to say about the face in the photo other than yes, she did recognise the person. They'd been at school together; played in the same hockey team. Yes, she did know the woman's name and yes, the woman had once visited the Hardisty home.

Albertina was nearly bursting to tell her side of the story. Eventually she could wait no longer.

"Dat gal come to dis house waving a piece o' paper and saying Mista Hardisty left dis 'ouse to her. Not a nice gal … very arrogant!"

"Why did she have the will?"

"Say she find it in de safe."

"What did she do with it?"

"I took if off her an' I tell her I mekk sure it be delivered to Heaval and Comp'ny, solicitors. I tell Mista Hardisty about my boy one time an' he tell me he use dat firm o' lawyas."

"And did you?"

"Yes I did. I ask my son Tobias to take it to work and post it to the Wraith offices of his comp'ny. Tobias, he works in de Leeds branch." Her chest swelled with pride in her son's status.

Sandra had not heard from Heaval and Co. or any other firm of lawyers. That part of her head was still buried in the sand. Taking her cue from the widow's expression, Andrena nudged her vacant colleague.

"Interesting. Come on you, it's time to go." She put on her hat. "Let me know if there are any more developments."

"I knew that black-haired bitch was a wrong-un. Where's that solicitor's office? She said as they walked back to the car.

A quick stroll down Wraith High Street led them to the lawyers' premises. Both sides of the discussion were curt and non-committal, but Andrena deduced that the firm was dealing with the Last Will and Testament of the first Mrs Hardisty, having only lately been informed of her demise by a young woman who had come across Fergus Hardisty's will in the safe at Hardisty Incorporated Holding's headquarters.

The partners had agreed that there could have been a conflict of interest, and so the recently-delivered document purporting to be Fergus Hardisty's will had been rejected.

Andrena, was stumped for now, but she would ferret out the truth one way or another, she was determined.

22

Simon knew his mum and dad were right about Sandra. She was damaged goods, no matter how much he liked her and wanted to kiss her again. Simon had rarely been away from Wraith except for school camping trips in the Dales or the Peak District, and he remembered with fondness his dad's stories about the travel and adventure involved in an army life. If he got tied down with Sandra, there'd be no adventure or excitement for him. He was dimly aware that joining the army was not something to do for fun; that adventure was not its main purpose; that battles, injury and death might be involved, but surely it must be better than spending the rest of his life in Wraith?

After a few false starts, he chose what he knew was Albertina's day off, borrowed the ladder and set off to clean the windows of Snellington. He did a few other houses before bracing himself to knock on Sandra's back door. He could feel himself blushing already.

Sandra did not get many callers and was wary.

"Who is it?"

Simon cleared his throat.

"It's me!"

The door flew open. Somehow he was in her arms – or was it the other way round? She pulled him inside and closed the door behind him. Sandra had been waiting for this moment. Had been determined to stay strong and aloof. To tell it like it was. There had been no hugs or kisses in her plan.

Simon's plan had been something similar. The things that had to be said didn't seem to matter for a while, but the voice at the back of his head was whispering, "*This is not why you came here.*"

Sandra had more strength of purpose. There was coffee to be made and biscuits to be offered. She pulled away and busied herself with the mugs and milk. Sitting across the table, she took Simon's hand in hers.

" We need to talk, Simon."

The coffee was hot. She blew on it. He hoped she wasn't going to propose.

"How do you feel about you and me?"

What answer did she want? What answer did she expect? He was stumped. His eyes showed his embarrassment. Sandra took the lead.

"The thing is, Simon, I really, *really* like you. I ... I suppose I *love* you." She paused. "I've never said that to anyone before."

Silence. His face reddened further. He studied his mug of coffee. "OK."

"But I've *been* married and I didn't like it. I don't want to get married again ... or not for a long, long time."

Married? No one had mentioned marriage! Simon was just worried about getting tied down too soon.

"I don't want to get married either. I think I might love you, too, but I don't really know what it means. Mum and Dad love each other, and I love my family, and I get a funny feeling when you and I are together, but I'm only seventeen ..." His voice tailed off.

"Exactly the right answer!" She did not often sound

triumphant. "You're too young for a serious relationship, and I don't want another one for a very long time. Simon, there's a world out there we need to explore. I need to find out who I am and what I want out of life now I've been given a second chance."

Simon's sigh of relief was audible. He stared at the table, rotating the mug back and forth in his hands.

"There's so much to see. I might end up coming home to Wraith, but I want it to be a choice, not…not…"

"Inevitable?" Sandra offered.

"Exactly."

She was so much cleverer and better with words, he thought, but if they did ever get together, he'd want to be her equal. The thought stuck in his mind. He'd never yet had an ambition in life – had been content to take each day as it came – but now the seeds of something different had been sown.

They spoke quietly, mutual understanding and fondness deepening as ideas of separate futures surfaced. That could be set as an objective, something to be reached in time. No lifelong commitments yet, they decided, but no big separation either.

"We could go travelling…" she suggested.

"You need money for that."

"If I sell the house, I'll have plenty."

"Yes, but I can't live off you. That wouldn't be right. Where would you like to go?"

"We could start off by exploring Britain. I've hardly ever been out of Yorkshire, except for the Peak District."

"Me neither. What about transport?"

"We could use my car, although it would be more fun to go back-packing."

Sandra had never carried a rucksack in her life, but at that moment it was her dearest ambition. She wanted to join the booted and cagouled squads of hikers and climbers she'd seen on the moors during her childhood trips to Whitby and Hawes.

Simon looked up in surprise. He'd never thought of her as an outdoor type, but they could give it a go.

She walked through into the hall. He could see her rattling a locked door, then searching a drawer in the hall table. Having found what she was looking for, she stood rigid outside the locked door, key in hand. From the kitchen, he could see her tremble, could hear the rasping sound of her breath. She grasped the door jamb as her legs weakened.

In seconds he was by her side, supporting her with his arm.

"What's wrong Sandra?"

"Thus is Fergus's study," she whispered. "I'm not allowed in here. I was going to see if there's a map on his bookshelf."

"Why aren't you allowed in?"

"Fergus said it was private, and when I did go in once … it …was … it was very upsetting."

A sob caught in her throat.

"Do you want to tell me about it?"

"No. I daren't. I don't want to bring harm to you, like I did to my mother."

"Now let's not start all that again Sandra. What happened to her was not your fault."

He snatched the key from her hand, turned it in the lock and flung open the door. He stepped inside the room which had not been touched since the man's death. Even Albertina had been denied entry. Haphazard piles of paper covered the desk, dotted with shrivelled petals from a stinking vase of dead marigolds. The smell of rotting vegetation and rancid water caught his breath. He opened a window and emptied the vase outdoors.

Still, Sandra trembled on the threshold. Gently he drew her into the room, then into his arms.

"Fergus can't hurt you now. I'll make sure of that." He soothed her until the trembling stopped.

"Why not ask Albertina to give this room a good spring-clean next time she comes, and you could use it for something else." His mind was struggling to come up with a plan. "I know, we could make this our planning headquarters."

"Planning what?"

"Our travels. We could get a big map, decide where we'd like to go and what we'd like to do. It will take a while to plan, and I'll have to get another job to save up some money … and it will be a while before you sell the house. It'll be great."

She looked at him doubtfully.

"Let's do it Sandra. We'll tell Mum and Dad to give them time to get used to the idea. We'll explain that we'll be travelling as special friends. I think Mum and dad are a bit worried that I'll get married too young and regret it later.

"That sounds like a perfect plan," she agreed, spotting a large atlas leaning against the bookcase. Taking it up, she led him back to the warmth of the kitchen.

"I'll ask Albertina to help me clear out the room. It will be fun to make it our strategic headquarters." Sandra giggled. "This is the most exciting thing that's ever happened to me."

Delighted to see her joy, Simon hoped his parents would not prove to be twin flies in the ointment of her happiness. He would have to tell them tonight.

23

Relieved that there was to be no teenage marriage in the foreseeable future, Bob and Doreen demonstrated an acceptable degree of enthusiasm for the plan. Perhaps a long jaunt together would be a good idea. It would be a test for the youngsters, but they could always come home if they got tired of one another, or Simon could, at least. Sandra's house should have been sold by then. Word was that Pamela Pogson's spirit was on the mend, although of course she still could not see. Apparently, that Albertina woman was involved in the improvement somehow. With luck, after the trip Sandra would be able to return to her parents' home.

Reassured to some extent that their boy would not be trapped by early parenthood, Doreen and Bob quietly gave their assent whilst silently dreading the forthcoming empty nest. They smiled at the appropriate times and showed an interest in the plans, but knew that this was the beginning of an ending.

Sandra drove the research, for the first time in her life feeling like an adult who knew her own mind. Having discovered the joys of a good atlas, her mind awash with place-names from far and wide, she made it her business to discover as much as she could about each potential destination: nation status, climate, topography, population density, dominant religion, racial make-up and economic output just to start with. How could it be that she knew so little of the world? The image of a caged bird perched always in her mind's eye; as her learning increased, the caged bird began to flutter its wings. There came days when she would stare through the window at the birds feeding whilst tracking their migration routes in an unused ornithological ency-clopaedia she'd found in the study. How incredible it was that these tiny creatures had the skill and courage to cross oceans and continents, trusting in instinct and fellow-trav-ellers. If they could do it, could she?

She purchased more maps and books, cleared the study and manufactured a jokey label for the door.

EXPEDITION HEADQUARTERS

Planning and Preparation

Co-ordinator: S. Fownhope   Sponsor: S. Hardisty-Pogson

She made sure there was space below for other roles to be added from the list in her head, such as Financial Control, Health and Safety, First Aid, Vehicle Maintenance, Communications Officer … and more besides. Making lists and plotting routes made the trip a more serious prop-osition. Loving every minute, she came to realise she was good at this. Faint thoughts of a future career flitted across the back of her mind and settled quietly in a cosy spot labelled 'Later'.

Elation kept her awake at night, yet Sandra rose each morning fresh and eager to press on. Fergus's study was soon stripped of its expensive carpet and formidable furniture. Together they took an experimental drive to a Scandinavian retail outlet off the M62. Amazed by what they saw available at reasonable cost, Sandra had soon ordered enough pale wood, bright rugs and glowing lamps to transform the room into an exciting expedition headquarters.

Simon felt a little unease; he was still doing the window cleaning, but the money he earned mostly went to his mum. Sandra didn't care. She had some money and was happy to spend it. Gone was the dour, careful widow of a few weeks ago. Once Fergus's will was sorted out and the house sold, she was confident there would be enough money to do whatever they wanted.

One summer day, an official-looking letter addressed to Mr Fergus Hardisty dropped onto the doormat. Sandra stared, but let it remain on the mat. She felt a flutter of her former terror: dare she open the envelope? Albertina saw Sandra frozen with fear in the hall when she arrived for work.

"Pick up de envelope, San'ra."

Reverting to obedience, Sandra did so, trembling. Albertina gave instructions again.

"Now open it. 'Tis your job, San'ra. You are de widow and have de right to read what de letter say."

She did as instructed, her eyes blurred with unshed tears. "Please read it for me."

Albertina took the single sheet and scanned its contents. Shocked into silence, she had trouble making sense of it, being already aware that the first Mrs Hardisty had been dead for some time.

The letter informed Mr Hardisty that, as the sole owner of the family home, his wife Enid Hardisty had bequeathed the building, the land around it and its entire contents to several local charities, including the dog-and-cat rescue centre, the Anglican church, the Girl Guides and the hospice a few miles from Wraith. Only her jewellery was left to her daughter Francine, with the wish that it be worn regularly rather than stored in a bank vault and viewed as an investment. The £10,427 in her own personal bank account, of which her husband had been unaware, was bequeathed to their son Irwin, with the plea that he would use the money wisely and keep in touch with his sister.

Albertina had to sit down. The hand holding the letter shook. It took a while to grasp the significance of the paper she held. She studied the recent date and local address of the letter. The late Mrs Hardisty had been very precise in her wishes. No matter how many times Albertina read and re-read the words, it was clear that the woman had owned the house outright and Fergus Hardisty did not feature in the will's provisions at all.

Albertina would need to talk to her son Tobias about the situation. How come the late Mrs Hardisty's will had taken so long to be dealt with? How come? How come there had been no mention of Mr Hardisty, or of his own Last Will and Testament? She would telephone Tobias that very evening and get some answers.

Meanwhile, Sandra was waiting for an explanation, one that Albertina could not supply. She waited, wide-eyed, for the older woman to speak. Albertina sank onto a carved mahogany armchair in the hall, lost for words. She waved the letter towards Sandra.

"You need to read dis yo'self, Ms Hardisty. 'Tis a private, legal communication."

Sandra read it sitting on the bottom stair.

"I don't understand. Enid Hardisty died three or four years ago."

"But do you understan' who own dis house, Sandra? Not Mista Hardisty, but his wife."

"Does that mean it didn't become mine when Fergus died?"

"I don' know, Sandra. 'Tis too much for me. I need to go home, an' I need to be paid for de work I done."

The bills at home were mounting up, and Albertina had been counting on getting what she was owed as soon as Mr Hardisty's will had been dealt with. She was two months behind with the rent and the water rates had to be paid. Despondent, she put on her coat, picked up her handbag and went to the back door.

"I'm sorry, Sandra, but I cannot carry on like dis. I need a proper job with a proper wage, or I will lose my own home. I need to t'ink." Her weariness was palpable.

The threat hit home. Sandra pulled herself together and picked up the keys to the Mini.

"I'll drive you home. Please don't make any decision yet. Let's see what happens. I'll go to the solicitors' tomorrow and see what they say."

Sandra hadn't a clue what she would say to the lawyer.

"Will you speak to your Tobias and ask him what I should do?" she pleaded.

"I will see. I mus' t'ink 'bout dis too." She would ring Tobias later.

24

Having already decided to set the Last Will and Testament of Fergus Hardisty aside as suspect, Heaval and Co took their time in setting a date for Sandra's appointment. The practitioner dealing with the estate of Enid Hardisty had been hospitalised following a road accident. The second Mrs Hardisty was asked to bear with the company until things were back to normal.

On hearing the news, and after a few perplexed hours pacing the kitchen, Sandra determined on an alternative strategy. Immediately she set this into action, and began to look to the future,

Having lived on a shoe-string for months, she had enough cash left to escape the stress. She might as well spend it now, before the house was sold over her head. Who could tell where she would end up? Simon had saved a couple of hundred pounds from his window cleaning, money he'd planned to give his mum for his keep, but the trip must come first.

No one seemed to know for certain who owned the house in Snellington, and Sandra didn't plan to hang around waiting to be ejected. If she didn't get away soon she'd go crazy, for sure. She had to leave, even if it meant leaving Simon behind.

Energised, she spent the long evenings poring over atlases and route maps. Narrowing her target area, the diversity of the British Isles became a fascination. She ordered books from the library about myriad small islands she had never heard of. Her time passed quickly, absorbed as she was in places on pages as she had never been in school. Her heart lifted at each new discovery; excitement and the compulsion to escape empowering her research. She was drawn to ancient places and customs, wanted to see the archaeology and hear about aeons past.

Albertina watched the change in her employer with mixed emotions. It was good to see Sandra take an interest and show some enthusiasm, but there was still no sign of the wages the cleaner was owed. The little postcards in the Wraith newsagent's window offered no suitable employment … she knew nothing about mucking out horses and had taken in enough ironing already to last a life time. The permanent chicken factory advertisement was still there, but no. Albertina would not contemplate that, so she continued to make the twice-weekly visits to the house in Snellington, carefully keeping a record of what she was owed in the hope that something would change.

As her plans evolved, Sandra became more self-contained and self-assured, less reliant on others for support, a mixed blessing for those who cared about her. Albertina longed for someone to lean on at the same time as she yearned to be needed. Spending time with Pamela Pogson broke the week up a little and made her feel useful, but Pamela was not an easy woman to bond with. There had been no sharing of hopes or fears, the sort of sharing which can offer fresh perspectives and ease personal burdens.

Arriving in Sandra's kitchen one morning, she was surprised to see the table covered by a large map of the British Isles. Piles of books stood on the work tops. Sandra herself leapt up and greeted her with a hug. She looked bright-eyed and raring to go. This was a different Sandra.

"Wha's dat for, San'ra?"

"It's to say thank you for everything, especially for being my friend. I can't wait to tell you!"

"Tell me what?"

"I'm going on a long trip. Simon's coming too, I think, but I'm going anyway, even if he decides not to come."

Albertina's heart thudded in her chest. What would she do for money? What would she do for company, and how would she cope with the loneliness if Sandra went away? The girl saw the shocked expression and something like fear in the eyes.

"Sit down and I'll make you a drink. Then I'll tell you my ideas."

Hot drinks on the table, her face beaming, Sandra drew up another chair. Albertina found it hard to show any enthusiasm. She could only contemplate her losses.

"Albertina, I want you to move into this house when I go away."

"What? I cannot pay any rent, Sandra, an' I 'ave mi own 'ouse. Why do you wan' me to live 'ere?"

"This is my plan. I do hope you'll like it!" She was tense with excitement. "I'm working on the assumption that I'll be away for a year. Maybe by the end of that time the solicitors will have sorted out who owns what. Surely I must be entitled to something from Fergus's will ... perhaps even his businesses? In the meantime, I don't intend to spend a day more than necessary in this place, although I have taken it off the market."

Albertina gulped, saying nothing.

"I'd like you to move in here as caretaker. In the meantime, you could rent out your own house to earn some money. I've persuaded Dad that he should ask you to look after my mother for a few days each week. That would mean he could look for another job, knowing that a kind and capable person was caring for her."

"San'ra, where you gettin' de money to go travellin'? Only a few week ago you had lots o' bills to pay an' no money comin' in."

"Well … do you remember how you made me start opening all the mail that was addressed to my husband?" She avoided the name Fergus, which still made her shudder.

Albertina nodded.

"It took me a while and it was really hard at first. I spoke to your Tobias once and learned a lot. You were right to make me face up to my responsibilities. Trying to make sense of everything made me grow up quickly. One by one, I've been dealing with matters that I'd never known or thought about before." She looked Albertina in the eye. "That's all thanks to you."

She grasped the older woman's hand.

"One of the letters was from an insurance company talking about about changes in the terms of their policies. I didn't know anything about insurance. Had never given it a thought until then, but I decided to get in touch with the company to explain that Fergus is dea …no longer alive. I expected them to close the account and that would be that. But it wasn't."

Albertina waited.

"It turns out that years ago, Fergus had taken out a life insurance policy … when he'd just married Enid and way before he became a businessman. The annual payments were still being paid by direct debit at the time he died. The company think that, as Enid died before Fergus, and I was his wife at the time *he* died, all that money should come to me. They're still waiting for the solicitors to confirm, which could take months, but they say I shouldn't worry about not having anything to live on and can assume I won't be thrown out of the house at short notice.

"They say there's no reason why I can't go away for a while. Any letters can be sent to Mum and Dad's address while I'm gone, and I'll keep in touch from time to time for updates."

She sat back, relief and excitement sparkling in her eyes.

The cleaning lady wished her own husband had had the foresight to get himself insured. Sandra was ready to continue.

"After I'd dealt with that, I went through all the other letters one-by-one. I settled the bills, found details of bank accounts I didn't know about, all sorts of information about Fergus and his money. Then I got in touch with a solicitor, but not the one *he* used. Everything is in hand, so we can take our trip soon. I want to start with the islands. I've never been on a big boat, but once you start looking, you realise how important they are to our country."

She pointed to a small pile of brochures on a chair. "In these are the timetables for all the ferries that sail from Scottish ports, and that one there is about air transport. This evening, Simon and I are going to decide which island to start with." Her face clouded momentarily. "I never went on Fergus's boat and have always been a bit afraid of them, but we'll start with one of the bigger ferries and try to wipe the *Young Enid* from my mind."

Albertina looked puzzled.

"That was the name of my husband's boat. The one he died in. I can't spend the rest of my life being afraid of boats and ships and water because of that."

The silence lasted half a minute, Albertina leant forward to touch Sandra's hand.

"I am very proud o' you, San'ra. You becomin' a strong, grown-up woman." She squeezed the hand gently.

"Actually," Sandra smiled, "I'm quite proud of myself, too!"

*

In a matter of weeks the first leg of the trip had been settled in detail, the Mini was serviced and Ralph shared his patchy knowledge of car maintenance with them both. They bought a second-hand two-man tent, tested and deemed it too small, so a second, new one was acquired. Both potential campers agreed that some privacy might be a good thing, in the long run.

During quieter, solitary moments, Sandra wondered if travelling together was really a good idea. It would only be a true adventure, she would only be truly grown up, if she made the trip alone, and yet Simon had promised to look after and support her. It would be cruel to turn him away.

Detailed books of campsites and Bed and Breakfast accommodation, insect repellent, first aid kits, boots, sleeping bags, clothes and anything else that could be squeezed into the tiny vehicle were piled up in the hall of the house in Snellington. The date was set. Destination: Cape Wrath. They'd worked out a circuitous route and knew it almost by heart, if the maps were to be believed. They had plenty of time.

Albertina agreed to move into the house and advertised her own home as a short-term let. She was doing this for Sandra, not herself, although the money would be useful if she could find a nice tenant.

After much persuasion, Josie and Ralph had convinced Sandra's parents to make a special occasion of it and at nine o'clock one sunny spring morning, both sets of parents, siblings, neighbours and the new caretaker gathered outside the house in Snellington to wave them off.

Elation surged in Sandra's heart. Simon was worried about how to change a tyre if the Mini got a puncture, but kept it to himself.

*

At around the same time, WPC Andrena Cooper visited the offices of Hardisty Incorporated Holdings once more. This time, she invited the late Mr Hardisty's Personal Assistant to accompany her and her colleague to the force's HQ, in order to help with their enquiries into the death of Fergus Hardisty.

"Just to tie up a few loose ends," Andrena explained, po-faced.

"I've told you everything I know," Marianne insisted, but to no avail.

"We'll just go through it again in case either of us has forgotten anything."

Andrena sat alongside her boss as he sat back in his chair and studied the black-haired young woman, who was about the same age as his own daughter. He decided to give the junior officer her head and let her conduct the interview.

"Go ahead, WPC Cooper." He nodded his encouragement.

Andrena had been longing for this moment. She reached into the folder in front of her and removed a typewritten document.

"Ms Reid, please take a look at this document and see if you recognise it."

Marianne took the sheet of paper and looked. Her heart leapt. Her mouth emptied of saliva. No words came to her. She looked at the WPC, questions in her eyes.

"Your reaction suggests that you *have* seen that document before, Ms Reid."

A slight nod. The voice, when it came, had lost its assured tone.

"I found it in the safe at work, after Uncle Fer ... after Mr Hardisty died."

Her mind was swimming. How had the police got hold of the fake will? She remembered the Albertina woman taking it from her hands and shutting the door in her face. It was supposed to have gone to Heaval and Co. Marianne had been expecting the solicitor's call for weeks and had already worked out how she would spend her inheritance.

Having set the girl on edge, Andrena noted the response and moved on quickly.

She fiddled with some instruments on the desk before asking,

"We were very grateful for your co-operation last time we spoke, Ms Reid. There are just one or two loose ends we need to tie up before we close the enquiries into Mr Hardisty's unfortunate demise. I hope you don't mind going over old ground, just for the records."

Marianne breathed more freely. The daft bat of a policewoman had been well and truly hoodwinked by the fake will. She smirked to herself ... a curl of the lip that was not missed by WPC Andrena, who in reality was not such a daft bat at all.

"I'd like you to tell me about the last time you visited Mr Hardisty's boat, Ms Reid?" The question was asked with a sympathetic smile. "It must be painful for you to revisit happier times, but this won't take long."

Instinctively, Marianne returned the smile and nodded.

"Yes, very painful." She blotted her eyes with a tissue. What answer was the right answer? She remained silent.

"Can you recall when it was?"

"Not exactly."

"Although you did visit the boat on occasion?

"Only once or twice." Was that the right answer?

Andrena reached for a transcript of her notes and studied it.

"Just to be certain, did you visit the marina around the time of Mr Hardisty's death?"

"No. Definitely not. I think it was about two years before that – a family outing. He was my uncle, you know."

Her mouth was still dry but she was confident she could outwit this copper, who seemed to be making heavy weather of a few simple questions. It was all quite straightforward. Marianne believed she could do this woman's job with her eyes closed, but she wasn't keen on the uniform.

Andrena was fiddling with her equipment again. She turned the screen of her desktop monitor towards the interviewee and pressed a button.

"Just take a look at this footage, please, Ms Reid."

Marianne rarely wore her spectacles but fished a cheap red-rimmed pair from her handbag. Everything became clearer. The monitor was showing a still image of the entrance to the marina.

Andrena pressed a button and the video ran. Mostly there were no comings or goings through the entrance – just a few old men with rucksacks and a family with teenage children.

"What's this got to do with me?" She sounded disgruntled. "This is a waste of my time and yours."

There was something at the back of her mind, waking slowly like a hibernating bat in spring, whispering that she had blundered; that she must get out of that place. Marianne buttoned her jacket and collected her handbag from the floor.

"This is a waste of time. I have things to do." She pushed back the chair and removed her glasses.

Andrena looked across at her boss, who nodded that she should continue.

"Just a little while longer please, Ms Reid. Can you confirm that you recognise the location?"

"Not really. As I said, I haven't been to Uncle Fergus's boat for a couple of years or more, and I didn't spend my time there gawping at the entrance when I did. It could be anywhere."

With a sulky pout she looked like a spoiled child, Andrena thought as the video continued to run. Suddenly, she pressed Pause.

"Here we are, Ms Reid. Tell me what you see on the screen now."

Marianne squinted. She could see something reddish but didn't want to look.

"Perhaps with your spectacles would be better?" Andrena knew the girl was prevaricating.

The glasses were retrieved. There was no way out.

"What am I supposed to be looking at?"

"Do you recognise the person on the screen?"

"Can't say I do. It's a bit fuzzy. It's woman in a red coat but it could be anyone."

"Those glasses can't be very effective, Ms Reid." Andrena's boss decided to intervene. He crossed the room while removing his own horn-rimmed spectacles.

"Try these."

She had no option but to take them. She had no way out.

"Can you confirm that you are the woman on the screen?"

"I suppose so." She handed back the glasses.

"According to our notes, you told the constable you had not been to Mr Hardisty's boat for some years. Why did you lie, Ms Reid? Why lie if you've nothing to hide?"

Refusing to answer their questions, she stood to leave.

"Wasting police time and lying to the police are punishable offences. You'd do well to remember that, Ms. Reid. We might want to question you again in the near future, so please let us know if you intend to leave the area."

The boss's tone was firm but fair. He opened the door and accompanied her downstairs.

"We will need to speak to you again, Ms Reid. It might be a good idea to get yourself a solicitor." His satisfied smile was hard to conceal.

"Well done WPC Cooper. Nice one."

Andrena's glow intensified almost to ignition. She could feel her career taking off.

25

Around the time that Sandra and Simon were crossing the border between Yorkshire and the rest of the world, Marianne Reid was boarding a train to London. There was no way she was going to hang about waiting for more questions from the police. She hadn't really done anything wrong, although if she ever saw that Albertina woman again, she'd get a piece of her mind for not delivering the will to Heaval and Co. Anyway, Uncle Fergus had assured her that she'd be a wealthy woman one day. He just hadn't got round to making the new will bequeathing everything to her, as promised. Really, Marianne, had just been trying to carry out the last wishes of the dead man, she told herself.

She had only been to London once on a school trip and hadn't liked it much. Now, she was drawn by the chance of anonymity. She had enough money in her purse for a week in a cheap hotel room. How she'd get by after that she had no idea, although opportunities would abound, she had no doubt.

By the time the train reached Kings Cross, Sandra, Simon and the Mini were crossing the Scottish border. Simon had scanned the book of campsites they could reach before evening fell. The further they travelled from Wraith, the freer they felt. Anxieties quietened, surges of excitement came in waves as they talked more freely than ever before. That

271

no romantic commitment had been promised made things easier, they agreed.

For that first night, Simon chose a site close to the sea near Dunbar. Tents erected, Sandra slid into her sleeping bag exhausted. She was proud of herself and smiled as she slept. There was no rush. They could take their time before she needed to tackle Edinburgh and the Forth Bridge.

Days passed before they felt ready to make progress, then, decision made, with hearts in mouths they navigated the maelstrom of motorways and bridges until, at last, they emerged among glens and streams and vast swathes of seemingly barren mountainside, occasionally sighting the silhouette of a lone stag or cluster of hinds in the distance. Heading vaguely north, they stopped at will when a tiny village proffered refreshment, wildlife or a glimpse of history.

As their confidence increased, they camped at the roadside or even took shelter at a remote inn, always heading vaguely north until, on reaching the Moray Firth, a choice had to be made: east or west.

Sandra had read about the Moray Firth during her preparatory research: a good place for dolphin-spotting, according to the books. Where the road split, the map offered alternatives: left to Nairn or right to Forres, Lossiemouth and the wild North Sea. Sandra chose right.

She was tired. Although thrilled by their progress so far, it was time for another few days' rest. Signs of habitation reassured her. Maybe there'd be a Bed and Breakfast where they could have a nice meal and a hot bath. They were on the A86. She'd be able to locate their position on the map.

Ahead she could see a steep hill. She touched the snoozing Simon's arm.

"Simon! Wake up. I need you to keep a look-out. It's getting dark. I need you to read the directions." He woke with a start and read that they were approaching Cluny Hill.

"There's a tower at the top. It's called Nelson's Tower. Let's have a look." He was wide awake now.

"What does it say on that metal notice?"

She was feeling uneasy and alone. She slowed the Mini to a crawl and stopped to listen:

"Here was 'The Witches' Stone, a large lump of stone, cleft into three pieces and bound together with ancient metal bands," he read. "In earlier times, from the top of Cluny Hill suspected witches were rolled in stout barrels through which stakes were driven."

Simon read the words in a spooky voice, grinning. It was like an old-fashioned horror film, he thought; laughable. He didn't notice Sandra's silence at first. Not until he heard her chattering teeth and wheezing breath. She sat rigid as the darkness closed in. The engine was still running…

"I can't go on," she whispered at last. "You'll have to drive."

"What's the matter?"

"I daren't tell you." She was whimpering now.

"Tell me!" He switched on the internal light and saw the pallid horror of her face.

She covered her face with her shaking hands.

"I think … used to think … I was a witch."

"Why on earth did you think that?"

"Because I harm people. I don't mean to! My just being there makes it happen."

"Who have you harmed?"

"My mother, and … and Fergus … and there might be lots of other I don't know about. You'll have to drive us over the hill!"

They were both tired, he reasoned silently, climbing out of the car.

"Let's swap seats, but you do know that I haven't actually passed my driving test yet," he reminded her.

"I don't care. I'll take over again … as soon as … as soon as we get off … this hill."

The whimpers were louder now, the wheezing deeper.

He revved the engine and tried to remember what to do. Slowly they moved forwards. A tractor coming towards them blinded him momentarily before passing, but he engaged the correct gear and the car edged forward. Gaining confidence, he pressed the accelerator. The little car made its way forward and up the hill. Darkness was almost complete. Only a few stars twinkled between the clouds.

Yards from the summit, a blaze of light shone into the night sky. Suddenly its beam angled downwards as a tractor and trailer combination breasted the crest of the hill. There was no time to swerve. The tractor was on them in a second.

*

Eighteen-year-old Angus MacAutry was used to driving tractors, but this was his first accident. Clutching the steering wheel tightly, he watched the little car do a backward somersault down Cluny Hill. He'd lived in the area all his life and was familiar with the spooky tales about curses and witchcraft, but thought it was all a load of rubbish.

He flashed the lights a few times to alert other travellers. Jumping down from the cab, he followed the route of the Mini, dreading what he might find. His head hurt and his knee felt as though it had been hit with a hammer.

All was silent. Another car was coming, not a local vehicle. Angus flagged it down; explained the situation. Together they approached the wreck. The stranger fetched a torch and his phone from his car.

"Can you hear me?" he called. Angus was trembling. The older motorist took charge.

The passenger window had been open. With his torch, he

could see a hand, a moving hand. He took hold of it. It was warm and responded to his touch.

"Can you speak? What's your name?"

"Sandra." The voice was faint.

"Can you see the driver, Sandra?"

Sandra was able to turn her head an inch or two.

"He looks as if he's asleep."

A sob caught in her throat before she passed out.

Only seconds later, it seemed, the Mini was surrounded by lights and vehicles and people. There were sounds she didn't recognise, people in uniforms with things in their hands and equipment in bags; others who looked like country-men. The sound of a siren was coming closer. Metal doors being opened and closed. She had not heard Simon move or breathe. Where is he? Where has the daylight gone to? But all the people were busy with metal things and lights and shouting orders. Someone had wrapped her top half in a blanket. Another person cut through the door and gently eased her out onto a stretcher. She thought she might be in an ambulance.

Where was Simon?

She began to cry. The woman from the following vehi-cle tried to calm her down, but Sandra knew she *must* be heard.

"It's because I'm a witch." The tears flowed.

"Och now, dear, we don't believe in all that superstition nowadays," she lied. "Just you lie there nice and calm while the men try to cut your young man from the wreckage."

The words sounded alien. 'Simon' and 'wreckage' did not belong in the same sentence.

Another patient was being settled in the ambulance, but it was not Simon. Her eyes pleaded with the paramedic,

"Who is he? Where's Simon?"

There was no reply to her second question.

"This young man was also involved in the accident. He's going to be OK but we need to look after him for a while." The tractor driver was feeling weak at the knees and had been persuaded to lie down.

A paramedic appeared. His face was grave. He did not speak while checking Sandra's pulse and head wound. She had to tell them, tell them that *she* was to blame. If Simon was dead, she was his murderer.

"Is there a policeman here?" She tried again.

"No. They're on their way."

"I need to speak to them. I need to tell them it's my fault."

There was a grunt from the other casualty

"That's a relief! And I was thinking it was me driving the tractor." His words were difficult to understand through his thickening lips.

"No, it's my fault "

The male paramedic shushed her. He needed to get on with his work. His voice filled the emptiness with questions and instructions until inevitably, he paused for breath.

"Are the police here yet? I need to confess."

"We have more important things to worry about at the moment, my dear. I'm just going to give you a little injection to calm you down."

"I keep telling them that I'm a witch, but no one believes me…." she whispered as the needle went in.

*

Angus MacAutry was made of strong stuff. After fifteen minutes in the back of the ambulance he decided he was not in need of any more medical attention. He had things to do, livestock to attend to and places to go … not to mention a sweet new girlfriend expecting a sweet, starry evening up the glen.

Confident that his injuries were not serious, the paramedics let him go. Efforts to extract Simon and stabilise his condition continued. The female passer-by sat with Sandra, who was conscious and able to speak softly. Again she raised the issue of witchcraft.

"Bad things happen to people I love," she whined, "It's because I'm a witch. I saw the sign by the roadside and I panicked."

"That sign has been there for many generations, my dear. People who live round here are used to it. The poor wee women who were so horribly killed … it was back in the dark ages, nearly … they were just wise women trying to help others. You must put the idea of witches out of your head." She paused, wondering how best to carry on.

"An ancestor of mine was accused of witchcraft back in the 1600s. She was well-known among the crofters for her skill with herbs and medicines … curing sickness and healing ailing babies, ye ken?"

"What happened to her?"

"Well, of course someone accused her of witchcraft and she was rolled down the hill in a barrel, but she survived."

"Oh, that's wonderful! She must have been so relieved."

"Not for long, my dear. You see, in those ignorant times, people thought no one could survive the roll down Cluny Hill in a staked barrel except by magic. The innocent died during the roll. Those who survived were executed for witchcraft later."

Silence stretched between them. The woman recalled her understanding of the barbarous past and the traumatic consequences that dogged her family to this day. Sandra didn't want to think any more. Please let this woman be telling the truth … that it *is* all superstitious nonsense.

The ambulance rocked a little as the male paramedic re-entered.

"You'll be pleased to know that your young man is awake, dearie. We've stabilised his condition and we'll take you both to the hospital in town. You can stop worrying now. Just relax, and we'll get you there a s a p."

He turned to the helpful woman.

"Thanks for your help Mary Mac ... again. Is it the third time this year?"

"Yes. That young Angus isn't the only one to have driven too fast over the brow of Cluny Hill."

Pressing Sandra's hand, she smiled. "You must learn to forget the past, my dear. I can feel that you've been through bad times, but they were not your fault. Accidents happen because humans are fallible. We all make mistakes. Try to forgive and move on. Search for the goodness and honesty in people, and look with understanding on their flaws. I can sense that your young man is going to recover, but if the time comes to let him go, you must do so with kindness and no regrets."

A moment's silence followed, and she was gone.

"She's a nice lady," Sandra whispered. "She was very kind. Reassuring."

"Yes, she always is. She knows what it's like to be rolled down Cluny Hill in a barrel. Mary Mac appears whenever there's a nasty accident here. They say she's trying to make amends."

"I don't understand. Make amends for what?"

"For surviving the roll when all her cronies died. The story goes that she escaped execution by hiding in a dung cart."

He closed the doors. Both ambulances drove off. In one, Sandra wondered if she could carry on alone. Drifting in and out of consciousness in the other, Simon wondered how things had come to this.

Sandra tried to forget Mary Mac. She needed to see

Simon, but could not forget the instruction: "If the time comes to let him go, you must do so with kindness and no regrets."

He was badly injured. He would survive, but at what cost? How would his parents feel about her when they found out? They would blame her, surely?

She should have made the trip alone. She should not have put Simon in danger.

Maybe the thought had been enough.

It would be kindest to follow Mary Mac's advice and let him go, before more harm was done.

She would find the strength to carry on alone.